LURED TO PARADISE

PARADISE KEY SERIES

MACY BUTLER

PARADISE PRESS

Lured to Paradise

Macy Butler

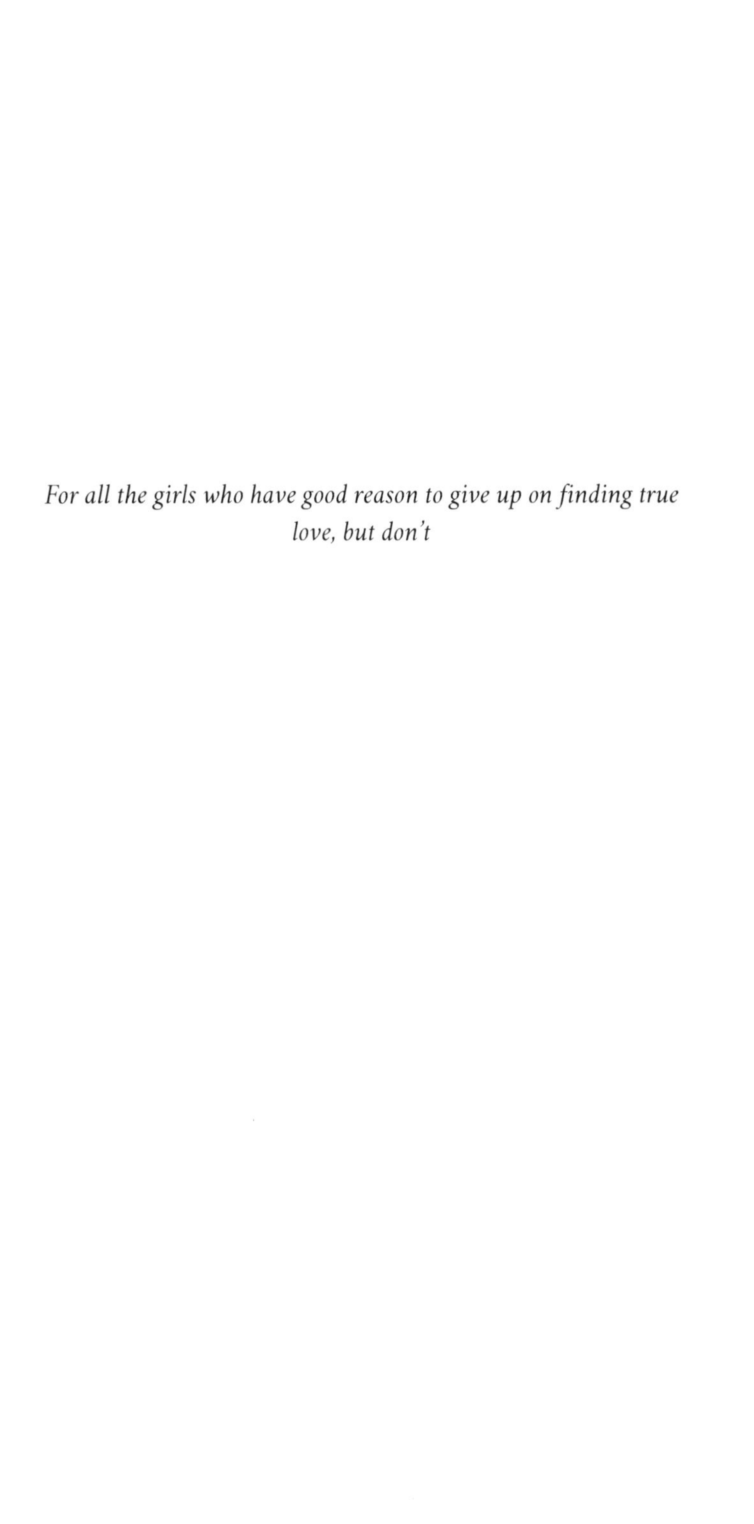

For all the girls who have good reason to give up on finding true love, but don't

CHAPTER 1

VIOLET

My phone buzzed on the desk distracting me from searching for the Parisian textile catalog that Clifton had given me yesterday. We were getting the resort ready for a photo shoot, and he wanted new drapes for the restaurant. I'd needed to order them yesterday. Even with express shipping and a seamstress on standby, it was highly unlikely they'd be finished before the shoot.

I'd find a way to pull it off. After all that's why Clifton had hired me as General Manager of Paradise Key. I'd jumped at the chance to help launch the luxury resort on his private island in the Florida Keys. Not even half a year later and we were already being featured in Condé Nast Traveler.

I was angry at myself for misplacing the catalog. Everything had to be just right when the photo crew arrived.

I glared at the phone, when it buzzed again. Of course it was my mother calling. I mentally counted to five before I answered.

"Hi, Mama. How are you?" *Where* was she, was more like it. The farm, the hotel, or her new condo in La Jolla?

"I'm good, dear. Just finished breakfast on the terrace." California it was.

"Oh yeah? Are you enjoying the new place?"

I held the phone to my ear with my shoulder as I rifled through the stack of papers on the corner of my desk.

"It's sublime. You have to come see it. Maybe next time I'm out here. I want you to meet my realtor. He's very handsome, and from a good family."

As long as he came from money, he wouldn't be after mine. I knew how her mind worked.

"I'm too busy for dating, Mama." Not that there were many chances for dating on Paradise Key, which was fine by me. I'd been burned enough to know better than to play with fire.

"You're gonna end up an old maid on that island of yours one day."

This was her biggest worry. At age thirty, I was getting perilously close to old maid status in her book.

I'd taken the job on Paradise Key rather abruptly after I caught my ex-fiancé cheating. The most upsetting part for my mother was that it'd been just three months before the wedding she'd planned to make the event of the century.

"That doesn't scare me, Mama. I like my simple island life."

My mother knew better than to hound me further. "How's the resort doing? Bookings are good for this season? ?"

"Yep. It's doing great. Plumb full for most of the rest of the year. But right now we're busy prepping for a shoot with Condé Nast in a couple of weeks."

"Condé Nast?" I could hear the excitement in her voice. Mentioning the prestigious travel magazine piqued her interest more than anything else about my job or my island lifestyle. "They're featuring the resort?"

I rolled my eyes. "Yes, Mama. A full spread."

"That's impressive. Your father will be jealous. Maybe you can put in a word."

The thought of making Daddy jealous gave me a pleasure I wasn't proud of. "I'm not sure how I'd work your hotel in Wyoming into an interview about Paradise Key, but I'll do my best."

"It's *our* lodge, Violet. You could just mention your rancher father and how he runs the hotel in Wyoming when they ask how you got into the business."

"So, I should lie?" How I got into the business had nothing to do with Daddy. And why she was looking out for him after the way he treated her was beyond me. I supposed living with a narcissist will do that to you.

"You said you were looking for a way to work it in..."

My eyes rolled again as I sorted through the stack of magazines on the coffee table in front of the sofa next to my desk. I could have squealed with joy when I found the textile catalog I'd been searching for. "Oh, thank God."

"See there, it's perfect."

We were talking about two different things, but that was pretty much par for the course with Mama.

"We'll see. I've got to run for now, unless there's something else." She wasn't usually one for small talk, so I figured there was a reason for her call.

"Oh." The line was silent for a long second. She didn't appreciate the snub, even though she hadn't been the least bit concerned that it was the middle of my workday. "Actually, yes, there is. Your father was hoping you could make it out to the lodge to discuss something."

"What?" Him putting her up to call me made my blood boil.

"He says it's important."

I bristled. "So important he couldn't call me himself?"

"Oh, you know how he is."

Controlling. Manipulative. Delegating every little thing that he could. Yeah, I knew.

"I don't have time for a trip to Wyoming. Tell him to call me if he has something to discuss."

"I wouldn't ask if it wasn't important. Please just go." Her voice was resigned because she knew as well as I did that he'd insist until I gave in.

"I just told you I have Condé Nast coming here in two weeks. And my assistant GM is on vacation. I'm more than a little busy. Daddy can call me or come here and talk about it after the interview."

I heard her draw a deep breath. "His cardiologist told him not to travel."

"Why? What happened?" That he might have trouble with his heart reminded me that he had one. "Is he okay?"

Her voice was somber. "He needs a bypass."

I straightened, glancing down at the catalog that no longer seemed important. "Oh. When? Is the surgery scheduled?" What was she doing in California if Daddy was sick?

"Next month. They said it's not an emergency, but your father wants to get things in order just in case."

I cocked my head, concerned. "What's that supposed to mean? He thinks he might die? That sounds pretty darn urgent." Something didn't add up, but that was often the case with Daddy.

My mother's voice was calm, too calm for the situation. "Heart surgery can be risky business. And we're not getting any younger. He's just being practical. He really wants to see you before the surgery."

I could tell by her collected manner that he wasn't in dire straits, but how could I refuse a summons like that? If she was instigating for him, she could be my buffer though. "I'll go if you'll meet me there."

My mother laughed before she crooned, demurely Southern, "You sneaky devil. You're too clever for your own good."

A sing-song tap on the door sounded before it swung open. I grinned at my best friend, pointing at my phone apologetically. "I've got to go for now, Mama. I'll see what I can do and get back to you with dates."

My lips fluttered in an exasperated huff after I ended the call. "Parents."

Corinne's eyes grew wide. "Ah. Are they threatening to visit?"

"Worse. I have to finagle a quick trip out to Wyoming."

"Shit. When?"

I noticed the catalog still in my hand. "I'm not sure. I'll have to figure that out. But first I need to order this fabric before I forget again. Sorry, just give me a sec." I scanned my email messages on my phone. "I've got the measurements here somewhere."

"Sure, take your time." Corinne plopped down on the sofa and picked up a magazine.

I pulled up the website on my laptop and placed the order. "Fabric for dining room drapes will be en route from Paris tomorrow. Now fingers crossed we can get it all done in time."

"You'll get it all done. You always do."

It often meant working ten hour days, but I loved it. "It doesn't help that Brian is on vacation for three more days. Or that Clifton wants to replace things that don't need replacing. But he wants everything to be perfect."

"Well, he *is* a perfectionist. And it *is* Condé Nast."

"*Pff*. Don't I know it. No pressure." I opened my eyes wide as I grabbed my sunglasses off my desk. "I need to eat. Have you had lunch?" What I really needed was a drink.

"Nope. You buying?"

"Clifton is." I winked before I slid my glasses onto my nose.

We took a two-top on the terrace of the bar and ordered two salads. I stuck with sweet tea even though I'd have preferred the Long Island variety after the call with my mother. "Is it terrible that I'm pissed off about being railroaded into visiting my father before his heart surgery?"

Corinne grinned. "Kind of, but I don't judge."

Corrine never held back. That was one of the many things I loved about her. "The cynic in me thinks he's playing the sympathy card to manipulate me somehow. That's the terrible part."

She waved off my guilt. "You have your reasons for thinking the worst."

She'd heard plenty of them. Corinne was the only friend in the Keys who knew how caddywampus my family was. There was no one else I'd tell about my father's infidelity or my mother standing by him, even if they had lived separately for most the last decade.

My island life would be a lot more solitary it it weren't for Corinne. Her friendship made all the difference, from the beginning. I felt like we'd known each other forever when we met my first week on the job. I opened up to her more than I had my lifelong friends about my heartache that was so fresh at the time. She let me vent my work stress, and let me bitch about my father trying to keep me under his thumb. All without judgment.

"Anyway, enough about that. How the hell have you been? It feels like ages since I've seen you."

Her face lit up. "Been great. Kind of hectic though, getting ready for Aquarius."

"Oh right. That's coming up soon isn't it?" I felt guilty that I'd almost forgotten her adventure was imminent.

Corinne was a marine biologist. She was headed for a research expedition on Aquarius Reef Base, the only undersea laboratory in the world.

She smiled, clearly a little awestruck. "Yep, only two weeks away. I still can't believe it."

"You are a rockstar. I'm bummed you won't be here for the Condé Nast interview though. I'm sure they'd want to feature our sexy marine biologist."

She looked down at her shorts and tank top. "I think National Geographic is more my style."

"Oh, shush. You clean up nice." Corrine was a knockout, even in a sundress and sandals when we went out on the town in Key West. "What does one wear in an underwater lab?"

"Basically this." Her hand fanned up and down her side. "Except on the dives, of course. I have a dry suit for that."

"I suppose fashion isn't a concern." I giggled. "But you never know. Are any of the other scientists hot?"

"Oh, God no." She cut into one of the giant prawns on the salads that the waiter had just delivered. "I do plan to get a new dress for my birthday party when I'm in Colorado though."

Right. I'd nearly forgotten her trip to Colorado as well. Was I a terrible friend? "Always good to take advantage of being back in civilization. Lord knows we don't have much shopping in the Keys. I'm sure you'll find something cute in Boulder."

"It's a quick trip but I'll make it work."

"You have a couple of days. Surely the visit with the shark scientist won't take up all of it." Corrine would be meeting with one of the country's premier shark experts to discuss a partnership on a research study.

"I'll only be with him for half a day, which will still be a trip. He's brilliant, but more than a little eccentric."

I laughed after I washed a bite down with a sip of tea. "Exactly what you'd expect from a shark scientist, right?"

She chuckled. "Yes, I suppose so. We are a strange lot."

"Normal is overrated. And boring. Keep being weird."

She shrugged. "It's the only way I know how to be."

"So is your birthday bash all sorted?"

"Yeah, I think so. I just met with Tessa. I've never had an event planner plan anything for me." She shook her head like she couldn't believe it. She's going all out. I'd be happy with a boombox, beer and pizza."

I chuckled. "Well judging from the purchase orders I've approved, you're getting a hell of a lot more than that."

"I know! I can't believe Clifton is so generous."

She'd probably shit a brick if she knew that he was in for well over twenty grand so far. "Well, he *is* a billionaire. But some of the stingiest people I've ever known are also the wealthiest. Clifton doesn't skimp on anything though. Especially when he likes someone."

"I still can't believe my luck. But I'll take it." She smiled. "When I came out here to survey the underwater space around the island before he could get the permits to build the dock, I was prepared to fight to keep him from ruining the island. Who knew he'd be a bigger environmentalist than half my team?"

"He's full of surprises all right."

Corinne beamed. "Speaking of surprises, I'm hoping to convince my brother to come for my party."

"Oh really? That's right, you said you might try to see him when you're out in Colorado." I'd forgotten that as well. It was settled. I was a terrible friend.

She nodded with a big grin. "Yep. Just for a night. Too bad there's no time for skiing."

"That sucks. The silver lining in my trip to Wyoming will be spring skiing."

Corinne flung her loose blonde curls over her shoulder while stabbing at another bite of salad. "At least there's that. And maybe it won't be so bad if your dad is humbled with health problems."

"Ha! The Grim Reaper himself staring my daddy dead in the eye wouldn't humble him." I felt bad for saying it out loud, but it was true. "I know it's awful to say, but I don't think that feeling his mortality is why my father summoned me. He's up to something."

"Well, I plan to shame my big brother into coming to my birthday party. So I can't say much."

"If you have to shame him into coming to an epic party on Paradise Key, there's something wrong with him, not you."

Her eyes rolled. "He's busy. But I'm hoping I can lure him with fishing."

"Ha. That's classic. You hate fishing." Corinne's soapbox against the fishing industry was a mile high and she climbed it every chance she got.

"But he loves it, and it's about damn time he visit." She grinned. "He's still single, you know."

She'd mentioned it on at least three occasions while not so subtly showing me his photos on Instagram. "You're as bad as my mama trying to set me up. I don't have time for men." Especially not my best friend's brother.

CHAPTER 2

HAYDEN

My phone ringing from the kitchen made me jerk, knocking the painted porcelain frame over the edge of the end table and onto the floor. My heart pounded at the sight of the shards of frame and shattered glass.

"Shit!"

I rushed to get the phone, cursing my clumsiness under my breath before I cleared my throat and answered.

"Hey there. You getting close?"

Corinne's bubbly voice made me smile. "Yep. Just pulled into Breck. I'll be there in ten."

"Good. Any problem on the pass? It dumped fourteen inches yesterday. I was hoping they'd have it clear by now." The mountain pass between Denver and Breckenridge got gnarly in the snow. But Corrine refused to let me pick her up in Denver.

"The pass was clear, but rush hour sucked. Bad timing."

"There's a pot of mom's stew on the stove." I'd made the recipe I knew was my sister's favorite.

"Good. I'm not built for this cold."

I chuckled. "We can make a fire if you want. Get off the phone and drive safe."

"See you in a few."

I took a broom and dustpan over to the scene of the crime to clean up the evidence. My face tugged in a wince as I carefully removed the glass from my favorite photo of my wife. I remembered snapping the picture of Jill grinning from ear to ear just after her first ultrasound. It was the happiest I'd ever seen her.

"Sorry, darling. It slipped. But the photo survived unscathed."

She'd still be sad that the frame she'd painted for Anabelle's nursery was beyond repair. I carefully placed the picture on the table before sweeping up the mess, muttering under my breath. "Why *that* picture?" I groaned with regret as I tucked it into the junk drawer. I'd have to get a new frame, stat.

Headlights turning into the driveway swept over the back wall of the living room. Wiping sweaty palms on my jeans, I went to the door and opened it before Corinne rounded the corner to the deck. I stepped out into the brisk evening air, the sun already gone behind the mountain peak to the west. "Howdy, stranger."

"Stranger is right. It's been too long." Corinne flung her backpack onto the snow-covered wooden deck as soon as she topped the stairs and threw her arms around my neck. The emotion of her embrace was so raw and real I had to take a step back. "Rough trip?"

"Other than the traffic?" She scowled before flashing the bright smile that had gotten her out of trouble a million times growing up. "I prefer island life."

She was blonder and tanner than ever, and I couldn't help but smile. "It seems to suit you. I never figured you for a Florida girl, but look at you. Living the dream."

"Pretty cool, isn't it?" Corinne beamed, arms wrapped around herself, shivering. "Are you going to invite me in? It's fucking cold."

I ushered her past the heavy oak door, chuckling.

Corinne dropped her bag onto the sofa on the way through the living room and followed me to the kitchen, huffing warm breath into her hands.

"The Keys have ruined me. I was bummed that I could only visit for one night before my meeting in Boulder tomorrow. But now I'm almost glad I don't have time to hit the slopes. I don't think I could handle it."

"You're tough," I scoffed. Tough was an understatement. Corinne's tenacity got her out of everything that her smile couldn't.

"You been shredding on the snowboard or sticking to skis this season?"

Neither was the truth. I hadn't been on the slopes all season, or last. But I couldn't tell my sister that. She already worried too much. "Mostly skis," I lied.

I chuckled at her rubbing her hands together as we reached the kitchen. "Island life really has thinned your blood."

Her brow creased. "I've gotten a thick skin working there though."

I cocked my head as I turned the corkscrew into a bottle of Cabernet. It was the first I'd heard her complain about the job she loved. "Why's that?"

Her lips twisted to one side, reluctant to admit. "It's not easy being the *inexperienced young woman* sometimes." Her tone shifted to give a sour flare to the descriptor she framed in air quotes.

My protective big brother instinct kicked in. "Who's giving you a hard time?"

"No one's giving me a hard time." Corinne punched my shoulder, more amused now than when I'd bristled at boys trying to make a move on her when we were teenagers.

By the time I went off to college, she was fifteen and taking care of them herself—and had been ever since. That's why her hesitation was surprising. "Then what's the problem?"

She shrugged but the concern returned to her eyes. "Just politics. The guys they skipped over to award me the post aren't exactly happy."

I looked up from pouring the wine. "You mean the guys you beat out for the opportunity? Fuck them. They're just jealous."

She bit her lip, looking skeptical. "Yeah, but I still have to work with them."

Corinne was so dedicated to marine biology I often joked that she should have been a Cousteau instead of a Kincaid. "Whatever. Don't let them get to you. You earned this."

She slid onto the stool at the breakfast bar, taking the glass I placed in front of her with a serious look. "Plenty of them are far more experienced."

I bet they didn't have her determination or her pearly whites. "They picked you for a reason." I eyed her gnawing her thumbnail. "Are you nervous about it—the expedition, I mean?"

Nearly two weeks underwater didn't sound like fun to me, but it was her dream come true.

Her back straightened, hand jerking out of her mouth to wipe her wet thumb on her jeans. "A little, of course. But mostly excited." When her signature smile returned, I relaxed.

"How's the meeting you have in Boulder tomorrow related to the lab?" I hadn't asked for details since we mainly communicated by text.

"I'm meeting with a professor, a well-known shark scientist."

My eyes widened. "In *Boulder*?" The nearest ocean was over a thousand miles away.

Corinne nodded. "He's *the* authority on shark fossils, too. That's actually huge here in academia, believe it or not. Anyway, he wants to bring me into a study and to collect some data for him when I'm down at the lab. That's what we're going to discuss."

I swirled my wine in any glass and grinned. "That's great, Cor. I'm proud of you."

"Thanks." She smiled, finally looking as confident as she normally did. I felt a nervous jitter as her eyes wandered over toward the living room. She paused for a second and I could tell by her tone she was trying not to sound judgmental when she said, "I see you haven't changed anything."

I averted my eyes to the pot of stew. "I'm hardly here."

"Yeah, you're traveling a lot lately aren't you? What's up with that?"

"Just the way it is." The truth was I volunteered to travel far more than was necessary. My employer saw it as drive, but I felt more like myself when I was on the road. "Two hundred days last year."

Corinne's face scrunched. "What's the point of living in Breckenridge if you're gone all the time? Might as well move to Denver. It's closer to the airport."

The thought had crossed my mind, but I couldn't leave the memories here. "It's good to be here when I am." I licked the spoon. "I think I got Mom's stew right."

"It smells almost right."

I grabbed the bottle of wine and splashed some into the pot. "There, that ought to do it."

Corinne laughed. "God, you remember Mom and Aunt Margaret cooking for grandpa's birthday?"

I smiled, recalling an epic night with the folks. "Yeah, Madge was so tipsy by the time we sat down to eat she could barely hold her head up."

My sister cackled. "I know. I was so confused then, wondering why everyone was laughing and silly. It was much later I realized that they were shitfaced."

"Madge especially." I grabbed the frame containing my dearest aunt's picture from the kitchen counter. "This was her seventieth."

Corinne laughed. "I remember. Barely." We'd all tied one on that night.

I scooped stew into two bowls and pushed one toward Corinne as I made my way around the island to sit beside her. "That was a good party."

"It feels like a lifetime ago."

Four years *was* a lifetime ago, with all that had changed in my life. "Life goes on." Barely for me at times but I tried to keep my struggles to myself.

After we finished the stew, Corinne led me to the couch, wine bottle in one hand and wine glass in the other. "My friends at the resort are organizing a birthday party for me."

"The eco-resort you were telling me about?"

"Yeah. Paradise Key. That's been a Godsend. Not only are the conservation dives I do for their guests extra income, the staff have become like family to me."

"Only you can make friends on a remote island." Corinne never met a stranger she didn't know.

She chuckled. "The general manager and I really hit it off. You might too." Her brows arched. "She's single."

My eyes rolled. "You're funny."

Corinne tucked her foot under her on the sofa and grinned. "Well, you can meet her if you come to my party."

Her birthday was only nine days away. "I can't go to Florida the week after next. I'm booked for the next couple of months."

"Can't you manage a weekend at least?"

I could, but the prospect wasn't appealing. "It's a four hour flight. And you're here now. A short visit so soon seems silly. I'll go another time when I can stay longer."

"It's perfectly acceptable to see your sister more than once every six months, you know? This is my third trip here in… how long's it been now? Over two years, hasn't it?"

Since Jill died. Two years, two months, and twelve days. I nodded. "Yeah, just over."

Her eyes flitted toward the wall full of wedding photos. She forced them back to mine again trying not to show judgment, I could tell, but it seeped through her crinkled brow. "You haven't been to see me in the Keys even once. A few days in paradise would be good for you. You can stay at the resort for free. It's normally two thousand dollars a night, so you shouldn't pass that up."

"That's tempting, but it's bad timing. Sorry, sis." I glanced up at the clock on the Wedding Wall, as Jill called it. "You must be getting tired. It's nearly midnight your time."

Her eyes narrowed. "You're putting me off. But I'm not giving up. It wouldn't hurt you to take a vacation and meet my friends." She smirked. "Especially Violet."

"The manager, I presume?" I shook my head, chuckling. "I don't need you to set me up. I do just fine in that department on my own."

"Yeah, right." She looked around the room. "Sure doesn't look like you're dating. You're living in a shrine."

I downed the rest of my wine. I didn't like this line of questioning. "I was on a date three nights ago, I'll have you know."

She huffed, disbelieving. "Oh yeah? Did you bring her home?"

"It was in Phoenix, so no."

"Tell me about her." Corinne said it suspiciously, like I'd made it up.

"She's tall, brunette, blue eyes. A flight attendant."

The details didn't seem to convince Corinne. "What's her *name*?

"Christy." *Or was it Crystal?*

One eye narrowed while her mouth drew to the side, smart-assed. "Let me guess, Tinder date?"

I shrugged, trying to act coy. "Maybe…"

"Hook-ups on business trips don't count as dating, Hayden."

If that was true, I hadn't dated at all. Even the repeats I kept at a two-time max.

Her gaze settled on the wedding photos again. "How do you stare at all this, all day?"

My throat constricted. "You know how Jill was with pictures." Some people have scrapbooks. Jill's was on display. Every special occasion was chronicled in frames on nearly every surface of every room. Birthdays, anniversaries, holidays, first dates, graduations, parent's retirement parties, and promotions.

"Yeah, I always thought it was a bit much, to be honest. But you don't have to keep it all out in the open now, Hayden. It can't be good for you."

What was good for me was that everyone usually left me alone. "The pictures don't bother me." Not like Corinne's nagging did.

Her head shook, resigned. "Alright, I'll shut up. You don't listen anyway."

I chuckled, relieved that she might actually drop it. "It runs in the family."

"Can't argue with that." She tipped her glass to finish the last sip of wine. Her eyes lit up when she set down the glass. "Why don't we go out for a nightcap? It'll do you some good to get out of the house."

I suspected she needed to escape the homage to my late wife as much as she thought I needed it. Either way, I was ready to be let off the hook. "Good idea." I squeezed her thigh. "There's a new wine bar I haven't tried."

"More wine sounds divine." She grinned as she jumped to her feet. "Mind if I freshen up first?"

"Of course not. You know where your room is. I should do the same." I stood to follow her down the hallway.

Corinne stopped at the first door on the left, glancing back at the closed door adorned with a floral wooden "A" across the hall. "Let me guess, still intact?"

My heart pounding in my chest rang in my ears with a dull thud as she stepped across the hallway and pushed the door open. The light of the hallway was enough to show the perfectly preserved nursery.

"Oh, Hayden." Her sad eyes turned up toward mine, full of the pity I'd come to despise from everyone who cared about me.

"You can donate this stuff to someone who needs it. But you need to get it out of here, Hayden. It's fucking creepy."

I rubbed the vein that protruded on my temple. "It's not creepy. It's Annabelle's room." Jill kept it intact, for the new baby we'd make someday, she'd said, so I saw it as a sign of hope at first. But when she'd spend hours in the rocking chair, I realized she was holding onto the past more than hoping for a future.

"Hayden, I know it was devastating to lose the baby after you guys tried for so long, but that was nearly a year before Jill died. And you know that I loved Jill, don't you?" She waited, eyes searching mine until I nodded. "You also know that she went a little cuckoo after the miscarriage, don't you?"

My instinct was to deny it, but we both knew the truth. Tears welled in my eyes as I nodded.

Corinne touched my arm with a rare tenderness. "Jill never got over it. But you still can. You must. None of this was your fault."

I'd been the one who'd insisted we go skiing, hoping it would make Jill feel better after so many months of depression. It was my idea to go to the top of the mountain that she never made it down, even though she hadn't been on the slopes all winter. It wasn't my fault that she'd somehow veered off the trail into a tree, but I'd taken her up there. But I couldn't tell Corinne that I still blamed myself. "I know."

My sister's warm smile melted the icy crust of guilt. "I can help you pack it up."

My fingers curled around her forearms. "I appreciate your concern. I'll think about it. I promise. Now can we talk about dessert? I'm craving something sweet." To overcome the bitterness.

I managed to keep Corinne talking about her work while we sipped a glass of Malbec. We were perusing the dessert menu when I recognized an old friend waving wildly from across the room. Todd Langley. I hadn't seen him in three years. Before that we were snowboarding together three days a week. After that last season, it all just fell apart. He was already headed toward us.

"Who's that?" Corinne looked up, grinning.

I stood and grabbed his hand, which shook mine firmly as his other hand patted my shoulder hard. "This is my buddy, Todd. He's a monster on a snowboard."

"Ha. You're better than I am. At least you used to be. God, it's been ages." He looked me over. "How the hell have you been?"

"I'm great. Just showing my sister around. This is Corinne. She's a marine biologist down in the Keys."

"Is that so?" Todd's gaze traveled up and down Corinne's front as she stood to shake his hand. I resisted the urge to fend him off. She wasn't a kid anymore and his attention might be just the distraction to keep her off my case. "The Florida Keys, huh? I've never been but I've always wanted to."

She flashed a flirty smile. "Can you believe my brother hasn't even come to visit?" So much for staying off my case.

"Well, that's a shame. But I can't say I'm surprised. We live in the same town and I haven't seen this guy in years." His eyes settled on mine, no longer concerned with flirting with Corinne. "I called several times."

After Jill died I ignored everyone who tried to reach out. What was there to say? "Yeah, sorry. I travel a lot for work now. I'm barely ever around."

"Well I'd love to see you when you are. Maybe we can go visit your sister in the Keys." He was back to flirting, so I was off the hook. "Call me sometime."

"I will, soon. Nice seeing you again, man."

He'd barely walked away when Corinne set in. "You really should come visit. I know it's soon, but please, please come to my birthday party. You could use a few days in paradise."

Her green eyes fixed on mine as I tried to refuse.

"I told you, I'm booked." It wasn't impossible since I arranged my own schedule, but she didn't know that.

"Please try. You'll love it. The water is crystal blue. And there's great fishing."

I chuckled. "You hate fishing." Saving fish and their habitat had become her life's work.

She smiled. "But you love it."

"I'll look into it, but don't get your hopes up."

CHAPTER 3

HAYDEN

I stepped out of the airport into the warm Florida air.

The luxury black SUV that waited on the curb looked like it was straight out of a motorcade. The driver leaned against the passenger door holding a sign bearing my name. He waved when he saw me staring. He couldn't have been more than twenty. "Mr. Kincaid?"

"Guilty as charged."

"Welcome to the Keys. I hope you had a nice trip." He took my carryon and headed toward the back of the car.

"Not bad at all," I lied, following him. Seven hours with a connection in Dallas sucked. I wiped the sweat beads from my forehead. "Hot out today for March, isn't it?"

"Hot out in March is normal in the Keys. That's why the snowbirds migrate here." He chuckled as he opened the back door for me.

My shirt stuck to my back as I slid into the seat. I wasn't expecting such balmy conditions.

The driver smiled into the rearview mirror after we pulled onto the highway. "First time in Key West, I take it?"

"Indeed. My sister lives here, up in Marathon actually, but it's my first visit to the Keys." At least Corinne wouldn't be able to hold it over my head anymore.

"Hopefully the first of many."

This trip should get me off the hook for while. But it'd be rude to say "I hope not," so I lied. "If I'm lucky."

Within a few minutes, the roadside businesses became sparse. A few minutes more and the two-lane highway lined by mangroves was virtually desolate. Crossing a bridge, water bluer than I'd ever imagined extended into infinity on both sides. The tiny strip of land wasn't much wider than the road at times and then turned to a dense mangrove hammock again.

A large rectangular sign warned *Key Deer Area Speeding Fines Doubled*. "What's a Key deer?"

"The tiny deer that live around here. They're protected."

I stared at the mangrove marsh out the window. They'd have to be small to get between the tangled trees. "How big is tiny?"

"About the size of a Labrador."

I chuckled. "Hardly worth hunting anyway then, aren't they?"

He didn't laugh. Tough crowd.

A few bridges later, we hung a left into a large paved lot with a sprawling thatched-roof pavilion. A carved wooden sign hung over the long dock extending out into the calm crystal water. *Welcome to Paradise.*

It looked more like the Caribbean than any place I've ever been in the US.

The driver came around to open my door but I'd already beat him to it. He carried my bag down to the dock.

"The boat will be here in a couple of minutes." He pointed to a shape on the horizon growing larger by the second. A pretty blonde in a floral dress appeared from the reception building, smiling as she handed me a tall glass of something that looked fruity, complete with a miniature paper umbrella. "Mr. Kincaid?"

I smiled as she handed me the glass. "That would be me. Does everyone get this reception or only the VIPs?"

"All our guests are VIPs on Paradise Key." At two grand a night she was probably right.

I sipped the refreshing concoction of tropical juices. She waited to take my glass when the boat approached the dock. The hospitality was certainly five-star.

She smiled warmly. "Enjoy your stay."

While I hadn't had much hope of that an hour ago, it seemed a far more likely possibility now. "That shouldn't be difficult. Thank you very much."

The boat picked up speed as we left the dock behind and cut through the surface of the shimmering sheet of glass stretching to the horizon. It was prettier than any postcard. Corinne was in her element all right.

A few minutes later the island came into view. My jaw dropped at the bungalows built out over the glistening water. There was no doubt about it—Paradise Key was aptly named.

The boat slowed as we turned around the back side of the island, skirting a sandy beach to land alongside a long wooden dock. A man in a white linen uniform helped me off the boat. "Mr. Kincaid?"

I was starting to feel like a celebrity with everyone knowing my name. "Hayden. And you are?"

"Manuel." He shook my hand firmly. "Mr. Barnes asked me to show you to the bar." Clifton, I presumed.

"Mr. Barnes must know me quite well, even though we've never met."

Manuel chuckled. By the time we reached the end of the dock, Corinne was trotting down the stairs of a gorgeous white house with indigo shutters. "Hayden!" She flung her arms around my neck, nearly knocking me over in the sand. "I can't believe you're here!"

"Me neither." I scanned the beach. "It's beautiful. And so are you. Did you get a haircut?"

Her fingers trailed over the golden waves on her shoulder. "I did. And a facial, manicure, pedicure and massage. Violet and I had a spa day yesterday, compliments of Clifton."

"Perks of private island life."

Her smile was brighter than the sun overhead. "There are many. You'll see." Her hand slid around my waist and she leaned into my side as she steered me toward the stairs. "Clifton can't wait to meet you."

The feeling was mutual. I liked him already.

When a tall, casually-dressed man of fifty at most stood from a table by the window to shake my hand, I did a double take. I'd expected someone older and more extravagant. Corinne's palm turned up. "Meet our gracious host and creator of Paradise Key, Clifton Barnes."

He shook my hand with a firm grip. "Hayden, I've heard all about you."

I threw Corinne a quick glance. Surely she wouldn't have shared anything personal. "I'd say you can't believe everything my sister says, but since she speaks highly of you, that might not be appropriate."

Clifton laughed. "She's honest to a fault."

Corinne made her opinions known. He seemed to know her well. "From what she says, she honestly loves Paradise Key, and I can see why. Thanks so much for inviting me. And for treating my sister so well."

He waved off the gratitude. "It's truly my pleasure." Clifton's smiling eyes lingered on Corinne. My overprotective big brother instinct questioned his motives. But if a handsome billionaire had eyes for my sister, and she was game, who was I to judge an age gap?

Clifton held out his hand to signal the door we'd just come through. "Shall we move to the terrace for a cocktail?"

While sipping rumrunners on the porch, Clifton described how he'd brought his vision of a luxury eco-resort to fruition. He wasn't afraid of hard work, that was for sure. I imagined he'd greased several palms along the way to make it happen. He was remarkably humble for a billionaire, but his money helped get him what he wanted. I wondered if that would be the case with my sister. She was far from a gold digger but that much money would tempt anyone. Their easy way spoke of mutual admiration. But it was hard to tell if there might be a spark of something more than that.

Corinne's face lit up in an even bigger smile and she waved, looking past me. I turned to see a woman in a brightly colored blouse—a splash of coral against the lush green of the tropical landscape. Slender, tanned arms swung at her side while long legs carried her in hurried strides.

"Finally. There's Violet."

Fuck, *that* was Violet? After Corinne had hinted heavily that I should meet her, I knew I'd better keep my distance. But the closer she got to us, the closer I wanted her to be. The layers of her raven hair seem to absorb all the light and reflect it back in an almost iridescent shine, like an oil slick.

Full lips painted the same shade as her blouse spread in a smile as she glided up the stairs. Oversized black sunglasses accentuated her delicate features. She looked like Jackie O in Nantucket.

"Sorry I'm late. I had some things to wrap up."

I was so busy staring that I forgot my manners. Clifton reminded me when he stood to greet Violet. "Doing your job is a good excuse, not that you need one."

I stood and extended my hand. "Nice to meet you, Violet."

Corinne grinned up from her chair. "Violet, meet Hayden." She said it with a teenaged playfulness that made my cheeks blush.

Violet pushed her glasses up onto her head and eyes so black they looked almost purple met mine as she shook my hand. "It's a pleasure. Corinne talks about you all the time."

Her thick Southern drawl that seemed mismatched to her exotic beauty caught me by surprise. I chuckled. “So I hear.“ I glanced at my sister. “Only the good stuff, I hope.“

Violet grinned as she took the seat across from me. “Naturally.”

The waitress had a rumrunner in her hand by the time I’d settled back into my chair, along with a fresh round for the rest of us. “So nice you could make it for Corinne’s big birthday bash. She was over the moon at the news.”

I flashed my sister a smile. “I wouldn’t miss it for the world.”

Violet looked admiringly at Corinne. “You must be as proud of her as we all are.”

A warmth stirred in my chest both for my sister’s accomplishments and the support system she’d found on a remote island. “She is the most impressive woman I know.”

Clifton interjected. “We’re lucky to have her. I’m lucky to have both these ladies here. Trailblazers.” Clifton smiled. “Violet is giving the whole resort a face lift before a magazine crew comes in a couple of weeks.” His gaze shifted to Violet. “You will most definitely get the credit when Condé Nast is here.”

“I’m just doing my job.”

“Superbly.” Clifton lifted his glass with a nod.

“Violet studied at Cornell.” Corinne smiled proudly at her friend. “And Princeton too, right?“

Violet waved a hand dismissively. “He doesn’t want to hear that.”

An Ivy League southern belle who looked like a Persian princess. Of course I wanted to hear more. "Sure I do. What did you study?"

"Tourism and Hospitality in undergrad. International Business in grad school." She said it like it was nothing to brag about.

"Top of your class at Princeton, if I recall." Clifton hadn't forgotten that impressive detail.

Violet's dark eyes rolled under a thick fan of long lashes. "Are you buttering me up for a favor? The flattery isn't necessary if you have another impossible task for me before the interview."

Sassy with her boss, she just got sexier.

Clifton's grin said he enjoyed the banter. "What you call flattery is simply the truth." Gushing compliments was part of his charm, but Clifton seemed sincere. He was smart enough to surround himself with people he admired. His was a bubble curated with competence. No dumbasses allowed. Must be nice.

Corinne must've worried I'd feel left out of the bragging when she blurted, "Hayden's a software engineer." It sounded mundane by comparison.

Clifton nodded. "Corinne mentioned you travel a lot for work. Anywhere exciting?"

"I have accounts all over the US. One city blurs into the next but I try to find excitement everywhere I go."

Violet flashed a smile. "I bet you have a nose for it."

I grinned before I sipped my cocktail down to the ice to keep myself from asking if she was implying that I could sniff out a good time.

Clifton chuckled as he stood. "I'm terribly sorry to have to leave you, but I have a dinner date with a local historian. They have a table for you on the terrace upstairs, perfect for sunset. Violet has your keys. She can show you to your room if you'd like to freshen up before dinner."

The sun was already low in the sky. I shook my head. "We don't want to miss sunset. And I'm famished." After two rumrunners on an empty stomach, Violet showing me my room could be dangerous.

CHAPTER 4

VIOLET

My face turned up to absorb the last of the sun's rays as the sky lit in a brilliant display. "I never get tired of this."

"It's spectacular." Hayden grinned. "Even more beautiful than I imagined."

I tried to ignore his aquamarine eyes lingering on me and the sharp angle of his square jaw. From the way Corinne smiled, I thought I wasn't imagining his attention. She smirked at her brother. "I told you you'd love it here."

Clifton had arranged a tasting menu with wine pairings. We savored samples of three appetizers with our best Pinot Grigio. Judging from the *mmm*s and *ahhs,* Hayden appreciated our award-winning chef's fare. Corinne beamed at her brother's delight.

Seeing her so happy filled my heart. Hayden was not only easy on the eyes. He was good company with his quiet demeanor that was more mysterious than aloof. Details had to be extracted.

I settled back into my chair after we finished the first course. "Breckenridge must be nice right now. Spring skiing is my favorite."

Hayden nodded with an easy smile. "As long as there's powder on top, it's my favorite too. Otherwise, the icy slopes kind of suck."

Corinne chimed in. "Violet's family has a ski lodge in Jackson Hole." I wished she hadn't reminded me.

Hayden's eyes lit up. "Oh, really? I love Wyoming. But I usually go in summer."

"Summer skiing is not nearly as nice." I chuckled. "But the hiking is gorgeous."

Hayden grinned. "And the fishing. Some of the best in the country."

"They say the same about the Keys." I smirked at Corinne. "But we don't like to talk about that much, do we?"

"I'm not going to bash fishing since it's why my brother *finally* came to see me." Her fingers ran across her lips like she was zipping them closed.

Hayden scowled but with a hint of a grin. "I came to see you, for your birthday party. But I do love to fish."

I chuckled. "Mountain fishing is a different animal."

Hayden's amused eyes twinkled. "Usually trout in my case. Do you ever go fishing when you're back home?"

I figured he meant Wyoming. "Home is Georgia. That's where I learned to tie a fly." When I was still the apple of my daddy's eye and he was still my hero. By the time he bought the lodge in Jackson Hole I was a jaded adolescent who knew him for what he was. A lying cheat. No one ever talked about that though. "I've done my fair share of fishing in Wyoming, too, but I mostly only go in winter now." For the holidays—when I had to.

He shook his head, mouth hanging open like he couldn't believe it. "You're missing out."

Corinne swirled her wine in her glass with a smile. "I don't know, winters are the best for skiing. Or spring in this case. I hope you get epic spring skiing this trip." Her gaze shifted to Hayden and she explained. "Violet has to go out for a quick family visit. If I weren't going to be sixty feet underwater I'd insist on going along for moral support. And the skiing, of course."

"I'd sure love to have you there, for both." I looked toward Hayden. "You must be on the slopes every weekend."

Hayden's eyes darted toward Corinne briefly before returning to mine as he answered. "Not so much anymore. I travel so much these days." He looked relieved at the interruption when the waitress brought our main course.

The sommelier poured from a bottle of Cabernet that I knew cost $500 wholesale. "The hint of currant complements the lamb nicely. I'll leave you the bottle." He smiled confidently but I could see the yearning for approval in his eyes. Even when I wasn't on duty, I was still the boss. Thank God for Corinne. She was the only person around regularly who wasn't constantly trying to impress me. Ironically she was often the person who impressed me the most.

She described the work they had planned in the underwater lab with childlike enthusiasm. "Fabien Cousteau said they collected ten years of data in their month on Aquarius."

Hayden grimaced. "That sounds exhausting. But I know it doesn't feel like work when you're doing what you love."

I chuckled. "I beg to differ. I love my job, but it's been feeling a lot like work lately."

His grin was as suggestive as his tone. "Then you're not doing it right."

I blinked, ignoring the heat rising to my face. "That's probably a fair statement. I'm just making it up as I go here."

Hayden shrugged off my modesty. "By the looks of things you're doing it well."

I tried not to let his compliments go to my head, but they stirred a flutter in my gut. "Appearances are everything in this business."

Corinne's hand covered her glass when Hayden tried to pour her another of the expensive Cabernet. "I have to drive back to Marathon tonight."

Hayden's eyes grew wide. He was surprised as I was that she wasn't spending the night. "Oh, I assumed you were staying here."

"I wish. I have a meeting with the Aquarius team at nine."

I blinked at her in disbelief. "It's nearly 10 o'clock." And she knew she could stay in a staff cabin anytime she wanted.

"I know. I need to run to catch the boat. I'll have to skip dessert. But I'll make up for it with lots of cake tomorrow. You two carry on." She shot me a smile.

Hayden looked around after Corinne walked away like he couldn't assimilate what just happened. His lips pursed before he declared, "Well, that was odd."

It wasn't odd at all though. It was all part of the set up. Get us liquored up before her hasty exit. I hoped she hadn't chatted him up about me. At least then it'd be easier to pretend like it wasn't a set up.

"It's a shame she has such a commute." It kept us from spending as much time together as we'd like. "If I had my way she'd live out here. But since she's also my lifeline to the rest of the world, I guess it's good that she doesn't."

"It must be tough living where you work. When do you get to unwind?"

"I'm not sure I remember what that means." I chuckled. "Corinne gets me off the island for a night out from time to time."

"It's the opposite for me. Since I travel for work so much, I make a point to go out as much as I can wherever I am. It keeps me from working all my waking hours."

I imagined him quite the playboy. He probably had a girl in every city. "Sounds exciting. I miss civilization sometimes, but after five years in Manhattan, I'm happy with the peace and quiet most of the time."

The sommelier returned to pour the dessert wines, with the waiter on his heels serving samples of the chocolate mousse, Key lime pie, and a divinely delicate miniature crème brûlée. Delaney was such a pro. The presentation itself was deserving of the Michelin star that she was in the running for. But the complex flavors she weaved into her beautiful creations was what set her apart. No one could eat her chocolate mousse without moaning out loud, which I did before I asked, "So what do you do to unwind when you're home?"

His shoulders stiffened briefly but then relaxed with his smile. "I'm there so little that I usually have to catch up on house projects on the weekends."

"Ah, that would explain no skiing then."

His smile was warm, but his eyes were sad. "I suppose it does." He took a deep breath, stretching his long legs out as he leaned back in his chair and patted his flat belly. "That is the best meal I've ever had in my life."

"Our chef is magnificent."

His green eyes settled on mine in the lull of silence. My heart pounded as I fought the urge to look away.

"Oh gosh, you haven't even checked in." My face flushed when I realized I still had to show him to his room.

His gaze didn't waver. "I'm in no hurry, but I'm not at work."

"Unfortunately I have a list of things I didn't finish today that I have to do before I can enjoy myself at the party tomorrow."

He held up his hand, understanding. "If you'll point me to my room I'll let you get some rest."

"Don't be silly. I'll walk you over there." I couldn't send him traipsing across the island in the dark.

Hayden held the door for me on the way out and complimented the grounds as we strolled the brick-paved path to the east side of the island. I realized he hadn't gotten a tour before I arrived. He identified several species of palms and tropical plants along the way.

"You know an awful lot about plants for a software engineer."

He chuckled. "I took a botany class as an elective in undergrad and loved it. Maybe that was my true calling."

"Tech is certainly far more lucrative. You probably made a good choice."

"Money's not everything." His grin sparkled in the moonlight. "I'm just kidding. I did find it fascinating, though. Take the violet, for example."

I cocked my head to listen as we walked.

"The ionine in them temporarily paralyzes your ability to smell the flower. So they smell sweet one minute, then like nothing the next."

I'd actually read that violets can short-circuit our sense of smell before. My namesake flower was one of the few plants I knew anything about. "Ah, yes, the ever-elusive violet."

I directed him to turn left off the path onto a wooden walkway that extended over the water. "Christ, this place is magical."

I laughed as I led him up the steps to his bungalow. "Wait until you see it in daylight. It's phenomenal."

The moonlight glimmered off the water on both sides of the small wooden porch, lighting the green in his eyes. My heart skipped a beat when he locked my gaze again, his voice peppered with confidence. "I guess I have something to look forward to."

I looked down, concentrating on keeping a steady hand as I tapped the key card on the reader. I avoided his eyes as I handed him the card. "Your bag should be inside. Let me know if there's anything else you need."

"Thanks, I will."

I smiled and started to turn away but his broad hand caught my elbow. I forced my gaze up to his.

The faintest smile lingered on his lips, like he was trying to hide it. "I'm sorry if my sister treating this like it was a blind date put you on the spot."

I was grateful for the darkness to hide my flaming face. "Corinne is just a tad delusional, but she means well."

Hayden let go of my arm, his smile spreading. "Pushy at times, but well-intentioned nonetheless."

"I doubt you need any help with that anyway." I don't know why I said it. I wished I hadn't immediately because it sounded like flirting, and I definitely wasn't flirting with my best friend's brother.

He chuckled smugly. "I do alright."

"I bet you do." My cheeks were on fire and I wanted to look away because he had Cassanova written all over his cocky face. But I kept a steady smile. "Don't worry about Corinne. I'm just ignoring it. We can just pretend that awkward little moment didn't happen."

He nodded with a shrug. "That's probably best."

And darn near impossible.

CHAPTER 5

HAYDEN

Still half asleep, I pulled back the curtains and squinted as my eyes adjusted to the bright morning sun. "Fuck me," I muttered as I took in the view of the terrace overlooking the bay, complete with a round cedar jacuzzi.

The luxurious room was more striking in the daylight. White linens covered the most comfortable bed I'd felt in years. A sofa the same deep blue color as the sea sat alongside a minibar that was stocked with miniature bottles of top-shelf liquors.

The Nespresso machine was a nice touch. I took a coffee out to the terrace, propping my feet up on the railing to soak up the sun. Calm crystal-clear water stretched out like a glass blanket.

With Corinne in meetings I had the day to myself. And this looked like the perfect place to spend it.

Eventually my growling stomach forced me to the restaurant. I regretted having practically inhaled the lobster omelette, wishing I'd savored it more when the best breakfast I could remember was finished.

I was signing the check when Clifton's smiling face appeared. "Good morning Hayden. Did you enjoy your first night on the island?"

"I did. Thank you again for your generosity. This place is amazing."

"Corinne mentioned that you like to fish."

"Love it is probably more accurate. Though I must admit I have little experience with ocean fishing. I got into flyfishing when I was in college in Boulder. But I've never been deep-sea fishing."

"Hopefully we'll remedy that."

"That's the goal."

"I'll have Violet arrange a charter for you."

"Oh, you are too kind. I don't want to take advantage of your generosity. Please don't go to any trouble. Corinne mentioned a charter out of Marathon."

"It's no trouble at all." Clifton patted my shoulder as he continued. "The charters that we work with are"— he paused to search for a tactful way of saying it—"a higher caliber experience. I insist. Violet will get back to you with the details as soon as she's got it booked."

"Thank you again." I winced internally at adding another task to Violet's workload that already had her a little frazzled. "You're too kind."

"We're all like family out here." He grinned. "So, by proxy, you are too. No thanks are necessary. Please—enjoy yourself."

"With this VIP treatment in paradise, that shouldn't be a problem. I'm looking forward to a relaxing day on your beautiful island."

"Let me know if you need anything at all. Or Violet. She'll be happy to help."

While I loved the idea of a gorgeous personal concierge, I wanted to keep her out of it. "I'll be fine."

The humid tropical breeze rustled my hair as I stepped onto the beige brick path to set out to explore. An enormous infinity pool looked like it disappeared into the tranquil bay. Another spot worthy of a visit for a pina colada from the tiki bar at its edge later.

I wandered on toward the white sandy beach I could see beyond the dock in the distance. A chocolate labradoodle bounded into the calm sea after a tennis ball that a smiling brunette chucked from the shore. She waved with expectant eyes. I raised my hand and waved timidly, thinking she had mistaken me for someone she knew before she said my name.

"Hayden, I'm glad to see you made it all right."

I cocked my head. "I did, thank you. And you are?"

"Oh goodness. Where are my manners? I'm sorry. She wiped her hand wet from the ball on her shorts before extending it to me. "I'm Tessa, the event planner here at Paradise Key. And happy to call your sister a friend. She talks about you all the time."

"Thank you, that's nice to hear." Even if it made me wonder what she might have said.

"She showed me your Instagram. That's how I recognized you."

"Ah." She must've scrolled through a bunch of photos of food and craft beers to find a face shot. My profile was mostly a chronicle of favorite spots I'd found in my frequent travels.

Social media was not my thing, but the updates kept my family happy. Bonus: it was a good reference for when I returned to a city to remind me of the places that had impressed me.

"Event planner, you said? Does that mean you arranged my sister‘s party this evening?"

"I did, indeed. In fact, I better get going. I have to be sure the stage is ready for the band when they get here."

"Oh nice. I didn't realize that there will be live music."

"There are two bands," she beamed. "But don't tell Corinne. We hired mariachis to surprise her with the cake."

"Your secret is safe with me. See you there."

Tessa clipped the leash onto her dog's collar. "Can't wait! Enjoy your day." She trotted down the beach around the mangroves, the dog running alongside.

I followed the path through the lush center of the island. The tropical vegetation was starkly different from the Rocky Mountain landscape I was accustomed to. Both beautiful in their own way, but after a harsh winter that didn't seem to want to give way to spring, the balmy island beauty was a welcome escape.

It was so hidden amongst the palms and dense landscaping that I didn't notice a second pool area until I'd nearly passed it. It was a much smaller pool, shaded and secluded by the trees. Yet another spot I could wile away several hours.

To think I'd been worried I'd be bored on a tiny island for four days. I looked forward to the fishing but had dreaded the down time. Not anymore.

Back at my stilted bungalow, I soaked in the Jacuzzi on the terrace until my skin was pruned. Then I started a medical suspense book I bought in Denver International while I dried in the sun.

I got so lost in the story I lost track of time until my dry throat alerted me that I was parched. No wonder. Two hours had passed. I chugged a bottle of Perrier from the mini bar before tucking my book under my arm and heading across the island to the pool bar.

I'd gotten deep into the book again when Corinne finally responded to my happy birthday text.

Sorry, I've been swamped. I hope you're having fun. Party's at six but I'll be there by five.

I chuckled at her worrying over me as I replied.

I'm having a blast doing nothing. Don't stress on your birthday. See you when you get here.

It was the most relaxed I'd been in years. I baked in the sun with my book until the sweltering heat finally got to me. I wiped the sweat beads from my brow and moved under the thatched shade of the tiki bar. It was piña colada time. The chill of the frozen concoction spread in my chest as I sipped and scanned the turquoise horizon.

The corners of my mouth tugged into a smile when I heard words I couldn't make out in the sweet Southern drawl I knew belonged to Violet. I spotted her approaching on the path at a determined clip. She had a serious look when she got to the bar, holding up a hand to apologize for continuing her phone call.

"I understand that, but we don't have two weeks. We need it here by the fourteenth at the latest. Make it happen."

Her dark brow creased, drawing in a deep breath as she listened. "I'm sure you'll find a way. Send it overnight as soon as you source it." She let out such a huff I thought she might deflate. But her eyes lit up in a smile. "You're just the man I'm looking for."

I cocked a brow. "You don't say? Maybe my sister was right after all."

Violet's tanned skin didn't hide her blushing cheeks before she snapped back into business mode. "Clifton asked me to arrange your fishing charter. I'm waiting to hear back from two of them."

I winced. "Yeah, sorry about that. I hope it's not too much trouble with everything else you're juggling."

She shrugged. "All part of the job. But I'm afraid it might not happen tomorrow. It's busy—spring break and all. But Monday shouldn't be a problem."

"No worries. A day to recover after the party probably isn't a bad thing."

Violet's smile spread. "Tell me about it. I still have a million things to do in the next two hours. Thank God I'm off tomorrow."

"I'd recommend a lazy pool day. And a piña colada." I grinned, holding up my glass. "Instant stress relief."

Visions of her long, tanned legs in a bikini made me shift on my stool.

"If I make it out of bed at all," she called, turning to head back to the main building.

Violet in bed all day was an even better vision. And one I knew I'd better get out of my head.

CHAPTER 6

VIOLET

The party was in full swing by the time I showed up half an hour late. Corinne was already on the dance floor boogying to an impressive rendition of Señorita by Shawn Mendes.

Tessa had outdone herself on the decorations. Red, white, and green streamers ran from a star-shaped piñata in the center of the room. The buffet table was set with steam trays for the taco bar. Rosa, the head server smiled as she approached with a tray of martini glasses with salted rims.

"Margarita?"

She certainly didn't have to ask me twice. "Si, por favor."

Even with a decent vocabulary and a lot of effort, I sounded more Southern when I spoke Spanish than I did in my native tongue. I sipped the drink down before I went to join the birthday girl on the dance floor.

"Happy birthday, beautiful. Your Mexican fiesta is amazing."

Corinne threw her arms around my neck, sloshing my drink onto the floor. "Thank you so much. It's incredible. I can't believe you guys did this for me."

"Thank Tessa and Clifton. My only role in this party was to show up and drink."

"Cheers to that!" Corinne clinked her glass to mine before finishing what was left in it in a single gulp. I scanned the crowd of scientific types around her. "Where's your brother?"

Corinne looked around before she shrugged. "He was just here. He said you had a nice talk after I left last night." Her brows raised. "Did you two hit it off?"

"Yes, we did have a nice conversation. But there will be no hitting it off, Madame Cupid. So you can knock it off."

She rolled her eyes and waved. "Lighten up. I'm just messing with you."

I looked back at the crowd. "Are these your colleagues?"

"Yep, along with a couple of the new Coast Guard recruits." She nodded toward the two handsome young men chatting with Clifton. "Maybe one of them will tickle your fancy."

Corinne knew that I hadn't had sex since I left Michael. Nearly seven months since I'd seen the texts on his phone that he'd tried to explain away. But it'd been easy to piece together evidence of the affair. Far easier than picking up the pieces of my broken heart.

Three of my last four boyfriends had cheated so it probably shouldn't have surprised me. But they hadn't put a two carat diamond on my finger. I suppose the silver lining was that

Michael's betrayal let me focus on what I truly loved—my job. Sex was the last thing on my mind.

I was glad Corinne had moved on from her brother to trying to set me up with Coast Guard cadets, but I'd like it better if she'd just stop altogether. "I can tickle my own fancy, thank you very much."

She chuckled. "It's not the same."

"My vibrator does not disappoint." That was more than I could say for any man I'd ever known.

Corinne bit her lip that curled into a mischievous grin. "Sounds like a great birthday gift idea."

We were giggling like schoolgirls when Hayden's deep voice interrupted from behind me.

"What's a great gift idea? I haven't gotten you anything yet."

A heat spread in my chest that flushed my face when I lifted my gaze to his aquamarine eyes.

I warned Corinne with wide eyes not to go there. She rolled her eyes before turning to Hayden. "You coming here is the best birthday present ever. But you can get us a round of Quitapenas if you insist."

Hayden winced, chuckling. "You're the birthday girl. Don't blame me for your sore head tomorrow."

Corinne and I danced until he returned with three tall shot glasses between his fingers. "Quitapenas, señoritas."

I spoke enough Spanish to know the name Quitapenas- *worry remover*- was misleading. Tequila took away your worries, but not for long. But I'd take temporary stress relief for now.

I took the lime wedge from the rim and held my breath as I threw back the shot. It went down smooth but the afterburn set in a second later. My face scrunched. "Tequila is never a good idea."

"Oh, shush. Tequila is *always* a good idea. Especially on my birthday." Corinne's eyes sparkled with the colors of the stage lights.

Hayden handed me a margarita from Rosa's tray as she passed. "Margarita chaser to top it off?"

I hesitated, knowing a glass of water would be the intelligent alternative. But it'd be rude to refuse, and a margarita sounded like more fun. "Sure, why not?"

Hayden seemed to loosen up when the liquor kicked in. We all did. That's the slippery slope of tequila. Liquid courage makes you forget your troubles. But the real trouble was that it usually made me forget everything else too. Restraint didn't even occur to me again until Tessa announced that it was taco time. Food was a good idea.

After wolfing down two chicken tacos and chugging a glass of water, I felt renewed.

The band kicked off again and we took to the dance floor alongside the crowd of marine scientists and dolphin trainers. Corinne was in her element. We danced like fools. Hayden's moves surprised me considering his somewhat conservative nature. But alcohol was good for shedding inhibitions.

It seemed like only minutes had passed when the band wound down another bluesy number and set their instruments down without a farewell. I looked around, confused until I spotted the mariachi band file in quietly through the kitchen door. They assembled side-by-side virtually unnoticed before they started strumming Feliz Cumpleaños.

Corinne's face broke into a broad grin when she turned.

"Oh my god. You know I love mariachis! I can't believe you did this!"

I smiled. "I might have mentioned it to Tessa."

Corinne basked in the serenade, unaware at first as Delaney approached. Her face lit up when she caught sight of the towering three-tiered cake aflame with twenty-nine sparklers. Delaney grinned as she pushed the cart to the end of the buffet table. We were drawn to the cake like moths to a flame.

When the mariachis finished the Spanish version, they played the English version of "Happy Birthday" so that we could all join in. By the time we finished the sparklers had burned down to nubs.

Corinne's hands covered her mouth. "Thankfully I don't have to blow out all those candles. It's nearly too many to count." She smiled at Delaney. "The cake is beautiful, thank you."

Delaney grinned and leaned in to hug her. "It's Gus's creation, but thank you. Happy birthday." She handed Corinne a triangular spatula. "You should do the honors."

Corinne carved out a generous wedge, handing the plate to Hayden with a smile. "You deserve the first piece for *finally* coming to visit."

I felt a tinge of jealousy at her genuine admiration for her big brother. My siblings and I hadn't drifted apart exactly. More like we'd scattered as soon as we could. Melissa left for boarding school in New England when she was thirteen. I barely knew her at age seven, and she rarely returned—only for holidays and the occasional obligatory family vacation, until she had a family of her own.

Clay stuck around until college. But even in high school he was so dedicated to academics that he barely noticed I was around at all. I was the athletic younger sister that probably reminded him of all the things he wasn't to our father. Mama drove me all over the state and clear to Florida for tennis tournaments while he flew off to national science fairs to win awards on his own. By then our happy family had all but disintegrated anyway, and no one wanted to talk about why. Dad bought the ski lodge and spent most of his time there, which no one seemed to mind.

When we were all together, though, we pretended like everything was normal. But pretending was as good as it got. There was never the sort of bond between any of us that I saw between Hayden and Corinne.

Hayden turned with his plate containing the giant wedge of cake, a joyful grin on his lips that flattened with concern when he looked in my eyes. "You alright?"

That's when I realized that tears had welled up in my eyes. I tried to blink them back but that only pushed them out. I brushed them away with my fingertips, sniffling. "Oh yeah, I'm fine. I just love your sister so much." The tequila was making me emotional.

"Someone loves her a lot to know that chocolate chip cake with fudge frosting has been her favorite since she was three.
"

"I didn't know it went back that far." But it was me who'd suggested the flavor.

"Our grandmother made this cake from scratch every year for her birthday since she was three." He eyed the giant chunk of cake. "Share this with me?"

"Good idea." I didn't feel much like sweets. After all that tequila all I wanted was more tequila. But I followed Hayden to the porch where we sat on the steps. I let him feed me a few bites of the birthday cake. The tiki lights lining the beach in the distance flickered off the black mirror of the bay.

After we finished the cake, Hayden set the plate off to the side. The silence was so comfortable it seemed totally natural when my weight drifted gently and slowly into his shoulder. And just as naturally, his arm moved up my back to draw me in closer.

"My sister is lucky to have you, you know?" His lips on my temple made me gasp a little before I swallowed it down. We'd only just met yesterday but I felt like I'd known him for years.

"She's lucky to have you too." So fucking lucky. "And we're both lucky to have her."

His fingers tightened around my shoulder and for a brief moment the smell of him was all that I could think of. Then I remembered that he was Corrine's brother and therefore absolutely off limits.

My back straightened as I turned to face him. "That's why this can't happen. You know that right?"

His hands drifted up in resigned surrender. "Yes, of course."

Neither of us wanted to jeopardize our relationship with Corinne. It was too important to both of us. *She* was too important.

"Good. Let's go dance." I jumped to my feet. "I'm ready for another margarita. How about you?"

"*Una mas* is a very dangerous thing, especially after you've already had *cuatro o cinco,* but I like danger."

I grinned at how easily the Spanish numbers rolled off his tongue.

Uno turned into *dos,* then *tres* margaritas that went down like lemonade as we danced to at least a dozen more pop tunes. Corinne had taken a liking to one of the Coast Guard cadets enough to let him dance close. When she didn't seem to mind his hands drifting, I figured the party would be winding down soon. The band seemed to follow her cues, wishing her a happy birthday before they bid us farewell.

I brushed back the strands of hair stuck to my face, panting for breath. "Maybe we should give your sister some privacy."

Hayden's lips spread in a relieved grin. "That's a fantastic idea. Nightcap on the beach?"

The night still felt young in our tequila-filled time warp. Hayden didn't want the party to end any more than I did. But being tipsy on the beach for all the staff to see wasn't appealing. Even if it was only the two security guards who might take note. It didn't feel right.

"Or we could make a nightcap back at my cabin. I have a hot tub." From the sultry sparkle in his stare, I realized the last part might've come out a little more suggestive than I'd intended. "I mean, just to relax and rinse off."

His warm smile relieved my embarrassment. "I didn't think otherwise. Sounds like a great plan." He held out his hand. "Lead the way."

I glanced at Corinne, engrossed with the Coast Guard hottie. The smarter plan would be to take my drunk heinie to bed but oftentimes the intelligent choices aren't the fun ones. I strolled confidently out the door ahead of Hayden.

CHAPTER 7

HAYDEN

I probably should've known better when Violet suggested tequila shots. Everyone knows they make your clothes come off, especially after half a dozen margaritas. And our clothes were already off, well, practically. Violet had changed into a one-piece suit but I'd had nothing but my boxer briefs to wear into the jacuzzi on her private patio.

The shots went down smooth with Pink Floyd tunes wafting up into the darkness. *Comfortably Numb* pretty much summed up what I had become.

As I settled back into the bubbling water, I pondered the ambiguous connection I'd noticed between my sister and Clifton. "I was pretty surprised to see Corinne flirting with the Coast Guard guy. I kind of thought she had a thing with Clifton."

Violet's face twisted as she shook her head. "Oh, God no. I mean he loves her, but like family. He would never."

I shrugged. "Goes to show what I know."

Violet laughed. "Corinne would never go there either. She has boundaries."

I chuckled. "I suppose we all do." The fire in her eyes as she reached for the tequila made me want to cross them all though.

Violet's shoulders swayed as she sang along with a Green Day song while pouring two more shots.

We laughed and sang at the tops of our lungs. The good time awakened a tingling in my groin but I was glad my cock was still sleeping soundly. It seemed to know that Violet was off-limits. But when her hand lingered on my chest, the boundaries we'd drawn blurred.

Our gaze locked for a long second and before I knew it her lips were on mine with a magnetic force. I tried to pull away but her hands slid over my wet skin, up my back and into my hair, holding me close as our tongues entwined. Any residual hesitation dissolved in the warm bubbles.

Arms and legs writhing, we swallowed each other up in desperate gulps. I struggled to hold one hand on the edge of the hot tub to keep us above the gurgling surface. When Violet started tugging at my boxers insistently, I had my wits about me enough to know we better get out of the water or we might drown. I squirmed over the edge and nudged her to climb out of the tub.

I took a step back, holding my hand up between us like it could stop the attraction. "Wait, didn't we say this can't happen?"

Her eyes leveled on me, defiant. "We're both consenting adults. We can do what we want. And I want to, don't you?"

The water drops glistening on her chest and the way she bit her lip made my cock twitch. "Of course I want to. You're fucking gorgeous." Not to mention amazing.

Violet grabbed my wrist and dragged me into her bungalow. "Stop thinking so much. We can be discreet. It's just sex."

I was good at just sex. An expert. But my attraction for her went beyond physical, and I could tell from the way she leaned into me like she belonged there earlier on the porch, that the feeling was mutual. My fingers wrapped around her wrists, squeezing to hold her at bay. "Maybe I should just go. I don't want you to do something you might regret." Or something that might end up hurting her. My sister would never forgive me.

Violet's steely gaze locked mine, determined. "The only thing I'd regret is letting you leave." She shook free of my hold and hooked the waistband of my wet boxers, grinning as she pushed them down to the floor. "But I'm not going to do that."

She stepped in close, her hands on my butt drawing my hips to hers. "I haven't had sex in a really long time. Will you just shut up and fuck me, please?"

Her demanding desire trumped all doubt. I wanted her just as bad, not just for the sex, but to know her more deeply. I couldn't resist.

Heat blazed in my chest as I tore the straps of her swimsuit off her shoulders, stopping to admire her full breasts glistening in the lamp light. "Fuck, you're beautiful." Her arms snaked up my back to pull her naked chest to mine as I pushed the suit over her hips. Throbbing with want, I was harder than I'd ever thought possible after all that tequila. I hadn't been this horny since...forever.

"You're the sexiest man I've ever laid eyes on, Hayden Kincaid. And I wanted to taste you on my lips the first time we spoke." She pulled me to her mouth.

I broke from the kiss to look into her onyx eyes. "I wanted to feel you all over as soon as I laid eyes on *you*."

We stumbled out of our clothes and over to the bed, laughing. Our wet skin stuck to the cotton sheets that smelled sweet like lilies. Or maybe violets. Our bodies pulsed with passion as Violet pulled me over her. Part of me knew it was wrong, but it felt so right. I couldn't bring myself to stop her as she reached to position my hard cock at her entrance. I groaned as I slipped inside her taut softness. I shouldn't be there, but she felt like home.

Violet's legs wrapped around me to pull me deeper. She moaned as I stretched her, slowly at first until I reached her limit. She clenched around me as I pressed deeper with every thrust. Sweat trickled down my cheeks and dripped onto her bouncing breasts as her moans filled the room. I blinked into her dark eyes and had to slow down when the urge to finish gripped me.

I held still, pulsing inside her, but I was too close to the brink. I slid out of her wetness and kissed a trail down her sweat-slicked chest. I lifted my gaze to meet hers, desperate with longing. She watched me part her folds and gasped when my mouth covered her silky sweetness. Her clit hardened under my tongue.

I licked her softly at first, then more determinedly. Her low moans made me throb. After several minutes, I attacked her clit with every move I knew. I thought she was close a few times, and even thought she was there once, but she never quite peaked. I figured it was the alcohol, but couldn't help but worry that I just couldn't crack her code.

I wasn't giving up, though.

My hand slid over her toned, tan stomach up to her nipple. I rolled it in my fingertips, squeezing harder as I raked my teeth over her clit. My tongue went into fifth gear, flicking so fast I thought it might cramp. But it paid off.

I held her bucking hips as her moans erupted, relentlessly provoking her sweet spot until she whimpered, "Yes, just like that." Her fingers curled into the hair on the back of my head as she called out, "Oh my god, Hayden. Oh my god. Don't stop."

I groaned into her dripping pussy, devouring her until she screamed. When her moans subsided, I loosened my grip on her hips and rolled over, thinking I'd better stop even though we'd already gone too far.

Violet laid panting for a few seconds before she rolled to her side. Her fingers trailed through my chest hair and down to my cock that still throbbed. "You worked awfully hard for that. Thank you." She took me in her hand, gripping my shaft. "But you aren't finished."

It wasn't a question and she wasn't waiting for an answer. She pushed up to her elbow and threw a leg over me. Dark strands of hair stuck to her breasts as she straddled me, reaching around to hold me in place as she lowered onto me. She was a perfect fit.

Violet ignored my attempts to control her pace. Her slender thighs glistened, quad muscles flexing as she bounced on my cock faster and faster. Her head fell back, oblivious that I was on the verge of losing control. I squeezed from the inside, trying to hold the eruption at bay. But so deep in her slippery pocket, I was beyond the point of no return.

My grip tightened around her thighs. "I'm going to come. You have to stop."

Wild eyes stared down on me as she groaned. "I don't want to stop."

I lifted her off me just in time, nails digging into her firm ass while I spewed onto my belly. She looked down at the mess I'd made with a satisfied grin.

My eyes narrowed at her. "You're dangerous." Irresistible.

She bit her lip, eyes dancing with a playful glint. "You're not really livin' unless you're livin' on the edge." She smiled before rolling over.

I staggered into the bathroom, as drunk on desire as I was on tequila. When I returned with a towel, Violet was fast asleep.

CHAPTER 8

VIOLET

My brain pounded against the inside of my skull like it was trying to get out. I took a deep breath to try to calm my racing heart as I surveyed the tangled sheets. Blurry flashbacks of rolling around with Hayden made my stomach turn over.

Fuck! What have you done?

I listened, thinking Hayden must be in the bathroom but there was only silence. I slipped my hand between my legs, feeling my swollen and slightly bruised sex. Goodness, me. I'd gone and fucked my best friend's brother after explicitly instructing myself not to at least a dozen times.

"Fucking tequila," I muttered as I pushed up onto my elbow and scanned the room. My swimsuit was crumpled in the middle of the floor, but there was no sign of Hayden. He'd apparently removed all other evidence of our indiscretion in his stealthy departure.

I fell back onto the pillow, empty inside. I wanted to scream at myself for being so stupid, but I wanted just as badly to have him there telling me it was okay. It wasn't just my mistake, it was ours. But he'd high-tailed it out of there to avoid the aftermath.

Hayden leaving without saying goodbye made me madder than a puffed toad. Probably because it reminded me of another coward who took off for Jackson Hole before the shit could hit the fan.

I blinked to focus on my phone. It was nearly ten o'clock. I squeezed my eyes shut, dreading the 10:30 brunch reservation. I couldn't not go. Then Corinne would know something was up.

My hands covered my face. I had to go, come hell or high water.

I grumbled every cuss word in the book as I showered. I'd known better. I'd forbidden myself from hooking up with Hayden because I didn't want it to be weird. But him just up and disappearing after we'd done the deed, that was beyond weird. It was rude.

As my soapy hands slipped over the sore spot between my legs I cursed my lady bits too. I'd been thinking with my vagina which hadn't had any attention in far too long. A heat stirred in my core, betraying the cool I tried to keep. The flashbacks of passion reminded me of what I'd been missing in all those months of abstinence. Hayden had been all that, and more.

Damn him. I didn't want to want him. But I still did. Even when soured by regret, the muscle memory of him inside me left me craving.

I missed sex. I missed intimacy. But I didn't miss the gut-wrenching disappointment I felt now, with Hayden for leaving and with myself for wishing he'd stayed.

Corinne and Hayden were already seated at the table by the window when I crossed the dining room. I couldn't help but notice him running his fingers through his tousled brown hair with an uneasy smile. But I shifted my gaze, determined to fix on his sister.

Corinne smiled up, lifting a mimosa with a shaky hand. "We survived."

"Barely." I glanced at the empty chair beside her before I sat. "Where's the young Coast Guard cadet?" I chuckled, keeping my eyes on her. "Did he survive?"

"He did." Corinne smirked. "But I don't know how he managed to make it to work this morning. Sucks to be him." She turned up her mimosa with a grin. "Good thing we can take it easy today."

I sat gingerly on the seat across from Hayden, eyes trained on Corinne to my left, pretending not to feel Hayden's gaze. I huffed, doubtful that today was going to be the least bit easy. "I'm certainly not up for anything difficult." Like saying goodbye or a conversation about the biggest mistake I'd made in years.

Corinne nodded. "I'm feeling it too. Hence, the mimosas." She glanced down at her glass and took another sip before turning to Hayden.

"I was planning to take you out in kayaks, but that may be a little ambitious. Let's see how we feel after food."

Paddling in the sweltering sun sounded dreadful in my current state, but doing it with Corinne and her brother in the current circumstances sounded downright torturous. I raised my brows doubtfully, shaking my head.

Hayden's laugh was nervous and a little louder than it should have been. Trying to get my attention, I imagined. "I'm fine with just relaxing." His voice raised another decibel when he asked, "Did you manage to sleep off all those margaritas?"

I finally looked at him, trying not to glare. "I must've slept like a rock. I don't even remember saying goodbye last night. I clearly overdid it." I cleared my throat, picking up the menu to break his gaze. "But I think it was the tequila shots that got me." I glanced at Corinne. "I told you tequila is always a bad idea."

Corinne laughed, tipping her glass. "I didn't exactly twist your arm. But I do recommend a mimosa. They make everything better."

I eyed her drink that didn't seem the least bit appetizing and picked up a glass of water from the table instead. "Oh, I'm not blaming you. I'm fully responsible for my bad decisions." I smiled up at Rosa as she approached to take our order. "I'll stick with coffee."

I could see the sting of my "bad decisions" remark in Hayden's face as he stammered. "Coffee sounds like a responsible choice. I think I'll make it a double though." He chuckled but it fell away, dry.

I shrugged, avoiding eye contact again. "You don't have to be responsible. You're on vacation. Do what you want." I pretended to focus on the menu while the bitterness churned in me. "I'm in the mood for something sweet. Might help get the bad taste of hangover out of my mouth."

I could feel Hayden's eyes on me when I looked up at Rosa. "The French toast, please."

Corinne didn't seem to notice my scathing undertone, wrinkling her nose. "The OJ and Prosecco is all the sweet I need. I'm going with greasy. The bacon gruyere omelette is calling me."

Rosa turned toward Hayden. He handed her the brunch menu with a grin. "The lobster omelette I had yesterday can't be topped."

Rosa smiled as she took the menu. "When something's that good, once isn't enough."

My eyes darted to Hayden's smirk at her apt remark, my face flaming red. He looked away to keep from cracking a bigger smile, I could tell.

The innuendo went right over Corinne's head. Thank God.

She asked her brother, "Did you talk to Clifton about fishing?"

"No, but I talked to Violet yesterday." His smile flattened on his lips but still danced in his eyes when he turned to me. "Did you hear back about tomorrow?"

I nodded, determined to keep my seething in check. "I managed to book you with a boat out of Big Pine. We've never used them before, but they have great reviews. I'm sure you won't be disappointed." I glanced at Corinne. "Well, you might, since you're not really a fishing fan. But these guys are some of the best in the business, so I'm sure you two will have fun."

"Yeah, about that." Corinne looked painfully apologetic when she paused. "They had to rearrange our training schedule around a scientist who's now leaving Tuesday. There's a module we have to complete now on Monday, which is tomorrow." She squinted, as though getting the timeline straight in her head was taxing. "I'm afraid I won't be able to go fishing after all."

Hayden blinked at her for a second but quickly shrugged it off. "No worries, sis. I know you'd rather be working than fishing anyway. I don't need a chaperone."

"Of course not. I wasn't exactly looking forward to fishing, but I hate for you to go alone. Violet, you like to fish. Maybe you can go in my place?"

I stared at Corinne, concentrating on keeping a steady mask of calm. "I'm afraid that'd be tough. I'm pretty swamped."

Hayden's hands flew up, trying to halt her insistence. "I know you are. I certainly wouldn't want to make matters worse for you."

His patronizing tone irked me further, but I just smiled and seethed. "That's very kind of you. So considerate."

Corinne shot me a confused look, finally seeming to notice my sarcastic edge, but still undeterred. "I know you're busy. But can't you squeeze it in? It'd be fun and I wouldn't feel so guilty for having to ditch Hayden. Please? Pretty, pretty please."

Hayden cleared his throat, his face turning beet red as he shifted in his seat. "It's really not necessary. Don't insist, Corinne. There's nothing to feel guilty for. Shit happens."

Corinne didn't miss a beat. "Yeah but sometimes cool shit happens when you're spontaneous. Come on, Violet. You know you'll love it." She grinned. "And it's my birthday. Just this one favor."

I knew all about what could happen when you're spontaneous. I took a deep breath, my face softening with the shame that she was oblivious to the reason for the tension in the air, the tension I'd created by screwing her brother. "Don't give me a guilt trip. That's not fair."

She smiled, satisfied she'd gotten to me even if she didn't know how or why. "It would mean a lot to me."

And with that I was determined to protect what was important. "Then I'll figure it out."

Corinne reached across the table to squeeze my hand. "Thank you."

I managed to get through half the platter of French toast and berries with a smile on my face. Corinne was bubbly herself after two mimosas and suddenly energized. "The water's flat calm today. How about a paddle out to the little islands?"

I shook my head instantly. "I'll pass. If I'm fishing tomorrow, I have some work to get done today."

Hayden's eyes narrowed at Corinne. "How far away are these islands that are even smaller than Paradise Key?"

"Not far. It's super easy with no wind." Corinne scowled. "You used to be adventurous."

"I'm still adventurous." His eyes flitted to flirt with me once more. "I've learned not to underestimate the treasures of little islands." He was still smiling more than I'd have liked when he looked back at his sister. "I'm game."

Corinne beamed. "You won't regret it."

Hayden huffed out a laugh, eyes swinging to hold me in the stare he didn't even try to hide. "I never regret a good time."

My breath caught as I stood to make my escape. If we carried on like that Corinne was going to catch on fast and there was no need for that. “You two have fun. I’ll be in bed with my laptop.” *Regretting the good time I wished I could repeat.*

CHAPTER 9

HAYDEN

I watched until the front door closed behind Violet. Her pissy attitude baffled me. She almost acted like hooking up wasn't *her* idea. She certainly seemed to blame me for something. And being forced to go fishing tomorrow didn't help matters.

I sighed at Corinne. "I know you mean well, sis, but I wish you hadn't done that. It wasn't really fair to Violet."

Corinne waved off my concern with a chuckle. "Oh, lighten up. Violet's fine. She loves fishing as much as you do. And you two get on great. I'm not trying to set you up. I promise. But I'm sure you're going to have a blast."

From the looks of things, I was afraid the blast would be a full-on blow up. This was not good. I had to let Violet off the hook or she might never forgive me.

"I'll be right back." I rushed out the door and down the steps, trotting to catch up with Violet on the brick path toward her office.

"Hey, Violet." I called ahead, resentful of the desperation in my voice. "Wait up."

She glanced back over her shoulder but kept walking.

I slowed from a jog to a walk, trying to match her hurried pace. "Sorry about that back there. I feel like Corinne manipulated you into agreeing to fish tomorrow. I totally understand if you don't want to go. Don't sweat it."

She stopped in her tracks, leveling her eyes on mine. "Oh, did you change your mind and decide you'd rather be alone?"

I eyed her, not sure where she was going with the sharp remark. "No. I just don't want you to feel pressured to do something you don't want to do."

"Ah. Definitely wouldn't want that, would we?"

"Wait a minute, you aren't suggesting that *I* seduced *you*, are you?" Surely she remembered that she was the instigator in the hot tub. I'd tried to keep my hands to myself.

"I'm not suggesting anything of the sort. Like I said, I take responsibility for my bad decisions." Her hands waved to point both index fingers at herself accusingly.

I licked my lips and rubbed them together to keep from smiling at how "bad" sounded like "bed" in her Georgia twang. But it stung in my chest that she thought of what happened between us as bad. Maybe we shouldn't have done it, but it was good.

"What's going on here? Why are you so angry?"

She planted her hands on her hips. "Oh, I don't know. Maybe I don't like waking up to an empty bed with a splitting headache and no one to talk about the colossal mistake I just made—*we* just made," she hissed, wide-eyed.

I processed what she'd said. It hadn't occurred to me when I left that she'd be upset. It seemed like what she wanted. "You're mad because I left? You were out cold and I thought we were supposed to be discreet. Wouldn't it be more awkward if I stayed?"

"Well, it feels pretty darned awkward now, doesn't it?"

"It doesn't have to." I reached for her arm.

But her hands flew up off her hips to warn me to keep my distance. "You're right. So stop making it weird. I agreed to go out tomorrow because my best friend asked me to. She'll still be my best friend after you're gone and none of this will matter."

I winced at the searing remark but Violet didn't flinch as she continued. "Let's just pretend the mistake didn't happen and move on."

I wasn't sure how *I* was making it weird when *she* was the one upset.

"It didn't feel like a mistake. I'm pretty sure you had as great a time with me as I did with you." When her face flushed, it was confirmed. The corners of my mouth tugged despite the effort to keep a straight face. "Is that what you're mad about? It was better than 'just sex', wasn't it?" She was mad because she liked it.

For a second I thought she might give in and admit it, but she iced over. "Whatever it was... what it *is*, is over. Please don't let on to Corinne. And forget it ever happened."

I held up my hands and took a step back.

"If that's what you want." It wasn't gong to be easy but I hated to admit it was probably for the best. "Of course I'll continue to be discreet."

"Yeah, you're real good at that." I didn't know how she could sound so sweet and be so mad at the same time. A deep breath seemed to help her regain her calm, or pretend to at least. "See you on the dock at eight tomorrow." She turned on her heel, as angry as she'd been when we'd started and leaving me just as confused.

Corinne was walking out the front door as I headed up the steps. I wondered how much arm waving she'd seen. She watched Violet disappear down the path. "All good?"

"Yeah, she said it's no big deal. I just wanted to be sure."

"That's sweet. But I told you. It'll be fun. You'll see. Now let's get you out to the little islands. They're spectacular."

CHAPTER 10

VIOLET

Babysitting my best friend's older brother? Annoying. Babysitting my best friend's older brother whom I'd accidentally slept with? Awkward as fuck.

But I'd gotten through worse, and I'd get through this.

I showed up at the dock ten minutes early to introduce myself to the crew.

Hayden strolled down the dock in board shorts and a T-shirt with a relaxed grin. "I thought I was early."

"Well, it's a private charter and you're the only client, so whenever you show up, we go." I turned to motion toward the captain. "This is Tony, *Captain* Tony, an offshore fishing legend in his own right. He's reported to have caught the biggest marlin in the Florida Keys."

Hayden's eyes lingered on mine before he addressed Tony. "A modern day Hemingway, are you?"

Tony chuckled. "Maybe so. But all my fishing stories are non-fiction."

Hayden said with a smile, "I'm hoping for a couple of those actual-fishing-stories today."

Tony patted his shoulder. "I can't promise you a marlin, but I can promise you a good day of fishing."

Hayden's palms turned up and I wished his easy grin didn't make me want to smile too. "I'm just happy to be here."

Captain Tony nodded. "Good."

I couldn't say the same, but I managed to smile. Tony told us to get comfortable so we could get underway. That was a stretch. I focused on Paradise Key growing smaller on the horizon behind us, and thought I was successfully masking my annoyance until Hayden approached to ask if I was okay.

I pulled my shoulders back and nodded to convince us both. "I'm fine. Just doing my job."

"Yeah, I feel bad about that. I know you're busy. And I know this is uncomfortable. I didn't mean to put you in this position."

"It's okay, I'm sure we can behave like responsible adults as long as there's no tequila involved. It'll be fine. I'll do my job and you'll get some world-class fishing. Just relax and enjoy." He was the client. His pleasure was our goal, but I tried not to think about that as he replied.

"I'm definitely getting the better end of the deal."

I smiled, but I knew we'd both gotten more than we bargained for from this situation. It was going to be a long day.

Luckily Captain Tony lived up to his reputation. We hooked three sailfish in as many hours, along with several tuna and dolphinfish. My love of the sport took over as I scurried from one rod to another when they were all buzzing with fish on. Hayden had an enthusiastic grin plastered on his face for hours as he learned intently from the first mate. The awkwardness waned in the thrill and the fun of a perfect fishing morning.

After I'd struggled to pull in a 30-pound yellowfin, Hayden marveled. "You're a fucking pro."

"Hardly. But fishing's one of the few things my daddy taught me well. And living here hasn't hurt." I handed him a Coke from the cooler and leaned back to let the sun warm my face. The exhilaration of the long fight with the fish still buzzed through me.

Hayden's arm waved out toward the blue that stretched for miles. "You do have the advantage that this is your backyard."

I took a big sip from the can of Sprite I enjoyed before I answered. "Paradise has its advantages and its limitations. But it's still paradise at the end of the day."

Hayden's eyes sparkled the same turquoise as the ocean as he said with an easy grin, "As long as the advantages outweigh the drawbacks, you can't go wrong."

He wasn't talking about us, but it reminded me that I'd managed to go way-wrong with him, no matter how delicious the advantage of fantastic sex after a long drought. The risk of creating a rift with my best friend wasn't worth it, but Hayden was a cool guy and there was no reason we couldn't be friends. When I finally loosened up, the small talk came easier. The afternoon passed in a blink, hauling in one fish after another.

Hayden sat so close our knees touched for the ride back to shore but it wasn't the least bit awkward. It was as familiar as he was. I was deep in a descriptive tale of trout fishing days with my father when we crossed the wake of another big sportfisher.

The roiling waves pitched the boat to throw me off the seat and practically on top of Hayden. I caught the rail behind his head to steady myself, but, looking into his eyes, I felt anything but steady.

I settled back onto the seat beside him, brushing my hair off my face. “Sorry about that. Caught me off guard.”

“If letting your guard down lands you in my lap, you won’t hear me complain.”

His crooked grin sent a tingle between my legs. I raised a brow to remind us both of the boundaries we’d crossed. “Yeah, well, I’ve learned my lesson there. No more of that.“

“I know, but a guy can dream.“ His sexy smirk made my stomach flip. I couldn’t do flirty banter with him. We were supposed to be pretending like nothing had happened.

But then his hand landed on my thigh and a searing heat spread underneath it. What was uncomfortable was how comfortable it felt.

My heart sped but I kept a steady gaze on the horizon. The memories of our drunken encounter were fuzzy but the intimacy we’d shared was still there, clear as a bell. Hayden was so easy to be with it made it hard not to want to.

He was like mercury—shiny and shimmering and tempting to touch, but dangerous.

Even if Hayden wasn’t Corinne’s brother, there was no future. He lived across the country and probably had a harem of women he was stringing along. If I’d learned anything from my collection of exes with roaming eyes, it was how to spot them.

A relief spread over me as the resort dock came into view. I'd managed to keep my hands off Hayden if not in my mind. At least now there'd be no more alone time. Hayden touched my arm as I stood, sending a surge through me as he spoke.

"Thanks for coming out today. I really enjoyed it."

I shifted, reaching for my bag as an excuse to avoid his gaze. "You're welcome. It was great. I enjoyed it too." I pulled my phone out of my bag as the first mate secured the dock lines. There were three texts from Corinne. I glanced up to see Hayden checking his phone as well. "Did Corinne ask you about dinner in Marathon too?"

"Yes she did. Always the planner. You up for it?"

At least there would be chaperones. "I'm not sure. Let me see how things are here."

"Hopefully you won't have too many fires to put out." His grin made a warmth spread from my belly up to my cheeks. There was only one fire I was worried about snuffing.

I stood quickly to put space between us. Clifton waved from the end of the dock, ready with a list of questions for me, I imagined. I clambered off the boat and strolled three steps ahead of Hayden.

Clifton wore a broad smile as we approached. "Did you get lucky today or did the big one get away?"

Hayden smiled. "We were lucky just to be out there. But we did a lot of catching, which is not always the case with fishing." He chuckled. "It was fantastic. Thank you again."

"Well I'm glad to hear it." Clifton glanced my way. "I hope you enjoyed it as much. Because I got a call from Dan Pinder this morning. They had a cancellation tomorrow."

"Oh." I'd been trying to arrange a charter with his operation for weeks.

"I'd like you to check them out. Are you two up for another trip tomorrow? Conditions are supposed to be perfect."

I just blinked at Clifton for a long second. He couldn't be serious. But he was. And I really didn't have a choice. We needed at least five charter boats for a group coming from Texas next month, and this was a top choice to add to our roster.

The universe had a sense of humor and it was testing my resolve.

I managed to keep an even tone and a straight face but I was dying inside. "Then I guess we're fishing again tomorrow."

Clifton put his arm around my shoulder. "I know it's a hectic time. But Brian will be back at work tomorrow to pick up the slack. And I reviewed the preparation for the Condé Nast shoot. Thanks to your organization it seems like we're just waiting on shipments at this point."

"It's not quite that simple. But you're right. We're fairly well prepared." I took a deep breath before giving him an affirmative nod. "I'll make it work."

Clifton's hand squeezed my shoulder "I know you will. Thanks for being so dedicated." His genuine smile eased my annoyance. "I'll leave you two to it. Have fun tomorrow."

Hayden's grin made it hard to keep my composure as he tried to keep me from leaving. "The tiki bar is calling my name. Shall we have a drink before we get ready for dinner?"

I couldn't let liquor anywhere near my lips in his company or they'd be all over his. "As tempting as that sounds, I can't. In fact, if we're going to be out all day again tomorrow, I think I have to pass on dinner to catch up on a few things."

He nodded understandingly but didn't try to hide his disappointment. "That's a shame. But I understand. Sorry you're stuck with me again."

He didn't look the least bit sorry though. My eyes narrowed. "Are you?"

Hayden nodded, trying not to smile. "Not really. I kinda feel like I won the lotto, to be honest. But I don't want to cause you any trouble."

It was a little late for that. But I could keep it professional as long as there was no tequila involved. "It's fine. It'll take you an hour to get from here to Marathon, so just keep that in mind if you're going for that cocktail before dinner."

"Ah. I suppose I'll skip it. Won't be any fun without you anyway."

Butterflies stirred in my stomach again. He wasn't making things any easier. "See you tomorrow."

I could feel his eyes on me as I walked away but I didn't dare look back. I'd successfully thwarted temptation, but it'd gotten tougher by the minute. Tomorrow I had to do it all over again.

CHAPTER 11

HAYDEN

Sipping coffee on the terrace over the calm water, my face warmed in the rising sun. Corinne's observation last night kept replaying in my head. I was like a different person when I was away from home.

Other than the one time we'd met at our folks' in California, this trip was the only time I'd seen her outside of Colorado since Jill died. I spent plenty of time away from home myself, but that wasn't any more real than talking to the photographs at home.

I felt more like my real self on this little island than I had in years.

Corinne was disappointed that Violet didn't join us, but at least she didn't seem to suspect that we'd hooked up. My mind fixed on the picture of Violet under me, though. I wanted more of her. Even with my two-time-max rule, we were still allowed one more. If it were allowed—which it wasn't.

Tempting as she was, Violet was not a physical indulgence. She was not a Tinder date. She was my sister's best friend and getting involved with her would create all sorts of problems for everyone involved when things went sour.

Violet had made it clear that it was over, and I knew it was for the best. The charge that spread through me when I recalled our heated romp made me want the chance, though. But I had to let it go.

It was a shame, really. I hadn't enjoyed another woman's company like that in years. Who would have thought that fishing expertise would be so sexy? I guess the attraction was that she liked what I liked and did it even better.

I'd never had that with another woman. Even with Jill, our only mutual interest was skiing and that was more mine than hers. But Violet was different. She could teach me a thing or two.

Birds chirped in the trees on the walk across the island. I stopped short when the dock came into view. A gorgeous Viking that must've measured at least 70 feet sat regally at the end, straight from a postcard.

Violet was the dark-haired siren of the sea that should be perched on its bow. instead she was standing on the dock with a big smile talking to the captain, I presumed. She waved me over.

"This is our guest, Hayden. He's more of a fly fisherman but he proved himself by landing two sail fish yesterday. I think he's ready for a marlin."

Her happy demeanor was a good sign that she wasn't enormously annoyed at having to accompany me again today. I flashed Violet a smile before I stuck out my hand for the stocky gentleman to shake. "Nice to meet you. And you are?"

"Daniel. Daniel Pinder. At your service. I'm afraid the marlin have been few and far between the last few weeks. But you never know."

"I'm feeling lucky." I raised a brow, flicking my gaze toward Violet. It was impossible not to flirt.

The captain clapped his hands together. "We better get a move on. This is a late start to get all the way out to The Hump."

A crewman held out a hand to help Violet aboard. Geared out in stylish fishing shorts and shirt, she looked like an ad from an outdoors magazine again today. She spryly stepped on without assistance.

The captain climbed up to the flybridge as they cast off our lines.

"They made us a full breakfast." Violet slid the glossy teak door open and extended her arm to allow me to step inside the cabin ahead of her. I scooted around the upholstered bench seat at the teak table that was set for two. "This is a nice surprise."

"I think they're trying to impress us. But I'm glad. I didn't have time to eat. You?"

Even now that we were alone, Violet seemed more relaxed than when I'd left her yesterday, acting like nothing had happened. I smiled, patting my belly. "Same."

A crewman served us plates of eggs and toast with a bowl of fresh fruit on the side. Light fare was smart for a day at sea.

"How was your dinner in Marathon last night?"

"Best fish sandwich I've ever had in my life. And good fun seeing Corinne so excited. I can see why you didn't go though. I wasn't back at the resort until midnight."

"See, it's not so easy living on Paradise Key."

"No kidding. Thankfully she's coming back to the island this evening. You'll be there for dinner?"

"I worked until after midnight myself last night, but I'm all caught up so I should be able to swing it." Violet bit her lip before asking, "Did Corinne grill you about us?"

I shook my head. "No, not at all. I don't think she suspects a thing."

The crease in Violet's brow relaxed. "Good. Let's keep it that way."

"Of course." I'd keep our secret, but watching her pop a strawberry into the lips I wanted to kiss, I couldn't help but secretly hope we could do it again.

After breakfast, we went out to get acquainted with the rest of the crew. They had four lines in the water and seemed perturbed not to have had a single bite.

The first mate took off his cap and wiped the sweat off his brow. "It's a slow start today, but that's fishing. All or nothing sometimes." He reached for one of the rods. "You familiar with these reels?"

He showed me how to use the bail lock. Violet didn't need instruction. The second mate fitted us both with fighting belts.

After several minutes of silence on the rods, the captain called down from the bridge, "We should follow the birds. Get those lines in."

The first mate grabbed a rod and started reeling as hard as he could. I went for another but he stopped me. “Nah, leave that one. We’ll leave two in to troll over to the next spot. You can get that one if you want.”

I went for the reel he nodded toward and wound in the line. Violet stood back, watching with a smile.

The mate’s voice bloomed from the stern. “Lines up, Cap.”

Violet threw me a bottle of water and grinned as the boat got underway. “A good captain can read the birds.“

I nodded. “They’ve got the better view.“

“There’s always someone—or some*thing*—that can see things more clearly from their perspective. It’s a test of ego to defer to that sometimes.”

I wiped my mouth with the back of my hand and chuckled. “Waxing philosophical are we?“

Violet’s head fell back with her easy laugh. “Surely you’ve spent enough time in waders to contemplate thinking like a fish.“

She was right. Getting out of my own head and into the minds of the fish I tried to trick into a bite was part of the magic of those hours in frigid mountain streams. But I’d never thought of it that way until now. “They’re smarter than we think.”

“Humans have a tendency to overestimate our own intelligence and underestimate that of pretty much every other living thing.“

I nodded, taken by the profundity of her words. “We have a superiority complex, that’s for sure.“

The loud whirring sound of a reel unwinding made my head jerk around. The first mate jumped to his feet and lurched toward the rod that was bending under the force of whatever was running away with the hook. He yelled up to the captain. "Fish on!" and flipped the bail on the reel before he lifted the rod out of the holder, but it nearly yanked free from his hands as soon as he did. The second mate jumped behind him and wrapped his arms around to help hold the rod. Violet and I hurried to the side to see what was on, but the line disappeared into the sapphire depths without a trace. Whatever it was, it was deep and running for its life.

The captain steered the boat toward the fish to help get slack in the line. But progress came in inches and there must've been a half a mile of line out.

Violet tapped my shoulder, handing me a belt. Hers was already secure.

"You don't want to just watch, do you? This could be a long fight."

Violet braced her thighs against the padded gunnel and got into a rhythm of leaning back and then releasing forward to reel a few inches at a time. Her face twisted with determination. She wasn't going to let the fish win. But after fifteen minutes or so, sweat trickled down the sides of her face. The first mate asked if she was ready to hand it off.

"I could go for a little longer. But there's no sense in tiring myself out too quick. This might take a while." She called back over her shoulder, "Hayden, are you ready to give it a go?"

She caught me off guard. I assumed the first mate was going to take over. I had my belt on, ready to go, but I didn't want to be the idiot that let the big one get away. “I might need some instruction.”

“C’mere.“ The first mate cinched the belt tighter around my waist. “Stand like Violet with your thighs against the pad. Bend your knees—a lot. You’re gonna need to lean back with all your body weight once she hands it off.”

He stepped one foot between mine and then leaned into Violet to take the rod. She kept hold while he shifted it over and got it locked into the holder in my belt.

The force of the yank when they released took me by surprise. If I hadn’t been braced on the gunnel I might have gone over. My abs screamed and my biceps burned after just a couple of minutes. I didn’t know how Violet had managed for as long as she had. I grunted through gritted teeth, pulling with all my might. “Holy shit. This thing must be big.”

The first mate rasped, “Seems like it. But you never know. Sometimes the little ones put up a bigger fight than you’d think.”

My arms felt like they were turning to noodles by the time the first mate offered to take over. We passed the rod between the four of us, scurrying from one side of the boat to the other while the captain steered to keep us lined up with the fish.

Violet seemed to have superhuman strength packed into her thin frame. She was reluctant to hand the rod over every time. I watched her technique, more fluid than even the trained professionals, and learning from her made me better with every turn. By the fourth time they handed me the reel, I wasn’t afraid I’d fuck it up.

It felt like a relay race, handing off the baton. Between turns, the crew made sure we hydrated, a good thing since the baking sun had climbed higher in the sky. While the second mate had the rod, Violet plopped down on the bench seat. I stepped over her long, tanned legs to sit beside her. "What do you think it is?"

Violet's lips pursed and drew to one side as she squinted. "Hard to say. Could be a shark. That wire leader is thick."

"Fuck. What do we do if it's a shark?" Pulling Jaws onboard didn't sound appealing.

She answered, "Cut the line once we get him close."

The thought of all that work to not even land the fish was a little depressing. "I hope it's not a shark."

"I know you're hoping for a marlin." Her hand landed on my knee, sending a surge through me. "Whatever it is, we'll probably have to let it go."

The long fight seemed futile to end only with a photo and the memories of the chase, but the thrill was what made it addictive. Just like Violet. With her so close, all I wanted was to reel her in. Even if I couldn't keep her.

She squeezed my knee. "You're up next. You up for another round?"

My heart pounded in my chest as I peeled her fingers off my leg to take her hand. "I'm ready when you are."

Her mouth twisted in a crooked grin. "I was born ready." She hopped up, shaking my hand free.

The captain called down from the flybridge. "He's closer to the surface. I saw a shadow. He's big."

I stared out to where the line disappeared in the water as we backed down on the fish. When I saw a shape break the surface, I shouted, "Holy shit, there it is!" Silver and blue glinted in the sunlight. I couldn't believe my eyes. Was that what I thought it was?

"Looks like your marlin." Violet leaned in, squeezing me in a side hug.

The first mate offered me the rod. "You want to reel him in?"

A nervous flutter rose in my chest. "I don't want to let him get away."

Violet pushed me toward the gunnel. "Then don't let him get away."

Every muscle in my body tensed as I cranked the reel. It seemed to take forever before the fish surfaced again, now much closer. Violet stepped in behind me, gripping my shoulders and leaning back to keep me from going over. My arms felt like they might give out but I pulled and reeled with adrenaline-fueled determination.

Bit by bit, I brought him in until he was a few yards from the boat. The fish thrashed, wild silver streaks just below the surface. Time seemed to slow down. I was awestruck. I didn't realize I was speaking my thoughts until I heard my own voice. "Fuck, he's beautiful."

When the first mate leaned over the gunnel and cut the line, it felt like a bad dream. The marlin did a quick U-turn and disappeared into the depths. I stood watching for several seconds, not wanting to believe it was over.

Violet patted me on the back. "Good job. You got your marlin."

I stepped back, unsteady on my feet as I found the seat. "That was incredible."

The crew put the lines back in the water while I recovered. The fish hit immediately after the big guy was gone. Four tuna and three mahi mahi were easy catches and hardly notable. That's the thing about incredible experiences—nothing compares after them.

Violet and I did the dance of keeping our distance, but in the post-marlin euphoria, we both let our guard down. The magnetic attraction came from her side as much as mine. Her hand lingered when helping me with the reel.

We didn't look away from the smiles or the spontaneous laughter. I didn't want it to end, any of it, when the first mate announced we'd be heading back soon.

"If you're hungry, lunch is waiting. I didn't figure you'd want to eat while the fish were biting."

I hadn't once thought of food in the thrill of the day. "You were right about that. But I'm starving now."

Violet concurred. "Me too."

The first mate motioned toward the door. "The table's set. Go on in."

CHAPTER 12

VIOLET

The bottle of white wine chilling on the dining table set for lunch was tempting. But so was Hayden. That's why I knew I'd better be careful.

I'd been lighting up like fireworks every time he brushed up against me, which didn't happen as often as I wished it would. He'd been so respectful that I almost wanted him to be out of line. But that's why I had to be careful. No more alcohol and bad decisions, thank you very much.

The A/C in the cabin felt heavenly. My body ached from the hours of reeling but was still charged with the thrill of the marlin fight.

I felt like I was melting into the seat when they served us a delectable fish in butter and caper sauce over a rice pilaf with fresh steamed vegetables. The second mate was obviously out of his element, awkwardly twisting the corkscrew into the bottle of white wine. He was more suited for catching fish than fine dining service.

I started to refuse the wine, but he'd struggled with opening the bottle for so long I thought it'd be rude.

A little glass wouldn't hurt. But he poured it like a sailor pours whiskey—hard and heavy, and darn near to the brim.

After a few bites, Hayden set down his fork to take a sip of wine. "Thanks for being so patient with me today. I learned a lot."

I paused before scooping another bite of fish onto my fork. "This crew is top notch."

"You handle a rod as well as they do, or better."

I chuckled but thought better of making a joke. Sexual innuendo was probably a bad idea after that tall glass of Chardonnay. "Our haul today was exceptional. I hope you don't get your hopes up thinking that this is how it's always going to be if you ever come back."

"Oh, I'll be back. But don't worry, I'm good at no expectations."

"I bet you are." I doubted expectations were an issue in his string of women scattered around the country.

He leaned back, his long legs stretched out under the table to the right and his left arm resting on the back of the settee behind me. "Less disappointment that way."

My expectations had always gotten me burned. "There might be something to be said for that."

His head fell back as he blew out a long breath. "There's something to be said for air conditioning."

I nodded, sipping the chilled Chardonnay like it was lemonade. "The heat out on the water is no joke."

He lifted his head and grinned. “Especially with you around.” His flirty eyes stayed locked on mine as he swallowed the last sip of his wine.

I pretended to glower at him, but my lips curled into a smile. “Don’t you start.” I slapped at his chest, leaving my hand there long enough that we both felt the spark it ignited.

Hayden licked his lips. “I was thinking more along the lines of finishing what we started.”

So much for pretending nothing ever happened. And so much for self-restraint after a half a bottle of Chardonnay.

When his arm moved to my shoulder and squeezed, I relaxed into his side with a sigh. “You weren’t supposed to do that.”

“Well that’s true of a few things isn’t it?” His finger lightly traced a figure-8 pattern on my arm just under my sleeve, sending a chill up my spine.

I sat up straight, remembering the rules I’d set for myself. “Yes it is. But we’ve got to behave. I’m still at work.” And he was still my best friend’s brother.

“Sorry, you make me want to misbehave.”

I stiffened under his arm that lingered around my shoulders. “Yeah, well, that hasn’t gone so well so far.”

He raised a brow. “Maybe we need a do-over. Sober.”

I shook my head, pulling away. “That’s a bad idea.”

“Bad ideas are usually the most fun. Corinne’s not coming until seven. Can you think of a better way to spend the next few hours?”

My heart raced and my face flamed. But the door sliding open saved me.

The first mate smiled. "We'll be docking shortly, if you want to get your things together."

Get ourselves together was more like it. I jumped to my feet like a cat on a hot tin roof. "Oh good. Do y'all need any help?" I knew they wouldn't but it was an excuse to escape temptation.

"No ma'am." He stepped aside to let me pass. "I cleaned the fish for you. There's a lot of it."

"Oh, you guys should keep that. Take it home and share it with your friends and family."

He shook his head. "You earned it. Since we couldn't keep the one you fought the hardest for, you might as well enjoy the ones we did." He opened the cooler and pulled out two enormous bags, handing me one that weighed every bit of fifteen pounds.

"Holy Moses. That is a lot of fish. I'll pass it on to our chef. Thank you."

Hayden was thumbing through bills in his wallet when I turned. He pulled out four crisp hundred dollar bills.

The first mate beamed. "Thanks, buddy. We appreciate it."

"You earned it. Thanks for a fantastic day. I'll never forget it."

"I bet you won't." The mate's wide grin shined through his whiskers as he took the cash and handed Hayden the other bag of fish.

Captain Dan climbed down off the flybridge to say goodbye. Brian was already halfway down the dock heading our way. "Oh good, I wanted to introduce you two. Brian is the assistant GM and will probably be the one calling to arrange for that group from Texas next month." I stepped off the boat ahead of Hayden.

"Brian, this is Hayden, Corinne's brother who's visiting from Colorado."

Brian nodded with a smile. "Nice to meet you. I hope you've enjoyed your stay."

"More than you can imagine."

Heat spread through my chest, but I stayed focused. "And this is Captain Pinder, the owner of Sea Time Charters. Fortunately they're going to have two boats for our Texas boys next month."

Brian extended his hand. "Excellent. Nice to meet you, Captain. I'll be in touch next week to iron out the details."

"Looking forward to it." Daniel smiled as he turned back to me. "It was a pleasure having you aboard. You rival the best female anglers I've seen, and I've seen a few."

He just had to say *female*, didn't he? It galled me like no tomorrow that men qualified compliments with gender. Worst part was that they didn't even realize it. But I was used to it, and I handled it with the Southern grace my mama taught me.

"That's high praise. Thank you, Captain. And thanks so much for fitting us in today. It was a treat being out with your expert crew." I should've said male crew, but I was a lady and held my tongue. Dressing disdain in a pretty wrapper was a Southern talent.

"You enjoy the rest of your day, Miss Violet." I figured he imagined me sipping a mint julep by the pool.

"You, too." It was harder than it should have been not to roll my eyes. Must've been the wine.

I heard Hayden thanking the captain as I started down the dock with Brian, who apologized for being gone for five days at a critical time.

"Don't be sorry. You're entitled to time off." Even if it was bad timing with Corinne's birthday bash and the photo shoot prep.

"Fortunately, it seems like everything is coming together for the shoot. The fabric you ordered arrived from Paris and is already with the seamstress. Honestly, there doesn't seem to be much more pending for now. Clifton is up in Islamorada at the residential development, so he's clearly not concerned."

There was little to be concerned about because I'd already done it all, but I didn't need to toot my own horn. The results spoke for themselves.

Hayden trotted up beside us with a silly grin on his face. I figured he was still on the marlin high. But boy was I wrong.

He was overly-serious when he said, "Are you able to come to my room to help me with that issue now?"

I felt lightheaded—probably from all my blood leaving my brain because I couldn't think of a single reason not to. Or a single word to utter. Hayden just smiled like he knew a secret no one else did.

CHAPTER 13

VIOLET

Brian chimed in after I didn't answer in my tongue-tied fluster. "What's the problem? I'll be happy to take care of it for you."

"Thanks, Brian. It's just a little tech hiccup. Mr. Kincaid is having trouble connecting to the WiFi. I'll get it sorted." I wasn't sure what I was thinking. I was pretty sure I wasn't thinking at all.

The heat burning between us tempted me closer, but I kept a professional distance and measured steps to keep from breaking into a jog.

I kept my eyes straight ahead so as not to give into the temptation to curl under his arm as we walked the path past the bar and restaurant.

"Well played, Mr. Kincaid."

Hayden's voice was clearly amused. "The Hail Mary. Low percentage is better than no percentage when the clock is running out."

He was leaving tomorrow. And it wasn't like we hadn't already done it. I couldn't argue with his logic.

As we turned down the more remote path toward Hayden's room, I finally let myself glance over at him. His flirty grin stoked the fire that'd been smoldering in me as he spoke.

"Sometimes you've just gotta throw it out there when you've got nothing to lose."

Trouble was, we had plenty to lose. Screwing my best friend's brother could screw up our relationship. Which was exactly why I wasn't going to do it in the first place. I hadn't meant to when I did. This time I didn't have tequila to blame. No, I stepped over that threshold into his bungalow of my own volition, my desire greater than all the risks and doubts.

I told myself it was just sex that I craved, but the spark in Hayden's turquoise eyes when he talked about things that mattered made me want to know him deeper. That's why I was there.

Once inside his bungalow, I shot a warning glance. "Not a word to Corinne."

Hayden closed the door, locking my gaze, gliding with confident strides until he was so close I could smell him. "I'm not thinking about Corinne." His eyes wandered down my chest, hungry. I fought the urge to turn away, suddenly bashful. Had I forgotten how to do this?

He reminded me with the whisper of his touch. A knuckle trailed down my cheek, a tingle in its wake. His determined gaze was equally tender when his finger hooked under my chin, tilting my face for a better angle to peer straight through to my soul. My legs felt like they might give way, and for a moment I wished they would so he'd have to catch me. And as though he sensed my ache for his arms around me, Hayden drew me into his musky-scented heat. "I haven't stopped thinking about this since I first held you in my arms."

I had to find my breath to push out the words, "Me neither."

Our lips parted, tongues dancing with an ease far more familiar than a drunken one-night-stand. In effortless synchrony, the rhythm drove us deeper into the kiss.

Hayden pulled back enough to slip his hands between us to unbutton my fishing shirt. When he reached the top button, I reluctantly released his lips to pull his shirt over his head.

We stared for a second, panting and connected in the burning desire that brought our mouths crashing back together like cymbals. We slinked and spun, strewing a trail of clothes to the bed. Hayden hugged me tight as he backed up to the edge.

Eyes sparkling blue in the soft afternoon light, he kissed down my belly as he lowered to his knees, pausing to smile when he reached what we were both waiting for. Cupping my ass, he nuzzled his nose into the tiny trimmed triangle of pubic hair, his mouth hovering over my shaven lips. Hot breath huffed from his throat, teasing my throbbing parts.

I moaned, desperate for his touch, and louder when I finally got it. He grinned up at me, groaning as his tongue burrowed between my lips, flicking my swollen clit that almost instantly fired lightning bolts up through my core.

Hayden tapped the back of my thigh, signaling my leg over his shoulder, eyes smiling when I complied. He devoured me with ravenous groans that vibrated through me in an electric buzz that heightened when his fingers slid inside, thrusting as I clenched to hold them.

My nails buried in the dark brown waves of his hair, helping me balance on one leg while my hips swirled under his tongue. When he found my nipple I lost all control, gripping his fingers as the wave washed over me.

"Oh my god, Hayden. Fuck yes." He watched as my face twisted, licking me furiously. His obvious enjoyment in pleasuring me took me to another level I didn't know existed. My scalp tingled, electrified like the rest of me. I twisted my fingers in his hair, holding him in place while I moaned until the contractions finally faded.

I was lightheaded and breathless and wondering where he'd been all my life when he released me slowly, my trembling foot finding the floor. I sank into the pillowy soft edge of the bed, my knees too weak to support me. I'd never come so hard. Ever.

Hayden stared down with amused eyes as he stepped in close. Tenderly brushing the hair from my eyes, he said, "Well, that was easier when we're sober."

"You feel everything more when you're sober." Not just the orgasms. Everything.

The pull I felt to Hayden went far beyond physical.

Him staring up into my eyes made me dream of long walks on autumn evenings, of counting the leaves on a neighborhood sidewalk, of backyard barbecues and card games with neighbors. All the things I knew we'd never have but I wanted with all my soul in that moment of bliss.

In my ecstatic euphoria, I dreamed of doing this over and over into eternity.

"That's a good thing, isn't it?"

I wasn't sure yet if everything he was making me feel was a good thing, but there was no denying I wanted more of it.

"It sure feels good right now."

The sight of his waiting cock woke me from the daydream- a that dream could never be. But the passion that stirred between us, that was real. It was all I could see, or smell, or think.

Even if there was no future, I wanted all I could have of him now, every inch of him.

I wrapped his long shaft in a fist, craving the taste of him on my tongue. His breath caught when I slipped my mouth over the smooth head.

I worked his shaft as I took him slowly at first, and then deeper into my throat. His fingers snaked into my hair, groaning as I did my best to swallow him. I wanted all of him but he was too much. I pulled back, coughing.

Hayden chuckled, his fist tightening at my scalp to stop me when I tried to take him into my mouth again.

"Come here, gorgeous."

He pulled me into his arms, kissing me as he cupped under my ass to lift me. My legs wrapped around him, clinging as he climbed onto the bed.

As soon as my shoulders hit the pillow he filled me, scratching the itch I'd fought all day. I crossed my ankles behind his back to pull him deeper into my wetness with a delicious lip-smacking sound. I clenched with his groans as he thrust harder and deeper. His rhythm increased until he halted abruptly, holding still for a second before sliding out.

"Fuck, your pussy is too goddamn perfect."

He stepped his knees back, giving himself a minute to recover. He was breathless and looked almost embarrassed at his excitement as his palms ran over every inch of me, taking a topographical survey of my contours. Then a flash of yearning lit his eyes.

"But I can't resist. I've been trying for days." He pushed my knees up as he entered me slowly. "I couldn't leave without feeling you again."

The word "leave" stung,

But I knew exactly what he meant. We couldn't leave it at a drunken romp that we pretended was a mistake. It was more than that.

I gasped. "You feel so fucking good."

Eyes locked on mine, Hayden guided my hand between my legs. "Touch yourself." He watched my fingers obediently find my clit as he thrust deeper. A tightening low in my pelvis made me grip him harder. His gaze lifted to stare into my eyes when another orgasm crested. My fingers moved faster over the swollen epicenter of the quake that rumbled through my core. I blinked to try to keep my eyes open and not miss the sight of him basking in my pleasure as I moaned. In the heat of passion, I said without thinking, "Jesus, Hayden. No one has ever fucked me like you do."

"That's good, gorgeous."

There was possession in his voice, like he'd successfully claimed a prize.

He bit his lip as he pulled out, grasping his shaft. He tapped my tingling clit hard three times before he spilled onto my stomach with a groan.

I could feel his arms quiver as his weight lowered onto me. His cum mixing with the sweat between us, we steeped in the heavy scent of passion. My heart was fuller than it had been in years, or maybe ever.

I was still trying to process the swarm of unexpected feelings when a knock sounded at the door. We still hadn't caught our breath. Hayden pushed into the bed to lift his chest. His eyes were wide as he whisper-shouted. "Fuck. Who's that?"

"Did Corinne come early?" I whispered as I slinked out from under him. Gathering my clothes off the floor, I scurried into the bathroom. "Pretend I'm not here."

CHAPTER 14

HAYDEN

I pulled my T-shirt over my head and tripped as I tried to get a foot into my board shorts on the way to the door. I stopped to tie the string at my waist and smoothed the wrinkles from my shirt before I cracked open the door.

I spoke loudly, hoping my voice would carry. "Oh, hi, Brian. What can I do for you?"

"Just making sure there's nothing I can do for you. Did Miss Monroe get you connected?"

I glanced back over my shoulder, relieved to see Violet appear from the bathroom door, even though her wide eyes flitted down to the button she hadn't yet finished fastening. "She did indeed. Everything connected beautifully." When I saw that Violet was ready, I opened the door further to not be suspicious. She stepped behind me confidently.

"I was about to head back to the office. I figured you'd be gone by now." Her velvety Southern drawl gave me goosebumps.

Brian shifted to let her pass.

"I was on my way out. I tried calling but thought you might be tied up with the issue here. I thought I should stop by to be sure you didn't need any help, or anything else from me before I left. We were supposed to go over the task sheet before day's end?"

Violet didn't miss a beat. "Yes, perfect. Let's do that now."

She turned to me with a smile from the porch, her cheeks still a deep red. "If you're all taken care of, I guess I'll see you at dinner later with your sister."

My smile was bigger than I'd hoped but I couldn't help myself. "I'm well taken care of, thanks to you. Sorry to keep you." I chuckled under my breath as I turned to Brian. "It's a good thing you caught her."

Violet shot me a glare over her shoulder as they started down the wooden walkway. "I told Corinne I'd meet you guys at seven. See you there."

I made myself a vodka tonic from the mini bar and plopped down on the terrace over the water, still charged from the secret sex. Why was doing what you shouldn't always more fun?

I thought I'd get my fill having Violet one last time. But we'd fulfilled the two-time-max and I was nowhere near full of her. My body still pulsed with the memory of her, yet it begged for more.

But it wasn't just the sex. Violet was the whole package. Fun and adventurous, confident and accomplished, and funny as fuck. She made me want to break all the rules. She'd been stuck in my head for days.

I muttered toward the pelican bobbing in the bay, as though he was the one who needed reminding, "There's a reason for the two time rule."

I wasn't ready to break it. Especially not with my sister's best friend. Thank God Corinne would be there to keep me in check tonight.

I sipped my drink, watching the changing colors of the sky reflect in the water. It was close to sunset. I'd better get moving.

The tingle of Violet around me still surged as the warm shower ran over me. My cock stood again at the thought of her, and I'd have jerked off, imagining I could take her as often and as long as I wanted, if my phone wasn't ringing from the vanity. I grabbed a towel and squinted through the steam at the screen.

"Hey sis, you here already? I lost track of time. I'll be right there."

Corinne groaned. "I wish. There's a total shit show on US-1. The drawbridge is stuck open and I'm at the Reef Base headquarters just *north* of the bridge."

I blinked, shaking my head to try to make sense of what she'd said. "Wait, what are you talking about?"

I heard her sucking in a deep breath before she spoke more slowly. "I'm at the Reef Base headquarters up in Islamorada. It's literally just north of the only fucking drawbridge on all hundred-and-twenty miles of the highway. I'm staring at the damn thing, still wide open. It got stuck an hour-and-a-half ago. They've called the Army Corp of Engineers, but who the fuck knows when they'll get it fixed? It's a disaster. Traffic must be backed up for thirty miles in both directions by now."

"Oh, shit. Wow. That sucks." When an avalanche closed the pass in Colorado, it was a similar sort of shitty. "I guess you won't be making it here for dinner then?"

"I'll be lucky to make it home to Marathon at all tonight. But, yeah, dinner is out. I'm sorry."

I was disappointed we'd miss our farewell dinner. Then I realized I was also losing my chaperone.

"Not like it's your fault, sis. I'm fine here. Don't sweat it."

"How was fishing today though?"

I grinned. "Fan-fucking-tastic. We caught a marlin after fighting him for hours. Coolest thing I've ever done." I was tempted to tell her how impressive Violet was but thought better of it.

"Ugh. Torturing a creature for hours just to turn him loose. Glad you enjoyed."

I rolled my eyes. "Why'd you even ask?"

"I don't know. You know I hate sportfishing. I'll shut up about it though. At least it got you to come visit the Keys."

I winced. "Your birthday was excuse enough. Although I may have to come back to try fly fishing for sailfish. The captain on the boat today told me about a family operation out of Islamorada that specializes in it. Rodman, I think he said? Apparently one of them is the best around. You ever heard of them?"

"Oh I've heard of them alright. The Rodman brothers are the *worst* at trying to roll back marine sanctuary restrictions."

I wished I hadn't mentioned it. "Oh. No more fishing talk then."

"Listen, if it brings you back down here, I won't bitch. Did Violet have fun or was she stressed about having to be out on the water all day again?"

"I think she had fun." My face heated at her recent moans echoing in my mind.

"Good. I'm glad she's there for your last supper at least."

I sipped my cocktail. "Yeah, me too." Except for not knowing how I was going to resist her.

Corinne sighed. "Assuming they get this bridge fixed, I'll leave early in the morning to take you to the airport."

"Aren't you an hour-and-a-half away? Seems silly for you to come all this way, and then go further south just to drop me in Key West if your work is up there. Do your thing. I'll be fine."

She groaned. "I want to say goodbye. Who knows when I'll see you again."

I smiled, touched. "I'll FaceTime you from the airport tomorrow. And it won't be long before I'm back. I promise."

"I hope not."

I pulled on my last change of clean clothes and rushed over to the restaurant, five minutes late.

My breath caught in my chest when I spotted Violet talking to the chef at a table across the room. Her hair fell over her shoulders in shiny black waves.

The way her face lit up with a smile when she saw me approaching made my heart race. Not kissing her again wasn't going to be easy.

CHAPTER 15

VIOLET

The shit-eatin' grin on Hayden's face as he strolled across the restaurant made me forget what I was saying to Delaney. My smile spread despite my effort to keep it in check. "'Bout time. I thought you guys stood me up."

He pulled back the chair beside me and looked me in the eye as he said, "Never."

I was pretty sure my panties were wet from the tingle that spread through my pelvis as he continued. "But unfortunately Corinne's still in Islamorada. Apparently the drawbridge is stuck?"

Delaney interjected, reminding me she was there. "Oh that sucks. Shoot, I'd have offered for her to stay at our house, but it's south of the bridge anyway so that's no help."

I blinked, processing it all. Corinne wasn't coming. Hayden and I would be alone. My panties were *definitely* wet.

Hayden responded to Delaney when I didn't. "You live all the way up there?"

"Most of the time I do. I stay here when I work a few long days in a row."

I clarified for Hayden's benefit. "Delaney and her fiancé live in Paradise Palms, Clifton's residential development."

"Ah. I bet it's gorgeous if Clifton had anything to do with it."

Delaney beamed. "It's amazing." She turned back toward me. "And seriously, even if we're there, you are always welcome to stay if you're up that way and don't want to come all the way back down here. The house is huge."

"Thank you. I might just take you up on that." I glanced over at Hayden. "Delaney's making today's catch for dinner."

"Fabulous. I can't wait to see what's in store."

Delaney grinned. "You might be sick of fish by the time you leave."

"Never. Especially when it's better every time."

Delaney bit her lower lip. "Hopefully we can keep that up." She clasped her hands, bowing her head to excuse herself.

"She's so humble. Even with winning several awards recently, she doesn't seem to recognize how amazing she is at her job."

"Talented and humble is far better than mediocre and cocky."

"True." Most of the men I'd dated fit in that category. I didn't want to think about them, though.

"Really sucks about Corinne. I know she must be bummed to miss your last night." I wouldn't miss having to pretend, though. And it was a bonus that Hayden and I had the night alone.

"Yeah, she was pretty upset about it, but that's life in the islands, I suppose." He shrugged.

"I guess the silver lining is that we have the night alone now. I certainly didn't expect that." I hadn't expected another minute alone with him, let alone a whole night.

"Neither did I." Hayden answered tersely before smiling up at Rosa who set a plate of tuna between us. He didn't exactly seem overjoyed at our surprise night alone. Maybe he was just hungry like I was.

The appetizer was divine, and sure enough Hayden loosened up after he got a little food and wine in his belly. "What an awesome last day. Thanks for coming with me."

"Thanks for making me come." I grinned as I swirled my wine. "All three times."

Hayden opened his eyes wide in mock surprise but the smile he cracked gave him away. "I'm shocked at such a crass remark from a Southern belle."

"Even debutantes have a wild side."

"You've already surprised me in that department." His gaze fell away, wandering the room.

He seemed off—nervous or tired, or something. Whatever it was, he was reluctant to engage in sexy banter. So I changed the subject.

"It's too bad you're leaving tomorrow. With the wind picking up it would be perfect to try out our new Hobie cats."

"You sail?" He shook his head like he didn't quite believe me, chuckling under his breath.

I tilted my head, questioning his amusement. "Yeah, why?"

He looked me in the eye before shaking his head again. "You just got even more perfect."

My stomach fluttered with the thought that he ever considered me anywhere near perfect. "I take it you like to sail?"

"I love it. My dad had a little 21-foot Catalina when I was a kid."

"My dad taught me on a Sunfish first and later on Hobies."

"Mine's a monohull man, through and through. But I always gravitated to catamarans when he used to take me to boat shows to tour fifty-footers, dreaming about sailing the South Pacific someday. We'd pour over charts, plotting the course he wanted to make to Bora Bora. *That* never happened, but the boat shows were fun." He shrugged and sipped his wine with a somber smirk.

"You never know, he might still do it someday. Dreams don't expire."

"Nah. He doesn't even talk about that dream anymore." There was a tinge of sadness in his voice.

"How 'bout you? Do *you* still dream about it?"

"Maybe. I mean, yes. Maybe not the Pacific but I'd love to sail the Caribbean someday."

"Then you should."

"That's a little complicated from Breckenridge. I haven't sailed since I left California. But you never know. " He chuckled. "Where'd you learn to sail?"

"Back home in Georgia, first on the lake. But then when I was ten or eleven we chartered a boat off of Jekyll Island on the southern Georgia coast. Three days just Daddy and me. When I was in college he tried to get the whole family to do two weeks in the BVI's on a big cat. But being trapped on a boat together—even in the crystal waters of the eastern Caribbean—didn't sound much like a vacation to any of us but Daddy."

Hayden's brow cocked, questioning. "Your dad sounds pretty awesome."

"He has his moments. But they aren't all peachy."

"Oh yeah, why is that?" Hayden paused, raising a hand. "I mean, if you feel like sharing. I don't mean to pry."

"I guess I lost a lot of respect for him when I was old enough to see that he wasn't exactly a devoted husband." I swallowed hard, washing the lump in my throat down with a sip of wine.

"Oh, I'm sorry to hear that. But your parents are still together?"

"On paper, yes. But they're rarely in the same state. They haven't been together-together for years."

Hayden shrugged. "Whatever works, I guess?"

"I try not to think about it much." I laughed but it came out dry. "Probably explains why I chose to live on a remote island."

Hayden forked another piece of tuna. "Not a bad choice."

"I'm dreading the trip to see them in a couple of weeks, to be honest." I bit my lower lip, embarrassed. "I'm sorry. That must sound awful."

He smiled back with sympathetic eyes. “I’ve pretty much avoided my family for the past couple of years too, so I get it.”

“Why’re you avoiding yours?“ From what I’d heard from Corinne, they had a normal, functional family.

“After my wife died they felt so sorry for me it was awkward. I guess I just don’t want them in my business.”

I knew from Corinne he’d lost his wife in an accident a couple of years ago, which must’ve been awful for him. But I knew from experience that pity doesn’t feel nice. I’d gotten plenty of it. I forced a smile to try to *not* seem sorry for him.

“Fair enough. Even though I’m sure it was nothing by comparison, I felt like that after my last break up.” And the one before that. Poor Violet, cheated on again. I shoved a big bite of fish in my mouth to stop myself from saying more.

“A rough one, I take it?”

Thankfully my mouth was full so I nodded and grunted, “Uh huh.” Hayden didn’t press for details on that dreary subject. We ate the sashimi appetizer in silence. Finally, I took another sip of wine to try to attempt small talk again.

“Sounds like work keeps you busy. So at least you’ve got a good excuse to keep your distance.” I leaned in like I was telling a secret. “That’s usually my excuse too.”

Hayden laughed, pouring us both another glass of wine. “You can only work so much, though. I need to get out to California to see my folks again soon. Sometimes you just gotta do it.”

“Yeah, don’t remind me.” I moved my small plate to the side to make space for the gorgeous fish entrée Rosa set in front of me. Before we dug in, I said, "You're in for a treat. This is the dish that won Delaney her first award—the one that put her on the Michelin radar. It's got a kick though. I hope you like spicy."

Hayden's brow waggled over his blue-green eyes alight with mischief, finally. "You ought to know I like it hot."

I raised a brow. "I got that impression."

"You know what's hot? A woman who loves to fish."

"I'm glad you think my tomboy ways are sexy."

"Everything about you is sexy, Violet." He sounded almost sad when he said it, but my body lit up like a Christmas tree.

"I could say the same for you, mister. And you're a pretty good angler too."

His sheepish grin made me want to slink over and climb up in his lap, but I kept my cool as we laughed over fishing stories from the past two days while savoring the delicious dinner.

When Rosa asked if we'd like dessert, I shook my head. "I'm too full." Key Lime Pie wasn't what I was hungry for. I was happy that Hayden declined dessert as well. I wanted to get out of public so I could get my hands on him again.

Rosa disappeared with our plates, leaving us in what quickly became an awkward silence. Hayden's mind was somewhere else as he fiddled with the napkin on the table in front of him. Food coma, maybe?

After what felt like ages waiting for him to make a move, I finally spoke up. "The night is still young. Want to try the hot tub, sober?" I eyed the empty bottle of wine. "Mostly sober."

Hayden looked like a deer in headlights before his gaze fell away. He drew in a deep breath but nothing came out but hot air.

The rejection stung in my chest like a poker from the fire.

CHAPTER 16

HAYDEN

Every cell in my body screamed for Violet but I was as mute as a mime. How could I explain what she made me feel and that I had a rule in place precisely to avoid feeling?

Her pained dark eyes were fixed on the napkin she methodically folded in her lap as she spoke. "If you're tired, I'll let you off the hook and we can call it a night."

She was gracefully giving me an out. But I didn't want off the hook. I wanted her to reel me in. Two times was already too many and not nearly enough. Resistance was futile.

"I don't think we'll make it to the hot tub, gorgeous."

She lifted her gaze, blinking and confused. "Yeah?"

"Yeah. Let's get out of here."

Her smile spread as she jumped to her feet. I nearly had to jog to keep up with her long strides.

When she stopped at her door the moon shadow accentuated her high cheekbones. It made my stomach flip over itself. I stepped behind her, sliding my hand around her waist while she pulled her key card from her purse. Her weight settled back into my chest with a sigh before she pushed the door open.

Violet paused as she started through the door and turned with an embarrassed grimace. “Shit. My place is a mess.” She scurried around collecting clothes that were strewn over the sofa. “I couldn’t decide what to wear tonight.”

My eyes swept over the light purple dress that fit her like a glove. “Good choice.”

She slid open the door to her bedroom and relocated the armful of clothes to the chair beside her bed. “My place is so small I have a hard time keeping it tidy.”

I chuckled. “My place is huge and I have the same problem.”

She looked around the kitchen and living area. “It’s not much but it feels a lot more like home than the plantation house in Georgia.”

It felt more like home than my sprawling mountain house in Colorado too. “A big house doesn’t make a home.”

She looked up quizzically. “What does? Three kids and a white picket fence?”

“Not for me.” That hadn’t been my dream even when I’d tried to make it so. “I could be happy living on a Catalina 21 if it was moored in the right spot.”

“I guess anywhere can be home as long as you love where you are.” She turned and glided over to the bar by the window overlooking the sea, leaving me to ponder the truth in her words.

After scanning the assortment of bottles on the shelf she asked, "Tequila?"

"Uh," I studied her face for a second before her lips parted in a grin.

"Just kidding. Champagne?" She bent over to pull a bottle from the mini-fridge.

Thank fucking God. "That sounds like a safer bet."

"And more appropriate to celebrate our bonus night. Although I thought for a minute there that you'd regretted our do-over this afternoon."

"God no." One last time was becoming a theme.

Violet peeled back the foil around the neck of the bottle and twisted the wire cage off the cork.

"I hate to admit I was kind of glad when you told me Corinne wasn't going to make it. Selfishly, of course." She pressed her thumb under the edge of the cork and squealed when it shot across the room.

I held the crystal flutes for Violet to fill. "You shouldn't second guess fate." I'd tried—and failed—enough to know it has its way whether we like it or not.

Violet set the bottle down and took a glass. "My mama always said not to burn bridges, but here's to a broken one."

I chuckled as she clinked the edge of her glass to mine. "You're a firecracker, aren't you?" I couldn't mimic her accent but the cadence of her drawl was infectious.

Violet's head tilted back, her long kissable neck trembling as she cackled. "With you I'm more of a Roman candle than a bottle rocket, I'd say."

My eyes narrowed, trying to discern the joke I'd missed. "How's that?"

"One fiery ball after another versus one shot and done."

I shook my head, laughing. "Why'd you say 'with you'?"

"Because that doesn't happen with just anyone. I haven't had more than one orgasm during sex in years."

My eyes widened to match my grin. "Really?"

"My ex thought his work was done after one." She winced, biting her lip. "Sorry, that's TMI."

"Doesn't bother me." Although why anyone would cut sex with her short was unimaginable. "Certainly his loss."

She clinked my glass again. "You can say that again." She swallowed half the glass of champagne in one swig. "To think I nearly married him." She chuckled. "Can't second guess fate."

I took a deep breath, trying to forget why I'd stop believing in fate before her. "Life has many turns, and it doesn't always turn out like we thought it would."

"Yep. Many turns. But if you keep turning in the same direction you go in circles."

I laughed, matching her pace with the bubbly and nearly finishing my glass. "I feel called out."

"Well if the shoe fits"—her eyes danced playfully—"maybe you should zigzag more."

She had no idea how much she was making me change my pattern right then. But damn if I wasn't happy she was. I chuckled. "Good advice. Makes you harder to trail, too."

She smirked. "I bet you're good at that. Shakin' the pursuers."

Now I definitely felt called out. I didn't stick around long enough to let them catch my scent. I smirked, running my fingers into her silky back hair. "I'm not sure if that's a compliment or an insult, but I'm going with the former."

She pressed her lips together, shaking her head. "Why do you have to be so darn cute?"

I traced the angle of her jaw up to her full lips as they parted in a sigh. Her dark eyes bottomless pools, beckoning as I spoke. "Why are you so darn gorgeous?"

I pulled her close, my lips meeting hers that were as sweet as honey. My heart throbbed as her hands ran up my back. Her sweet scent made me hungry for more. I needed to taste her, all of her.

I lifted her off her feet and set her on the countertop, our lips still locked in a passionate fury. When I tried to pull away, her legs wrapped around me and her fingers dug into my back to hold me in place.

I ran my fingers up the back of her neck, tightening around her silky hair to pull her head back and force her to release me. She stared with dark eyes full of want as I loosened my grip on her hair, trailing my fingers down her long neck.

"I want to kiss your other lips, beautiful."

She sighed, wanting it just as bad. I crouched between her knees, pushing the hem of her dress up over her tanned thighs. I moved her purple lace panties to the side, my mouth watering as it hovered over her perfect pussy. She leaned back to give me easier access, and gasped when my tongue parted her lips. I licked in long, slow strokes until I felt her clit harden.

Her heels dug into my back while my tongue flicked faster. "God, Hayden, that just makes me want you inside me."

I wanted the same, but not before I made her come all over my face. I smiled up, licking her hard and fast until her face twisted in pleasure and her moans erupted. Her nails buried in my scalp as she screamed my name.

She was still shuddering when I released her. I smiled up into her eyes before I growled, "God, you're delicious."

She sighed, breathless. "I love what you do to me."

I grinned.

"I love doing dirty things to you." What she did to me had me all tangled up inside and it scared the hell out of me.

I pulled back, her feet still on my shoulders as I unzipped my shorts and pushed them to the floor. Standing slowly, I gauged whether she was flexible enough to attempt what I had in mind as I stepped closer, pushing her legs higher into the air. I slipped my finger under the lace of her panties to hold them to the side. Her eyes locked on mine, her feet beside my ears, I slid into her. It felt like time slowed down and she felt like heaven opening up for me. My fingers dug into her firm ass, pulling her closer as I pressed deeper.

Violet's eyes lit and her smile spread when I pulled her hips off the counter and she slipped further onto me. I carefully stepped out of my shorts and away from the counter before pumping my arms to lift and lower her on my cock.

Her moans on my ear sent shockwaves of shivers through me that gave me superhuman strength. She felt light as a feather in my arms but I didn't want to keep her in the contorted position too long. I lowered her back down on the counter and wiggled my shoulders so that her feet fell to the sides.

Kissing her neck while her pussy pulsed around my throbbing cock, I groaned just below her ear. "You feel incredible."

She whined almost like it hurt, "God, so do you Hayden."

I pulled her hips forward again, gripping under her ass. "Hold on, beautiful." I carried her to the bed, feet wrapped around my waist in a hug more comforting than a favorite blanket.

Violet lifted off me, sliding down my chest like the soothing rub after a band aid is ripped from a wound. Biting her lip, she unbuttoned my shirt.

I pulled her dress over her head, slipping my fingers into her bra to twirl one nipple. Her breath caught before she kissed down my chest. She sat slowly on the edge of the bed, her eyes as black as night locked on mine as she wrapped her fingers around my shaft.

Licking her lips, she cooed. "I've never really enjoyed this before, but I love it with you."

I tried to contain my gasp when she took me into her mouth. "Well, you could have fooled me. You're really fucking good at it."

She swallowed me deeper with every pass. I wanted to tell her that I'd never enjoyed this as much with anyone, ever.

But the thought of baring my unquenchable desire scared me as much as feeling it did.

Her dark eyes staring up took me from in-control to teetering on the edge in a matter of seconds. I pulled out of her mouth and hooked under her arms to push her further up the bed to the pillow.

Her eyes glimmered with a seductive playfulness, enjoying the gentle manhandling, it seemed. Grabbing her ankles, I pushed her feet toward her until they almost touched her butt, tapping her softly.

"Lift your hips."

Her smile told me that she liked being told what to do.

I stepped my knees between hers and held under her hips, entering her slowly. I tried to contain myself but the urge for more drove me to push harder and faster when her moans sounded more like pleas with every thrust. The throbbing tingle in my cock intensified with the intoxicating desire in her glazed-over eyes. Holding back became impossible. I had to pull out to make it last.

The disappointment in Violet's desperate moans fueled my need to please her. She gripped the two fingers I slipped into her wetness from the inside with muscles I doubted many women even know they had.

I slid my knee under her ass to support her weight when I felt her knees quiver. Placing my free hand low on her flat stomach, I applied pressure as I pumped into her furiously, curling my fingers back toward me to try to find her G spot. Her moans strung together, hips thrashing as I pushed harder and faster.

Holding her hips, I pumped relentlessly, watching her face until I was sure she was almost there. "That's it, come for me, beautiful."

Watching Violet come was the prettiest sight I'd ever seen. Her eyes drifted half-open, dazed at first, but then they grew wide, looking surprised and confused. I wondered why until I felt a warmth flow onto my hand and down my wrist.

It took a few seconds for me to register what had happened —a phenomenon I had never witnessed. The liquid kept flowing, a sloshing sound around my relentless fingers. I only slowed when her moans faded, finally pulling my drenched hand away.

She gasped. "What just happened?"

I grinned. "I think you squirted."

Her eyes grew even wider before she shook her head, blinking in disbelief. "What? I don't squirt."

I held up my glistening hand. "Seems you do." When the cool air hit my thigh I realized the liquid had dripped down my leg under her. I touched the wet spot on the sheet. "And quite a lot, it seems."

She blinked faster but her voice came out slow. "How did you do that?"

"No idea. It's new to me, too." I slid my knee out from under her and climbed over her, smiling into her confused eyes. "But it's the hottest thing I've ever seen."

I tapped my erection on her mound to prove it. "Wetter is better, beautiful."

She rolled her lip between her teeth as I slid inside. "I love what you do to me."

"I love doing you, beautiful." The truth was that she was *un*doing me, and I loved it just as much. I pumped into her wetness at a steady pace to make it last. Our bodies moved in sync while the sounds of our heavy breath filled the room. We were so connected in that moment that it seemed like we might last, too.

One more time was never going to be enough.

CHAPTER 17

VIOLET

The Kleenex stuck to my belly when I tried to dab the sizable splatter Hayden left there. Tissues were not going to work for this. I turned the faucet and called through the open door out to the bedroom. "I'm gonna hop in the shower. You wanna join me?"

I cocked my head, waiting for a reply. Was Hayden already asleep? Ejaculation was nature's Ambien for men. Two minutes later, they were out like a light. But not Hayden, apparently, because he was standing in the doorway licking his lips with a glass of water in his hand when I turned. He drank me in with his eyes while handing me the glass. "You probably need to hydrate after that."

I glanced down at the semen glistening on my stomach and laughed. "We both lost a lot of fluid." I chugged half the glass of water and gave it back. "You coming in?"

Hayden finished the glass before stepping close behind me while I adjusted the water temperature. The heat of his words tickled my neck as his hand slid down my belly. "I hate to wash you off me, and me, off you."

My head fell back onto his shoulder, my body pulsing with want again. "God, that's hot."

"You're hot." He kissed a trail up my neck to my ear. "So fucking hot I can't think straight when you're in the room."

When I turned to meet his gaze, my head spun so suddenly I thought I might faint. I steadied myself on the marble shower wall. "I haven't thought straight since I met you, Hayden Kincaid." And I never would again as long as he was in my head.

In a desire-filled daze, I lathered my favorite body wash in my hands. Hayden's hands slipped around my ass to pull me close while I washed the remnants of him from between my breasts.

"A shower now will save me a few minutes in the morning, which means more time in bed with you. He scooped a dollop of suds from my tummy on his fingertip and wiped it on the tip of my nose. "And I'll take all of that I can get."

I didn't want to think about him leaving but when I did I couldn't help but think how sad Corinne must be at not getting to see him before he left.

"I wish I could take you to the airport tomorrow since Corinne can't, but I've got a morning packed full of meetings after taking the day off today."

"Don't worry, gorgeous. I'll be back soon."

I tried not to sound too excited when I looked into his eyes. "Are you already planning your next trip?"

His confident reply quelled my doubts. "Fly fishing for sailfish. Visiting my sister. And her beautiful best friend. Those are three solid reasons to return as fast as I can. And not in that order." His lips twisted and eyes narrowed like he was thinking. "Actually, the reverse order would be more accurate."

Men can say all the right things after fucking you senseless but they don't always mean them. I wanted to believe him though.

"I trump fly fishing?"

His hands slid over my butt, pulling me closer to his chest. "You trump fly fishing *and* my sister."

I leaned into his sudsy chest, kissing his neck. "I won't tell her you said that." Which made me wonder what exactly I was going to tell her when I saw her. "I suppose escaping without a farewell avoids the awkwardness with Corinne, at least."

Hayden laughed, like it wasn't a serious concern. "It doesn't have to be awkward. We could just tell the truth. It was her idea after all."

Stiff in his arms, my eyes widened and I shook my head. "Yeah, no. Not just yet anyway." There was no reason to go there yet. This was barely happening, and whether it was going anywhere remained to be seen.

Hayden chuckled again, more guarded this time as he pulled back to look me over. "Well, she's definitely going to know when I come back to see you."

My stomach fluttered with a mix of hope and hesitation. "We'll cross that bridge when we come to it." If we ever did.

Hayden chuckled. "Good analogy." His lips brushed mine in a whisper of a kiss as he reached for the pump on the bottle of body wash on the shelf in the corner.

"I love lemongrass. What is this stuff?"

I remembered the bank holiday weekend during my semester abroad at Cambridge, when the body wash was the most sensuous thing I'd discovered. "It's my favorite." Hayden rubbing it all over me took it to another level.

The now-familiar heat that he ignited in me burned low in my pelvis, but I knew better than to go anywhere near his cock when I washed him. As much as I'd love for him to stay another day, I didn't want to be responsible for him missing his flight tomorrow. I draped my arms around his neck as the last of the suds washed down the drain.

"We better get some sleep. You have an even earlier day than I do tomorrow."

He grimaced. "I don't want to think about that right now." He planted a soft kiss on my forehead. "But you're right."

I wrapped myself in a towel as Hayden went over to inspect the bed. "The sheets are almost dry."

I forced my hands that wanted to wrap around his waist to stay at my sides.

"Are you sure that doesn't gross you out?"

He climbed right on top of the damp spot in the bed. "I'm positive that it's the hottest thing I've ever witnessed."

My brow cocked. "You didn't just witness it, you *caused* it."

He held up his hands. "Guilty as charged." Grinning, he motioned for me to snuggle into his chest.

I settled onto him, running my hand over his perfect pecs. “I’ll have to remember to put a towel down if you come back around.”

“*When* I’m back around.” He lifted his chin to kiss my temple. “Speaking of which, I have a new client in Miami I’ve been meaning to visit. If I can arrange it in the next couple of weeks, after your photo shoot, maybe you could meet me there for a night or two?“

I thought my heart might have stopped in my chest until I felt it racing. The hypothetical see-you-again-soon just became meet-me-in-Miami-in-a-couple-of-weeks. I lifted my head to look him in the eye. “Really?”

Hayden looked at me, amused. “Yeah, really. Why’s that so hard to believe?”

“Best not to count your chickens before they hatch.” All of it was too good to be true.

Hayden’s chest shook under me as he chuckled. “Where do you come up with these things? Is there an almanac of Southernisms?”

“If there is, my gram wrote it.”

“Well I’m not sure if this is the chicken or the egg, but I’ll call my client tomorrow to see when I can get it on the books.”

I laughed at his effort to keep up. “That metaphor doesn’t really work there.”

“I’m from California. Cut me some slack.”

He stroked my hair, staring deep into my eyes. “I’m going to make it happen, come hell or high water.” There was a question in his voice without seeing it in his eyes.

I laughed. Unable to look him in the eye, I snuggled back into his chest. "That's better."

Hayden continued, insistent. "I'm serious. I'll let you know as soon as I have the dates. I promise."

His arms tightened around me as I settled into his chest, breathless.

That he was planning our next meeting wasn't what was so hard to believe. That I believed him, was. So much for just sex.

CHAPTER 18

HAYDEN

I slipped my numb arm out from under Violet, careful not to wake her. Checking my phone on the nightstand, I blinked to bring the numbers on the screen into focus. 6:28. Two minutes before my alarm.

We hadn't moved in six solid hours. I'd stay in that bed with her for six more days if I could. Even if my whole body fell asleep and atrophied, it'd be worth it.

Unfortunately, I'd have a lot of explaining to do to the client I was supposed to meet for the launch in Dallas. "Real life" awaited but this felt more real than anything I was going back to.

Violet looked like an angel sleeping when I returned from the shower. Waking her seemed a sin but I sure as hell wasn't going to leave without saying goodbye again. I didn't have to wake her just yet though. And I didn't want to say goodbye at all.

I glanced around the room and followed the trail of clothes out to the kitchen. I pulled on my shorts on my way into the bathroom to take a leak. The faint scent of lemongrass still lingering in the air made my cock twitch in my hand. I shook it and tucked it away. There was no time even for a quickie if I was going to catch the boat in less than half an hour.

Stepping into the white marble shower, I lifted the bottle of body wash to my nose. My breath caught with a vivid flashback of her silky smooth skin under mine as we washed each other, still electrified from the best sex of my life.

I snapped a photo of the bottle before I washed my hands, wishing we had more time. But the boat was leaving at 7 sharp and I still hadn't packed.

Studying Violet in her peaceful sleep, I sat on the edge of the bed, committing every detail of her beautiful face to memory before I stroked her arm. Her eyes blinked open and the sweet smile on her lips made me want to kiss them.

"Good morning, beautiful."

She squinted and groaned. "Oh no, is it time?"

I touched her sleepy face. "I'm afraid so."

"Ugh."

"You don't have to get up though. I still have to run to my room to pack. And then go straight to the boat. Just stay here gorgeous. Get some more sleep."

She rolled over, pushing up onto her elbow. "No, I'm awake. What time is it?"

"6:40."

She sat up, clutching the sheet to her breasts, blinking. "I'll meet you at the dock."

"If you insist.."

"Of course I insist on seeing you off. But kiss me now, like you mean it. We won't be able to do that there."

My fingers trailed down her face and around to snake into her hair at the back of her neck. "My pleasure."

Her lips parted and our tongues fell back into the rhythm of the slow waltz they'd danced for hours last night. She dropped the sheet to wrap her arms around my neck, pulling me close. My cock pressed into my zipper when she tried to climb on my lap.

My shoulders drew back, creating distance so that her magnetic force didn't pull me in. "If we start that, I'm going to miss my flight."

She licked her lips, rubbing them together as she shrugged, more awake now. "Worse things could happen."

"Believe me, the thought has already crossed my mind. As much as I'd like to stay, I have got to go, for now."

"I know." The sadness in her dark eyes made me want to kiss her again, but I knew better.

"I'll see you shortly on the dock then?" It took all my willpower to stand up and walk away.

I shoved my dirty clothes into my carry-on and added my toiletries after I brushed my teeth.

The sun was just rising over the horizon when I stepped out onto the terrace for one last look around. A long huffing sound came from under the wooden slats beneath my feet. I leaned over the railing and watched the flat surface for a sign of the source. Ripples appeared before a gray shadow came into view. A manatee at least 10 feet long glided under the crystal water. When its head surfaced for another breath, I greeted it.

"Hey buddy." At the sound of my voice, the creature turned all its massive length to face me just a few feet from the terrace. "Nice morning out isn't it?"

I felt silly talking to the animal, but I didn't want it to leave. It stared up with wise eyes for a few seconds before its head dipped under the surface and it turned to continue its eastbound course into the rising sun.

"I guess you've got somewhere to be, too."

My carryon wobbled on the pavers as I hurried along the path through the center of the island. I pushed the handle down and picked it up to make better time, jogging past the smaller pool that I've never had a chance to visit. Next time.

Violet was waiting on the end of the dock in a white gauze dress fitting for an angel, with sad eyes that didn't match her smile. "Did you get everything?"

"I hope so. But if I forgot anything you can bring it to Miami soon."

"You're serious about that aren't you?"

"As a heart attack." I grinned. "Does that metaphor work there?"

Her eyes sparkled as she said in an even thicker accent than usual, "Well, I declare. I might just turn you Southern yet, California boy."

She glanced back at the boat. "They're waiting for you." Her fingers laced through mine.

My feet felt heavy, reluctant to carry me toward the boat. "I'll contact my client this morning. Hopefully I'll have dates for Miami soon."

Violet drew in a deep breath as we approached the boat. "I can't wait to see you again."

I handed my luggage over to the attendant. "Soon, beautiful. Soon."

Her arms wrapped around my neck. "It won't be soon enough." I wasn't sure if I should kiss her, but she didn't hesitate, raising on tiptoes to plant a soft kiss before stepping back. "Take care."

"You too."

I stepped aboard and turned as the boat pulled away from the dock. My heart raced, watching her wave goodbye. I shouted to be sure she would hear. "See you in Miami."

Violet cupped her hands around her mouth like a megaphone and screamed, "I'll believe it when I see it, California boy."

I shook my head and smiled but an emptiness opened like a chasm in my chest as she grew smaller in the distance.

The same driver who'd brought me was waiting in the lot. He nodded with a smile, taking my carryon from my hand to load it in the back of the SUV. "Did you enjoy your trip?"

"Even more than I expected."

On the plane, I tried to focus on spreadsheets for the project in Dallas, but my mind kept wandering back to Violet. When the captain announced our descent I began to think the flight was a metaphor because my mood dropped in sync with our altitude.

When we landed in Denver, I was so low it was hard to drag myself to my Land Rover in long-term parking. My heart iced over like the road on the pass, which was surprisingly treacherous in a fresh spring snow. By the time I reached Breckenridge, the town where I'd lived for eight years didn't even feel like home.

This wasn't like returning from my work trips. They were my alternate reality- long days getting shit done followed by nights out, meeting new people I'd probably never see again.

Returning to my reality where I didn't have to pretend was normally a relief. This time it was the opposite. I'd been away from home long enough to actually connect with myself. And someone else. That was the problem. I was the real me, going home with another woman in my head, and my heart. I wasn't ready.

I was disoriented and not sure where I was when I woke from a sailing dream, blinking through groggy eyes that finally focused on a Christmas photo on the nightstand.

Jill was glowing in an ugly sweater and an elf hat. I wore a Santa hat and a big grin. I remembered our first Christmas after the wedding well, but I couldn't recall feeling as happy as I looked in the picture. I rolled over, unable to look that version of myself in the eye with the ache in my chest that wasn't for Jill.

I'd tossed and turned all night, missing Violet's touch, as I had the night before. Rousing myself from the bed, I shuffled over the cold hardwood floor out the kitchen. I built a fire to cut the chill in the air while the coffee steeped in the French press.

Slumping into the sofa with a steaming mug, I ran through my mental checklist for my trip to Dallas tomorrow. I dreaded going back to full-on work mode after my island getaway, but I welcomed the escape from the guilty ache in my gut.

I needed to get started on the launch plan for the software that was going live tomorrow after nine months of prep, but I felt heavy and distracted by the strong desire to be anywhere but home.

I had to get out of my funk if I was going to be able to focus. Maybe some music would lift my mood. I scrolled to my favorite nineties playlist, and sure enough, two songs in and I was on my feet belting out Smash Mouth.

I stopped in my tracks when the song changed. The signature hard riffs of Green Day immediately took me back to the drunken hot tub sing-along with Violet, even though it was a different song. I laughed out loud recalling our inebriation as I strummed the air guitar.

When the singer got to the chorus I realized which song it was. Welcome to Paradise. My eyes were drawn to the flames burning in the fireplace and the heat of that first night with Violet flooded me. What I wouldn't give to be back in Paradise.

I picked up my phone to text Violet, hesitating at first since it was so early in the Keys. But I liked the idea of her waking up with thoughts of me. It was only fair since I couldn't get her out of my head.

Listening to Green Day thinking of you.

My smile faded when I glanced up at the photos lined like soldiers on the mantle. Memories past that were incongruent with hope for a future.

A ding from my phone snapped me from my melancholy. Hoping it was Violet made my heart pound. I turned my back to the judging stares on the mantle as if that could hide my longing for another woman.

It wasn't Violet. It was terrible news. My client in Dallas needed to postpone the launch until next week. I sank into the soft Italian leather of the sofa and picked up my coffee. Now I didn't even have an escape.

CHAPTER 19

VIOLET

Catching up on work was a good distraction from missing Hayden. Finalizing the last-minute details had consumed the last three days, but I'd somehow managed to get it all done in time to join Corinne for her final night on dry land. I stopped into the restaurant to get a spare key from Delaney on my way to catch the boat.

"Thank you again for letting us stay at your place. I'm sorry you and Simon won't be there though."

"I am too. Especially since there's a full moon party. You guys are going to have a blast."

"I've heard they're great but I've never made it up there for one. It's a hike. Perfect timing that Corinne is leaving from there tomorrow though."

Delaney smiled. "Give her a hug from me."

On the boat ride to shore, I texted Corinne.

On my way. Meet you at Morada Bay?

My nervous stomach churned. I hadn't seen Corinne since Hayden left. Keeping our secret didn't feel right but neither did telling her. There was no reason to distract her when she had bigger fish to fry. But really I was just a chicken.

I didn't want to jeopardize our friendship if things went south with her brother. Better to see how it played out in Miami, if that even happened.

The sun was already low in the sky when the resort car turned into the lot to drop me. Corinne was waiting at the bar with two cocktails in quart sized mason jars. Glow sticks shined green through the transparent orange liquid.

"What in tarnation is that?"

Corinne grinned as she shoved a jar into my hand. "Rum punch."

I took a sip of the fruity concoction through a wide paper straw. "This could be dangerous." I looked around for the rest of her crew. "Where are your people?

"Oh, everyone's doing their own thing tonight. I think we're already sick of each other. It's been a stressful few days." She drew in an exasperated breath. "Hopefully we won't kill each other down there."

I laughed. "I imagine it will be close quarters for six of you. But I'm sure you'll be fine. You're going to love it."

Her face scrunched. "I know. But I'm a little nervous. So let's not talk about it. Want to go check out the band?"

"Sure."

We made our way through the crowd on the wide beach over to the stage. It was impossible not to dance to the Caribbean beats that blared. I was sticky with sweat in no time flat and had downed more than half of my enormous cocktail after two songs. I motioned for Corinne to follow me down the beach so that we could hear each other talk.

Corinne stared out over the still water reflecting the orange-painted sky. "Fuck, I never get tired of this."

"Yeah, it's hard not to take it for granted sometimes though."

"Not tonight!" Corinne pulled out her phone. "Let's get a selfie."

I smeared the sweat off my forehead with the back of my hand as we posed, speaking like a ventriloquist through my wide-toothed grin. "I'm already a mess. I can't believe it's still March."

Corinne chuckled as she flipped through the photos. "This is the best I'm going to look in the next two weeks, diving eight hours a day."

"Good point."

She turned the screen toward me, smiling. "Oh, that one's cute."

"Not bad." Not great either but I looked less like a wet hound than I felt. She fiddled with her phone. "Sorry, just texting it to my family."

I bit my lip to keep from asking if she meant her *whole* family or just her parents.

She slipped her phone into the back pocket of her high-waisted jean shorts. "I still feel bad that I didn't get to see Hayden before he left. What a shit show that turned out to be."

"Of course he understood."

"Such bad timing. Thank you so much for keeping him company while I was so busy."

"It was my pleasure." My face burned red hot.

"He said he'll be back. I won't hold my breath for that after it took me a year and half to get him here." She rolled her eyes. "But you never know. After a taste of the Keys, he might be hooked. I hope so."

I did too, but I didn't want to talk about her brother. "It's good you *want* to see your family. I'm dreading the trip to Wyoming. But first I have to get through the photo shoot."

Corinne's hand flew up to cover her mouth, embarrassed. "Crap, I'm sorry. I've been so self-absorbed I didn't even ask how everything's going for you."

I laughed. "You don't have to apologize. You've been even busier than I have. Fortunately everything at the resort is all coming together. I think we're pretty much ready. Which is more than I can say about the trip to Wyoming."

"I can't frigging wait to see the article." Corinne beamed, fanning herself with her palm. "On the bright side you get to escape the heat for a few days after the shoot."

"At least there's that."

Corinne's eyes lit up as they followed a group of four guys passing. "Let's go to the bar. Time for another rum punch."

I chuckled, jogging to keep up as she high-tailed it across the beach. "You lookin' for some last minute lovin'?"

She shrugged with a smirk. "You never know. I'm sure Delaney wouldn't mind if we bring a couple of hotties home."

"You can if you want. I won't judge."

We were approaching the bar when she blurted. "You're the one who hasn't had sex in six months."

I shot her a wide-eyed glare. The four cute guys to her right exchanged glances. I wanted to bury my head in the sand when the nearest one turned and grinned. "Where are you guys from?"

Corinne wiggled her brows at me before answering him. "We're locals. How 'bout you guys?"

"Lucky ladies, living here. We're from Wisconsin where there's currently a foot of snow."

Corinne cooed. "Lucky you're here and not there then isn't it?"

"Sure is. Can I buy you ladies a drink?"

I started to refuse but Corinne was already nodding. "Of course you can." Great.

He ordered a round of six giant drinks.

"Have you seen the fire dancers over by the bonfire?"

Corinne's chin dipped, coy. "Not yet..."

I took a deep breath. What the hell was she getting us into? After he bought us $28 cocktails we were obliged to hang out for at least a few minutes.

We followed them to the other end of the beach where a beautiful girl in a bikini twirled a long baton with little flaming pots dangling from either end.

I stood off to the side, mesmerized by the dancer and half-listening to the small talk. Derek, the one who bought our drinks, explained that they were college buddies together for a bachelor weekend for Kurt, the shortest of the four. Eddie, the cutest of the bunch, was the only one who'd already tied the knot. "You think he'd know better. He's the lawyer." Derek laughed at his own joke.

When Ben, the tall one with auburn hair, said he had a hotel in Madison, Corinne patted between my shoulder blades. "You should talk to Violet. That's her business too."

I resisted the urge to glower at her, smiling curtly at Ben instead. Unfortunately, he took her advice and came over to chat. I kept my answers short and sweet about my hospitality degree and my job on Paradise Key. I was smiling and nodding at his drawn out explanation of how he ended up with a bed-and-breakfast when I felt my phone buzz in my hip pocket.

Butterflies stirred in my stomach when I saw Hayden's name on the notification. I turned my shoulders to hide it from Corinne's view before I opened the message.

You look beautiful. Have fun tonight. Wish I was there.

My face flushed as I lifted my eyes to Ben who still hadn't finished his story. Manners were the last thing on my mind when I held up my hand to interrupt, "Sorry, just a sec." I walked a few steps away to reply in private. As with all my messages in the past few days, I gave a toned-down and nonchalant version of what I was really thinking.

Me too. Miss you.

I held my breath when the dots indicated he was typing.

Miss you madly. Still trying to nail down Miami dates so I can see you again soon. Do you need a few days after your Wyoming trip before you can sneak away?

That would probably be the responsible way to arrange it, but I didn't want to wait any longer than I had to.

Nah. Just book it and I'll work it out. I'm sneaking to text you now so I've got to go.

Okay. Have a great time. And kiss my sister for me.

He finished with a kiss emoji and the laughing one.

I giggled as I typed my reply. *Funny.*

Corinne seemed to be enjoying the audience as the guys plied her with questions about her trip down to Aquarius tomorrow. Ben tried to strike up a conversation a couple of more times, bless his heart.

I didn't have the energy to feign interest. Hayden was in my head, as he had been nearly every waking moment since he left.

I was hoping Corinne and I might shake the bachelors when she said she was ready to dance again. But Derek was down to boogie and dragged his buddies along. They were nice enough guys, and not bad dancers.

By the time the band announced they'd be back after a short break, we were all sweaty and breathing hard. Derek put his arm around Corinne's shoulder. "Perfect timing. Drinks?"

She had a twinkle in her eye when she answered. "Thought you'd never ask."

All I wanted right then was a tall glass of ice water and a bed where I could dream about meeting Hayden in Miami, but I didn't want to be a party pooper.

While Derek ordered our drinks, Corinne dragged me off to the ladies' room. We filed in behind the dozen girls doing the pee-pee dance in line.

She grinned expectantly, "Well…?"

"Well, what?"

She rolled her eyes. "Ben is cute and he's totally into you."

"He's cute enough. But I've got too much on my mind to think about men right now." Namely her older brother.

"Well, it wouldn't hurt you to loosen up and have a little fun."

That logic had landed me in bed with Hayden.

"I'm not as much of a stick in the mud as you think. But I'm not into Ben." When I saw her disappointment I hurried to add, "Don't let that stop you from having a little fun with Derek before you go, though. He can send Ben home with his buddies and I'll give you your privacy. Delaney said her house is huge, so that shouldn't be a problem."

"Nah. I was entertaining the idea, but more for your sake than really wanting to."

"Aww, that's sweet." I smiled. "You're a better friend than me if you'd take one for the team."

"I mean, Derek's pretty hot. So it wouldn't be a big sacrifice. But I'd be just as happy getting a good night's sleep."

"That makes two of us. Derek will be disappointed though. He's been on your heels all night. You can blame me if you want."

She smiled. "I'll let him down easy."

I chuckled as we finally made it into the air-conditioned restroom.

Corinne didn't dally in letting the boys down. I was taking the first sip of my last drink when she stated matter-of-factly, "Thanks for the drinks, boys. We're gonna have to go after this one though. We both have early days tomorrow."

Derek seemed a little miffed but Ben was the one who voiced his disappointment. "Well, that's a shame. I was hoping to know you a little better, Violet." His imitation of my accent would have been endearing if my mind wasn't elsewhere.

The Uber ride was only ten minutes to Paradise Palms. Lights shone up the trunks of the tall palms lining the lane to the ocean. I'd only been to the development once, just after they'd broken ground. It was as magnificent as I would expect from Clifton.

Simon and Delaney's palatial house was equally stunning. Corinne stared down at the colored lights in the lap pool that laid parallel with the beach as we climbed the stairs. "We're getting in there immediately."

I glanced back over my shoulder. "I didn't bring a suit."

"Pff. Neither did I. You can keep your bra on if you don't want me to see your boobs."

I chuckled as I slid the key into the door. "It's too hot for a bra."

"Skinny dipping it is, then." Corinne shrugged with a grin. "Let's get a drink and head down."

"That rum punch did me in, I'm..." My jaw dropped as we walked through the open living room facing the sea. "I'm sticking to water." My voice trailed as I scanned the gourmet kitchen.

When I looked at Corinne her mouth was also agape. "Holy fucking shit! Delaney lives here?"

"Right? She struck the jackpot with Simon. Sexy as sin *and* a mansion on the beach." I pulled two bottles of Perrier from the fridge.

Corinne nodded when I questioned with my eyes if the nonalcoholic beverage would suffice. She twisted the cap off, grinning from ear to ear. "Don't forget the British accent. I was tempted to go after him myself the day we had that crazy dolphin dive, but when I saw how he looked at her, I knew he was smitten."

I nearly spit sparkling water through my nose. "Ha! I didn't know you liked Simon. You never mentioned. Then again I didn't know Delaney liked him either until she was moving in with him. I guess you both hid it well."

Corinne waved it off, leading me back out the front door. "I thought about it for a minute but it was already too late. He fell hard for our ginger beauty."

"I guess they both fell hard. He went all out to win her heart."

She looked up at the full moon that reflected in the pool as she pushed her shorts over her hips. "There's hope for us yet, Violet. If Delaney can find love on Paradise Key, so can we." She threw her top on the lounge chair with her shorts.

I didn't know what to call what I'd found with Hayden on that little island, but he'd taken a piece of my heart with him when he left. And not being able to tell my best friend was torture.

I hesitated, briefly bashful to get undressed but I quickly followed Corinne's lead. She'd already seen more intimate parts of me than my breasts. "You can get back to worrying about our love lives after you're back from the lab."

"If you keep putting it off you're going to be an old maid." She giggled, mimicking the words I'd told her my mother liked to harp on.

"That is the least of my worries." I rolled my eyes, chuckling as I stepped into the cool water beside her. "I'd rather be an old maid than stuck with a man who can't keep his pecker in pants."

Corinne knew me well enough to know I was talking about my dad as much as my ex. "Why do you think your mom never left?"

"Daddy has a way of getting people to do what he wants. He perfected it with her."

"But you said they haven't lived together for years. You'd think they'd want to move on with their lives now that their kids are all grown. I don't get it."

"Neither do I, hun. Neither do I."

We stared out at the full moon that lit the sky as bright as dawn.

Corinne chuckled. "I'm so glad we came home alone. This is way better than sex with a random stranger."

I cocked my head, not quite sure if it was a well-disguised jab for nixing her chance to get laid. "Is that sarcasm?"

"Nope. I'd rather be skinny dipping with you than getting screwed by a lawyer any day."

"Derek wasn't the lawyer." I cracked up, which set Corinne into a giggle fit. Before long we were both laughing so hard my side hurt and tears were streaming down my face.

It was a full two minutes before I could finally speak. "God, I love you."

She wiped the tears of laughter from her eyes. "I love you, too." When the chuckling died down and she'd regained composure, she said more seriously, "No, really. I don't know what I'd do without you."

I studied her face, wondering why she'd suddenly gotten sentimental. "Well, I don't plan on going anywhere soon."

"You better not. I kicked myself when you were out fishing with Hayden in my place and it dawned on me that if you did hit it off he might steal you away. Lucky for me there wasn't a spark."

I leaned back onto the pool edge, scanning the sky. Only the brightest of the stars shined through the moonlight and the still night swallowed all the sound like a vacuum. I didn't want to lie about the spark that had already ignited a wildfire, so I said something I knew to be true. "Your brother is a perfect gentleman."

"With you, I'm sure he was." You'd think from her grimace as she took a swig that the Perrier burned like whiskey. "But it's better for everyone that my plan to set you guys up didn't work. That man's got issues." She seemed to catch herself from bashing him further. "But, hey, we all do, right?"

I wanted to ask more, but if Hayden's "issues" were a string of women scattered around the Southwest like I'd suspected, I wasn't sure I wanted to know. "I've got a million issues." Hayden might make it a-million-and-one.

CHAPTER 20

HAYDEN

The doorbell interrupted my strained grunting as I struggled through the last two push-ups in my fourth set of 50. I looked up to see the big brown truck backing out of the driveway through the dining room window. I hopped to my feet and jogged to the front door. The air was still crisp but there was finally a hint of warmth. Maybe spring had arrived. The corners of my mouth tugged to a smile when I recognized the shipping address. Rue de Maisson, Paris.

"Perfect timing."

I carried the package to the kitchen and sliced the tape with a steak knife. The pump bottle was buried under eco-foam peanuts. I grinned at the label before lifting the pump to my nose. Only the faintest trace of lemongrass, but it was unmistakable. Violet's favorite body wash.

I couldn't wait for the water to heat, but I was so hot and sweaty from the exercise that I didn't need it to anyway. The cool water took my breath at first but it was tepid by the time I was lathered up in the silky foam.

The scent carried me back to the marble-tiled shower where Violet had washed me. And when I closed my eyes it was her hands sliding over my aching pecs, and down my abs, and along the length of my cock. It grew in my hand that instinctively gripped it tighter.

The shower was the one place in my house where I could think about Violet freely, and I did so—often. The aromatherapy took it to a whole new level. By the time I was finished my whole body tingled, and my legs trembled when I stepped out onto the thick terrycloth rug.

I chuckled to myself in the half-fogged mirror. "Hell of a way to start the day."

Wrapping my towel around my waist, I started down the hallway to the kitchen and averted my eyes from the flowered A on the closed door as I passed. With a fresh cup of coffee in hand, I opened my laptop to tackle my inbox.

My client in Miami had finally gotten back with dates. The only day that would work was next Thursday. "Shit." I muttered. That was the day Violet was returning from Wyoming, but we might be able to make it work.

The big gulps of coffee burned my throat before I hurried back to my room to pull on a pair of jeans and a sweater. I grabbed a jacket on my way out the door and hopped in the Rover. Halfway down the hill I called Violet on FaceTime.

My heart skipped a beat when her smiling face appeared on the screen in the holder on the dashboard. "Is this a butt dial?"

"No, of course not."

"I didn't think you did phone calls let alone FaceTime. But I'm pleasantly surprised. How are you, handsome man?"

"I was pretty fabulous before, but even better now that I see you."

"Where are you going?"

"To grab some breakfast." I could see she was in her office. "You working?"

"Triple checking that everything is ready for tomorrow."

I smiled at how cute the crease in her brow was when she worried. "And is it?"

She drew in a deep breath. "It damn sure better be 'cause if it's not done now, it's not getting done."

"What time will they be there?"

Her dark eyes widened. "All day long. The boat is meeting them at nine and they want to stay through sunset."

I winced. "Long day. You might even be glad to get away after that."

"If my dad hadn't convinced my mom to come two days after me, I might actually be looking forward to it."

"Maybe he just wants a couple of days alone with you."

"That's exactly what he wants. Divide and conquer, that's his MO."

I chuckled as I parked outside my favorite cafe. "I'm sure your pessimism is well-founded. But I hope it's exaggerated and you'll be pleasantly surprised."

She looked doubtful when she said, "So do I."

I sat there staring at how pretty she was and almost forgot why I was calling. "So you're flying back on Thursday?"

"If I last that long, that's the plan."

"Well, I got some news from Miami. The only day we can meet is Thursday. I'm trying to figure out how we can make it work with you flying back to Key West. I'd hate for you to have to drive all the way up to Miami that day or the next. If it works for you, I could just rent a car and drive down to Paradise Key Friday for the weekend."

"Or I could change my ticket and fly straight to Miami."

My heart beat faster. "Could you? Would you?"

"Damn right I would. I deserve an extended vacation after all I've put into the prep for this photo shoot. And I'll need one after five days with my father."

I laughed, relieved that she was as anxious as I was to make this happen. "If it's not too much trouble, that would be amazing. I can stay until Sunday."

"That sounds like a dream." She laughed. "Three days of heaven after six days of hell. I'll change my ticket as soon as we get off the phone."

"You just made my week. I can't wait."

"Me neither." She looked up toward the knock sounding at her door. "I'm really, really sorry to have to go because I've enjoyed this so very much. But Brian is here to go over some things. I'll talk to you after the shoot. I'll be covered up until then."

"Rock it, beautiful. I know you will."

"Thanks. I'll do my best." She kissed the air and smiled. "See you soon!"

I bounced into the café grinning from ear to ear. The owner nearly fell over when she spotted me.

"If I didn't see it with my own eyes I wouldn't believe it. Hayden, it's been a while."

I'd known Grace since my first week in Breck. But I'd only been in the café a handful of times in the past couple of years. "It's been too long, Grace."

"I'm glad you're back. What can I get you? The usual?"

My chest warmed. "Yep. To go please." When she looked disappointed I hurried to add, "I have to get back to work but I'll be back soon. I promise."

Violet's bright smile, dark eyes and infectious laugh were vivid in my mind on my way home. I could almost reach out and touch the high crest of her cheekbones. In less than a week, I would.

I was high on life, almost floating into the kitchen to grab a plate for Grace's specialty, a buttery croissant sandwich. As I slid it out of the paper bag, the engagement party photo on the countertop caught my eye. I smiled back at Jill. "I got the usual." It was her favorite too.

I chuckled at myself. I still talked to photographs of my dead wife and had to leave home to call the woman who'd made me open my heart.

Violet changed me. She brightened my world, made it vivid, technicolor. But something more had shifted. I got a chill when I realized what it was. My memories of Jill had become flat, two-dimensional like the photographs.

CHAPTER 21

VIOLET

The air vent overhead wouldn't open any further and the tiny stream that flowed from it wasn't going to cut it. The flight attendant smiled when she saw me trying to adjust it again. "It'll cool down as soon as we get moving."

I tried to keep my cool even though I was melting into the seat. "I dressed for Jackson Hole, not for Key West, so I'll be glad when we do."

She nodded, knowingly. "Happens to me every time I make this trip. But it's sure nice only having to pack a bikini and a sundress for my layover here."

I smiled, wishing I was in a sundress and not a sweater dress right then. "Are you based in Denver?"

"Yes. So this is a welcome escape from the cold. How about you? Are you heading home from vacation?"

I shook my head. "No, this is home now. But I'm going to visit my folks in Jackson Hole."

She reached up to close the overhead bin. “Nice. And lucky you on both accounts.”

I almost said that the latter was debatable but I decided to keep that to myself.

She clasped her hands together, asking eagerly. “Can I get you something cold to drink before we take off?

I pressed my lips together, contemplating. “A mimosa would be nice.”

“A mimosa is always nice.” She winked as she turned.

It was only 10 a.m. but I deserved a drink. That’s what I'd told myself when I had that last Mojito last night. Which was at least one too many. But we were in celebration mode after the twelve-hour day that we’d spent two months preparing for.

It was still hard to believe the Condé Nast shoot was finally behind me. Harder yet to believe that it had gone so perfectly. Every single bit of it. Even the parts we couldn’t control couldn’t have been better. It might have been the most spectacular sunset Paradise Key had ever seen.

The resort had only been open for seven months and we were already 80 percent booked for the rest of the year. After this article, we’d probably be booked out for two years.

By the time all of the coach passengers had boarded, the mimosa was kicking in. The sweet flight attendant brought me another without even asking. “How fortunate that your neighbor didn’t show.”

“A first class row to myself is a good start to a trip.”

Daddy had offered to buy my ticket but I wouldn’t let him—out of stubbornness more than anything. I should’ve let him since this trip was his idea. But I could pay my own way, first class, thank you very much.

I was on such a high from the shoot that being railroaded into this trip hadn't brought me down. The fact that I was going straight to Miami afterwards had a lot to do with my optimism. I hadn't stopped smiling since Hayden called.

I had tried not to get my hopes up. Even though we'd texted a quite a bit, I half-expected his promise to "be back soon" to fade into the distance between us after he got back to real life. I still couldn't believe it was happening and so soon.

My body buzzed with longing for him. My head buzzed after a third mimosa with the surprisingly delicious breakfast. First class was worth the investment, especially on a trip you didn't want to take.

The sweet flight attendant cleared my breakfast tray. "Would you like a pillow and blanket? We've still got two hours in the air. "

"I bet I can nap away most of that. Yes, please."

The cabin temperature had probably dropped by twenty degrees, but I was cozy under the quilted blanket with the fluffy full-sized pillow tucked between me and the window. I slept so hard that I was disoriented when the captain announced that we had started our descent.

The sun beamed in when I cracked the window shade to look at the clouds, but it seemed out of place. I felt like it was the middle of the night. Exhaustion had hit me like a ton of bricks. And the dread of being at my dad's lodge for five flipping nights made me want to curl up and go right back to sleep.

A forty-nine minute layover in Denver was cutting it close, but they weren't yet boarding my connection when I reached the gate. I looked out the gate window. Breckinridge was two hours away. Impossibly far, but that didn't keep me from wishing I could see Hayden. I pulled out my phone to text him.

Just got to Denver but leaving shortly

He replied immediately. *Are you still exhausted?*

I smiled at his concern as I responded. *Better after a long nap on the flight. How's your day going?*

As I watched the dots waiting for his reply, knowing he was typing his message from so near only made me miss him more.

Peachy ;-) Just booked a trip to Dallas BEFORE Miami. Crazy.

How the heck was he going to manage that? *When?!?*

Tuesday to Wednesday then Thursday to you :-). Tight but had to be done. Rescheduled from last week.

We were both going to need a vacation after this. *Can't wait!*

The gate attendant called a list of five or six names, standby I presumed, until she added mine to the list. I wandered up to the counter where the handful of others gathered.

The gate agent smiled curtly. "This flight doesn't have a first class section but since you were all on a first class connection we'll attend to you first."

"That's great, thanks." I started to walk toward the scanner at the jetway, thinking we were boarding, but she called me back, lowering her voice so only we could hear.

"Unfortunately we have a mechanical problem and we can't get another plane. We're pulling your luggage off now. It will be the first off at carousel six. We've already rebooked you on the early morning flight and made reservations at the Westin. Their shuttle will be waiting outside baggage claim."

One of the other passengers, a boisterous man in a cowboy hat and boots that had never seen a lick of mud, was agitated. "Isn't there another flight tonight? On another airline if you don't have one? I can't be stuck here overnight."

"No, sir. There are two other flights on other airlines but they are both oversold. It is not likely that we can get you on, but I'm happy to try to put you on standby for one of those if you prefer."

"Listen, darlin', I'm only gonna be in Jackson Hole for 36 hours. I need every single one of them. Do what you have to do to get me on a plane tonight."

"Yes, sir." She tapped her keyboard before looking up. "Would anyone else like to try for standby? The chances are very slim but you never know."

The chances that Hayden could drive in and meet me in Denver were better and far more appealing.

Another man raised his hand. "I'll try my luck."

"Okay, you two step over here"— she motioned to her coworker to her left—"and here are vouchers for the rest of you." She handed us each an envelope.

"We're terribly sorry for the inconvenience. Thank you for understanding. "

Alone time with my dad just got cut from two days to one. And I might get to see Hayden. There is a God.

I called Hayden, practically skipping on the way to baggage claim.

CHAPTER 22

HAYDEN

I did a double take when my phone buzzed on the table beside my laptop. Violet should be in the air by now.

"Hey there?"

I could tell she was smiling when she asked, "What are you doing tonight?"

"Uh… nothing much. Are you calling from the plane?" She couldn't have possibly landed by now.

"The plane is broken." She sounded on the verge of laughter. "My flight got canceled. I'm stuck in Denver for the night."

"You sound awfully happy about that."

"Of course I am. Want to meet up? They're putting me up in the Westin."

"Oh, wow." I looked at the spreadsheet on my screen. Fuck it. "Are you kidding me? I'd love to meet up. It'll take me a couple of hours to get there though."

"That's perfect."

Perfect indeed.

Passing the Wedding Wall on the way to my bedroom, guilt bit me like the chill of a winter wind. But I was too excited to lay eyes on Violet to let it take hold. I rushed into the bedroom to change into khakis and a button-down.

On my way out, I grabbed my sweater off the back of a stool and my keys from the kitchen island. I stopped and chuckled at the photo beside my keys. Jill and me with Aunt Margaret on the very same Christmas she'd given me the cable knit sweater hanging on my arm right then. Serendipity.

Fortunately Friday rush-hour was already past its peak by the time I got to the outskirts of the city. I dialed Violet on the car speaker. Excitement bubbled up into my chest at the sound of her voice.

"Hello, handsome."

"Hello, beautiful." My foot slipped off the accelerator like that might slow my racing heart. This was really happening.

Her voice was velvety. "Are you close?"

"Ten minutes. Are you ready?"

She cackled. "That's a loaded question if I ever heard one."

I laughed. "Sounds like someone wants to skip dinner and go straight to dessert."

"I'm craving dessert. But I want it all."

Her breathy words reminding me of all that I wanted with her made my chest tighten. "Good. I've got the perfect spot, as long as you're not starving. There might be a wait."

"Oooh. For the perfect spot, I can wait."

I'd rather ravage her in her room first, but then we'd miss dinner altogether. "Meet me down front so we don't accidentally get detained?"

"Good idea. My restraint clearly fails in your company."

I grinned. "Restraint is overrated."

Her voice turned coy. "I don't know…handcuffs and ropes can be kinda hot."

I swallowed. Was she serious? "Yeah? You like those do you?"

Violet laughed. "I don't know, I might. Just kidding, though."

I chuckled. "Stop turning me on and get your pretty little ass downstairs. I'm four minutes out."

"Oh yay!"

My chest swelled a little more with every passing block and I thought it might burst when I saw her. Standing under the lobby awning wearing a sexy sweater dress and the biggest smile I'd ever seen on her face, Violet was even more stunning than I remembered.

I put the car in park and started to open my door but Violet was already opening hers. I grinned as she slid into the seat. "Well, aren't you a sight for sore eyes."

Violet giggled. "Have you been googling Southern sayings."

"Maybe…"

Her smile spread even wider. "Well, you look finer than frog hair split four ways."

I laughed. "Never heard that one. What does that even mean?"

She looked me over, rolling her bottom lip between her teeth. "It means really good. So where is this perfect spot?"

"The oldest restaurant in Colorado. Don't expect fancy, because it's not. But it's iconic. And not far." I glanced down at the GPS and merged to the right lane for an upcoming turn. "I was tempted to take you to the Stanley but it's an hour and a half away."

"The Stanley? Rings a bell but I'm not sure why.."

"It was Stephen King's inspiration for *The Shining*. Based on the mostly-true-according-to-legend story of an innkeeper so haunted by the resident ghosts he gradually lost his mind."

She grimaced. "Living with ghosts might do that to you. Never read the book but that movie gave me nightmares for months when I was a kid." She wrapped her arms around herself like she was trying to keep the chill of the memory out. "I'm kind of glad you didn't take me there. Sounds kind of morbid."

I turned into the lot adjacent to the long free-standing brick building that was like a time capsule spared from modernization. "This place is a little morbid too."

Violet read the name from the red awning over the doorway aloud. "The Buckhorn Exchange?"

I swung the door open and held out my arm. "The one and only."

Her eyes grew wide as she scanned the tightly packed room of red and white checkered tablecloths and the walls covered in animal heads. "I see what you mean by morbid."

I was relieved when she laughed. "Looks like a big game hunting lodge."

"The elk steak is to die for."

"Now you're talking."

The hostess took my number to text when a table was ready. "We should have a two-top within an hour. You might find a stool in the saloon upstairs if you'd like to wait there."

Violet's hips moving under the fitted sweater dress as she ascended the narrow wooden staircase ahead of me brought flashbacks of that perfect ass on top of me. I had to force my eyes to hers when she turned.

"Looks like there's a spot over there."

We shuffled through the crowded saloon to the end of the small bar. "What are you in the mood for?"

She raised a brow. "You mean drinks?" She grinned. "An old fashioned seems appropriate."

I lifted a finger to signal the bartender and ordered two.

Violet looked around the bar. "So exactly how old is the oldest restaurant in Colorado?"

"Well, it opened in 1893, so, old. Teddy Roosevelt made it famous about a decade later, I believe."

She nodded. "Makes sense. He was a big hunter."

"The original owner ran with Buffalo Bill. Legend has it that Chief Sitting Bull dubbed him Shorty Scout. Apparently he was not a tall man, but was an infamously sharp shooter. Teddy Roosevelt hired him as a guide and they set off by train to hunt on the Western Slope."

Violet sipped her cocktail, pensive. "I love the history of the Wild West. The Gold Rush, shootouts, and saloons. It's way better than slaves picking cotton in the South. Although what happened to the Indians was also terrible."

"It's all an embarrassment when you think about it that way."

"Sorry. It's a sore subject for me."

"That's why you live on an island in the Keys and not the plantation in Georgia."

"Thank God for that. It's still pretty backward there."

"What's your place in Jackson Hole like?"

"Daddy's place?" She clarified. "Dove Creek is nice. Typical ski lodge feel."

I chuckled. "The idyllic man cave?"

She nodded. "Exactly. It's beautiful out there though."

I raised a brow. "Sounds like you might actually be looking forward to it."

"I look forward to seeing what my daddy's got up his sleeve. And to getting some skiing in. It'll be my last chance before Christmas."

I ran my finger down the side of my glass, trying not to think about her skiing.

"I hope you get some fresh powder." Really, I hoped she'd make it down okay.

Violet smiled. "You should hit the slopes in Breck before it's too late."

I nodded, my gaze wandering to the age-spotted mirror behind the bar. "I probably should."

I definitely should. But my aversion to the sport I used to love had only gotten worse with time.

My phone dinged on the bar. I read the message from the hostess. "There's a table ready in the rooftop garden, just out here."

The air was warmer than I expected when we walked out to meet the hostess in the garden. The large gas heaters standing between the tables did the trick.

"It's nice out here. Might be hard to eat an elk steak while staring one in the eye."

I laughed at her assessment. "The taxidermy is a little morbid."

Her lips pursed like the last of her drink was sour. "I've never understood it. Daddy's got a big buck over the fireplace in the lodge."

"Isn't that obligatory?"

"I know it's a trophy, but who needs reminders of death on the wall?" She scowled. "Seems crazy to me."

I scanned the menu intently, trying not to think of my home in Breck. "The Rocky Mountain oysters are a Buckhorn Exchange specialty. You feeling adventurous?"

She scrunched her face, disgusted. "Elk is adventurous enough for me tonight. And I don't think you need anything for virility."

She was right about that. I'd had a half-chubby since I saw her at the hotel. "In your company, I most certainly do not." I grinned. "How about the grilled duck breast appetizer?"

"Sounds great." Violet continued to peruse the menu. "Want to split the elk medallions—save room for dessert?"

"That's not the dessert I had in mind."

Violet's dark eyes danced with mischief at the innuendo. "We can have both."

I chuckled. The dinner conversation was easy, as was everything with Violet.

Her eyes lit up when she gave me the details of the Condé Nast shoot. But she seemed genuinely surprised that Clifton had given her so much credit during the interview.

"He said that I was the one putting Paradise Key on the map, not him. Ha!" Her eyes rolled up toward the sky at the preposterousness of it all.

I eyed her, skeptical of her humility that bordered on delusion. Of course he gave her credit. She was integral to the resort's success. "You do run the place. And in half a year you're already a world-class destination. Hence the Condé Nast interest in the first place…"

Clearly uncomfortable discussing her accolades, Violet changed the subject. "I wonder how your sister is doing down there."

"I imagine she's having the time of her life. What I wonder is when you plan to tell her that we're meeting in Miami, or *if* you do?"

Violet took a deep breath. "I haven't really thought about it."

I held up my hands. "I'm just curious. I won't say anything, of course, but I won't be seeing her like you will. Keeping it from her is going to feel weird, fast."

"That's the bridge we'll cross when we come to it. Remember?"

She didn't want to get ahead of herself. I got it. Better to see how it plays out before bringing Corinne into it.

"You're right. The bridges can wait."

But staring into Violet's dark eyes, getting a deeper glimpse of her with every minute that we shared, I had no doubt that Miami would leave me jonesing for my next fix. The Violet high was better than any drug I'd ever tried.

She placed her spoon on the saucer and licked her lips. "Secret soirees are sexier."

"Surprise soirees are the sexiest." I squeezed her hand. "You wanna get outta here?"

Violet cocked a brow with a smirk. "Does a bear shit in the woods?"

CHAPTER 23

VIOLET

Hayden and I giggled down the hallway like teenagers rushing to steal a moment. The day had become a surreal fairytale. Fated by the Gods.

The hotel room door had barely closed behind us before we fell into each other's arms.

It had only been two weeks since I'd seen Hayden last. I'd gone almost seven months with no sex and hadn't even missed it much before I met him. But after I'd gotten a taste, it was all I could think about. I craved him.

Hayden pulled me tight, squeezing the breath from my chest. Warmth spread from deep in my core. I wanted his hands on every part of me at once. My palms ran over the contours of his muscular back while his hands slid down to lift my sweater dress over my head.

The tip of his tongue traced his upper lip while he stared at my chest. "God, I've missed you."

I looked up into the turquoise eyes I saw every time that mine closed. "I've missed you too."

I unbuttoned his shirt while he unbuckled his belt, both of us eager to feel what we'd been missing. I kissed my way down his chest. His hips shifted when I reached the black elastic stretched over the tip of his hard cock.

Stroking him through the silky fabric sent an electric surge between my thighs. He throbbed beneath my tender touch.

Hayden helped to push his underwear down, freeing his gorgeous cock. I'd thought about it while I touched myself at least a dozen times since he'd left the Keys.

My fingers wrapped around his rock-hard shaft. I *needed* that inside me, but first I wanted to taste him. Oral sex was something I did because I thought I had to before. But I craved it with Hayden.

I dropped to my knees, cupping his balls gently in my palm. I started at the base of his cock and licked my way up to the head, circling it with the tip of my tongue. His gasp when I took him into my mouth made me even wetter.

I swallowed him slowly, eventually taking him deeper into my throat than I'd ever managed before. The tip of my nose grazed the delicious trail of hair that bisected his toned abs.

He pulled me up to my feet, smiling as he pushed my hair off my face. "You never cease to amaze me."

Hayden took me by the shoulders and sat me on the edge of the bed. When he stepped closer, I reached for him, eager to taste him again.

His gentle fingers hooking under my jaw stopped me. Grinning, he said, "My turn."

My knees fell open as he lowered between them. The backs of his fingers trailed up my thigh, kiss after kiss following in their wake. My fingers worked into his dark hair as his tongue found my folds.

I bit my lip and moaned when his teeth raked over my swollen clit. He teased and flicked over it relentlessly. When I started to moan, his hand moved to my breast, rubbing and squeezing before rolling my nipple between his fingertips. The louder my moans, the harder he pinched, until I was gasping between a string of "Oh my gods." He knew my body like the back of his hand .

He stood, grinning as he wiped his face with his wrist before motioning for me to stand. Pivoting my shoulders, Hayden turned me to face the bed then pushed gently with a hand between my shoulder blades. I lowered my hands to the bed, gasping as he filled me.

I moaned as he pounded me from behind, louder when his fingers found my clit. As the wave built inside me, I dropped to my elbows. My arms trembled as my whole body shuddered. It had been too long even though it hadn't been long at all.

I climbed shakily up to the pillow. I licked my lips at the sight of Hayden's chest in the lamplight as I laid back. He was the sexiest man I'd ever seen naked, by a long shot.

His gaze locked mine as he climbed over me and entered me slowly.

I sighed, full of him and full of hope. "I haven't stopped thinking about you since you left Paradise Key."

The corners of his mouth curled to a smile. "That's good because I haven't been able to get you out of my head either. And I don't want to."

The intensity of his stare sent a surge through me.

Hayden slid easily in and out of my wetness, pushing so deep that I groaned. He held when he'd reached my limit, pausing for me to stretch so he could push my limit a little further. There was more of him than I could take, which made me want it all.

My fingers curled around the bedcover as I hooked my ankles behind his back, pulling him deeper with every thrust.

We made love for what felt like hours, but I lost all concept of time. When he finally let himself finish, I could barely move.

Hayden brought a washcloth from the bathroom and cleaned me up, smiling tenderly.

With his sweaty chest pressed into my back, wrapped in his arms, I wished that I wasn't leaving tomorrow and that perhaps he'd never let me go.

I sighed, eyelids heavy. "This feels like a dream." A dream come true.

Hayden kissed my hair before he whispered, "I couldn't have dreamed a better surprise."

CHAPTER 24

HAYDEN

The bed was empty beside me but I could still smell Violet on the pillow. Steam clouded the only light in the room coming from the open bathroom door. I was tempted to join her in the shower, but she had a plane to catch. I rolled over with a groan, stretching my arms over my head after I sat.

I tugged the zipper of my khakis over the erection that the shower thoughts provoked. The sweet song Violet hummed in the shower made me smile as I unwrapped the paper cups and filled the miniature coffee maker.

When Violet appeared wearing nothing but a towel around her head, my breath caught in my chest.

"Well, hello handsome."

"Good morning, gorgeous. I slipped my arm around her waist, brushing her lips with mine as I handed her the cup. "It's shitty coffee, but it's better than nothing."

"Thanks." She climbed in the bed, leaning back against the headboard to cross her ankles, leisurely sipping from the cup. She didn't seem to be in a hurry.

"What time did you say your flight is?"

"It's at nine. But while I was in the shower, I got to thinking…" She blew on the coffee before taking a quick sip. "Seeing as how fate has already intervened and delayed my plans, it wouldn't hurt to delay them a little longer."

I cocked my head as I threaded my arms into my sweater. "What do you mean?"

"I mean, I'm already here, and so are you. If I *happened* to miss my flight, we could have another day. Maybe hit the slopes? I could book an afternoon departure tomorrow and you could show me your house in Breck."

Fuck. I hadn't seen that coming.

My throat closed and I felt the blood drain from my face in a cool rush of panic. I couldn't take her to Breckenridge. More and more I'd seen my house for what it had become: a museum of my dead wife.

And I certainly couldn't take her skiing.

"As lovely as that sounds, I can't today."

Violet's smile faded. "Oh. I thought since it's Sunday you might be free."

My clammy palms tightened around my sweater that was still stretched across my chest. "Sorry, I already have plans."

I realized how aloof it sounded when I saw the disappointment in her eyes. I swallowed hard as I slipped my sweater over my head and blurted out the first thing that came to mind.

"Family obligation. My Aunt Margaret's in town." I turned to gather my shoes and socks from the floor, avoiding looking Violet in the eye for fear she'd see the lie written all over my face. But she shrugged with a grimace when I looked up.

"Dang it. I was hoping you would help me procrastinate. But I guess I might as well get it over with." She kicked her legs off the bed and hopped to her feet.

My heart pounded in my chest but I kept a steady voice. "Sorry, beautiful, it's just bad timing. But I'll see you Thursday in Miami."

Her brow wrinkled briefly, but she shrugged it off. "Thank the Lord. That gives me something to look forward to."

My shoulders relaxed as I wiped my clammy palms on my khakis. "Me too."

When I dropped Violet at Denver International, I dreaded going home as much as she dreaded going to Jackson Hole. The stupid lie I'd told gnawed at me, but not as much as the reason I'd had to tell it.

I stopped in a diner on the way into Breckenridge and was just finishing my breakfast when a couple of old friends walked in. Mark and Melanie. I hadn't seen them since Jill's funeral.

Melanie was a wreck that day. She was Jill's closest friend, the one Jill had cried to the most after the miscarriage. And she looked to be at least six months pregnant.

They didn't see me at first and I was kind of hoping they wouldn't, but Mark spotted me as he scanned the room for a table.

Melanie's bright smile spread as she rushed over to greet me. "Hayden Kincaid. How the hell have you been?"

"Hi Mel, and Mark." I nodded at her husband who looked as uncomfortable as I felt. "I've been good."

Melanie looked me over with wide eyes. "We were just talking about you the other night. How you seemed to have disappeared off the face of the earth."

My chin dipped, embarrassed at all the unanswered messages that'd finally stopped. "I've been traveling for work nonstop."

Melanie quipped, "I was hoping it's because you have a new girlfriend."

My head jerked in surprise at the strange comment from my late wife's friend. "No, I've just been working a lot." I eyed her belly. "It looks like you two have been busy too."

Mel's tone softened. "Yeah, can you believe it?" She rubbed over the bump under her blouse. "It's funny that the first person I wanted to tell when I found out was Jill." Her voice trailed.

I took a deep breath. "She'd be happy for you."

"I know she would." She paused, smiling warmly. "She'd be happy if you met someone else too."

Mark shot her a look. "Babe."

"Sorry, I know it's none of my business. But you just looked at me like I was crazy when I suggested you might have a new girlfriend, so I thought you might need to hear it."

I blinked up at her, speechless, while Mark shifted uncomfortably, looking at the floor. Instead of changing the subject to break the awkward silence, Melanie tried to explain further. “We’re all worried about you, Hayden. No one‘s heard anything from you in two years. I know your buddies have reached out.” She looked to Mark for reinforcement but he stared at his shoes.

She continued, undeterred. “We just want you to be happy. And Jill would too.”

I cleared my throat but my voice came out shaky. “Thank you. I appreciate it. I’m doing all right. Really.”

Mark finally looked up from the floor, embarrassed and apologetic. “Come for a barbecue Saturday. The whole crew’ll be there.”

“Thanks, I’d love to but I’ll be in Miami, extending a work trip for an extra couple of days in the sun.“

Mark smiled. “Well it’s good to hear you’re taking care of yourself. I’ll call you the next time we’re getting together.”

I nodded. “I’ll go next time for sure if I’m around.” I doubted they believed me any more than I did.

The trip up the hill to the dream house Jill and I’d built when we first married felt like returning to prison after a furlough. I opened the windows despite the chill to let the stale air escape, but it was stagnant. Trapped. The pictures all around chronicled happier times, now only collecting dust.

Violet’s words from last night rang in my head. Why would anyone want reminders of death on the wall? Living with ghosts can make you crazy.

Preserving Jill’s memories was keeping me from making new ones, but I wasn’t sure I could bring myself to let them go.

CHAPTER 25

VIOLET

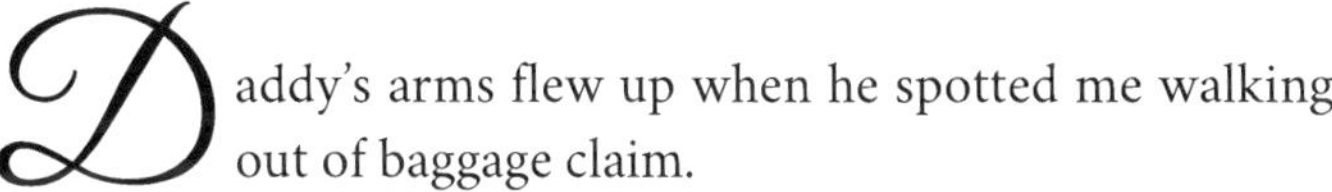

Daddy's arms flew up when he spotted me walking out of baggage claim.

"Over here, Punkin'!" He waved frantically from beside his big Dually truck. His giant grin made me feel guilty for dreading the visit.

"Hey, Daddy." I leaned in to kiss him on the cheek, but he pulled me into a big bear hug, lifting me off the ground.

Thankfully, he didn't seem the least bit frail, looking me over like he hadn't seen me in years. "'Bout damn time."

"I got here as fast as I could."

"I know. Just bad luck with the damn plane breaking."

I tried not to smile at what good luck it had been. "Yeah, but we've still got plenty of time. I'm here four more days." About three too many by my count.

He huffed as he wrested the handle of my suitcase from my hand insistently. "Thank the Lord for that."

I chuckled. Daddy was not a churchgoer or a praying man, but he did seem genuinely happy to see me. Which of course made me suspicious.

He rolled my suitcase around to the back of the truck, hoisting it up into the bed like it was light as a feather. Sixty years old and still strong as an ox and stubborn as a mule.

He filled me in on the latest news from the lodge, not that much had changed since I was here at Christmas.

"I gave Ezra the day off in the kitchen today so she could rest up before Irene comes. You know how your mama takes over that kitchen when she's here."

"Ezra will never live up to Mama's standards for southern cooking."

Daddy chuckled. "Well don't tell Ezra that. She's already nervous as a kitten every time your mother comes around."

"We having lunch there or are you gonna stop in town?" I heard my accent slip deeper into the familiar drawl of home even if we weren't in the South.

"Ezra made a big ol' pot of venison chili just for you when we thought you were coming yesterday. So we saved it."

I wasn't sure if that was intended as a dig, but I wasn't going to let him ruffle my feathers. "Chili is always better the second day."

Daddy reached across and patted my thigh. "Look at you—looking on the bright side. Must be all that Florida Keys sunshine."

My eyes slanted to study his face. He'd never been a fan of my choice to move to the furthest point from Wyoming in the lower 48. He'd practically begged me to come out and run the lodge when I left Michael. "It suits me well."

He smiled. "Well I'll say. You look pretty as a peach."

My cheeks flushed at the same compliment Hayden had paid me the night before. Heat rose in my chest but I had to put him out of my mind. I needed a clear head to see through whatever Daddy was buttering me up for.

"Thanks. You look good, too." I wasn't just being cordial. It was the truth. His smile was brighter than ever. Yet he was supposed to be sick? Something wasn't right.

"So, you saw a cardiologist, I hear."

"Oh, yeah. Seems I have little blockage"—he waved his hand—"nothing serious, though."

"Serious enough for a bypass?"

"No." He swatted like he was backhanding the exaggeration. "Not a bypass. They recommended a stent. I bet your mother made it out to be more than it is." His eyes rolled before they settled on me. "She's worried, but she shouldn't be. Neither should you."

I felt a little guilty that I'd never been worried, really. I figured his condition was exaggerated to persuade me to come out here, but it was surprising that it was Mama's doing. He sure as heck didn't look ill.

At least it was a fairly simple procedure he needed, and not open heart surgery. "When will you have the stent?"

Daddy shrugged like it didn't matter much. "In the next month, I suppose."

"And in the meantime…?" He was the kind of man who swung an axe for fun and spent most of his time on the mountain. "Are you supposed to limit activity?"

"The doctor said not to do anything crazy, so I'm staying off the moguls." He grinned. Even that was a sacrifice. Daddy liked adrenaline.

I eyed him, dubious of his compliance as a patient. "You're still skiing?"

"Only bunny slopes and cross country, real gentle."

I shook my head at his complacency. "As long as they say it's all right."

There wasn't any point in arguing that he should probably just take it easy.

Daddy dished out the chili and I helped him carry the bowls to the table. I savored the first bite. "God, that's amazing. I do miss this kind of food."

Daddy scooped a big spoonful of chili. "Are you tired of seafood yet? Must get old."

I smirked. "Does beef get old for you? You might ought to lay off the red meat, Daddy."

He laughed like I must be joking. "Clive is coming for dinner tonight. Chester will be with him." He looked down as he crumbled more Johnny cake into his bowl, trying not to smile.

He'd made a point of telling me Chester was recently divorced when I was here at Christmas. Was that what this was about? Surely he wouldn't drag me all the way back out here to set me up with Chester. He'd better not. "Is that right?"

"They just bought another thousand acres. I think Clive is trying to make the biggest ranch in the state."

"Well, good for them." I scraped my bowl with the spoon, grinning before I took the last bite. "I don't care what Mama says, this is the best chili I've ever had."

Daddy chuckled. "If your Mama was here you'd be singing a different tune."

"We all sing a different tune when Mama's around, don't we?" He could stay on his best behavior for a few days here and there. Somehow that was enough to keep her.

"She's got a feast planned for you. All your favorites."

My mouth watered at the thought of soup beans and turnip greens even though I was full to the brim. "I can't wait."

I laid my napkin over my bowl and pushed it to the side. My fingers laced together as I drew in a deep breath and lifted my gaze to look him dead in the eye.

"Are you going to tell me why you brought me out here?"

His look of shock and surprise was one I knew well and was not the least bit convincing when he said, "I asked you to come because I wanted to see you."

It was all I could do not to roll my eyes. My voice was steady even if my words were annoyed. "Quit beatin' around the bush."

"It's the truth. I did want to see you. We don't have to wait till holidays to get together."

I strained to contain my annoyance." You know the planes fly in both directions don't you? You can always come visit me in the Keys."

"Actually, I might be doing more of that soon. That's what I wanted to talk to you about. There's an interesting opportunity for us down there."

Us? Now the truth was coming out. I pretended like my mind wasn't already set, to hear him out. "What's that?"

"There's a condo hotel on the market down in Key West."

"Okay…?"

"It's 50 units, on the water with its own marina. It needs some work, but it's got good bones. I think with your eye for design we could do it up high end."

I shifted back in my chair, crossing my legs. "I'm happy to give you some advice when you get to that stage, if you do."

He smiled, eager. "I was thinking that you might want to run it?"

"I already have a job, Daddy." And I certainly didn't want one working for him.

"I'm not offering you a job, I'm asking you to be a partner. I'll put up all the money if you'll manage it. You'll be on the deed fifty-fifty. We'll split the profits, which should be sizable from the get-go, a lot more than they're paying you in that job, I'm sure."

I drew in a deep breath, careful of my tone as I spoke. "I make a pretty good salary, believe it or not. And I'm happy there. I'm not quitting my job, Daddy."

"You're too smart to be working for someone else. And for a salary." He said it like it was a bad word.

I was too smart to get caught in his web. "I have everything I need in the job you don't seem to think much of. I'm sure you can find a manager if you really want to buy the place."

He scowled. "Damn it, Violet. I'm trying to make a business with you. If you wanna live in the Keys, this is the perfect opportunity."

I put on the sweetest smile I could muster. "I already have the perfect opportunity. And I prefer to keep my business separate."

I expected him to blow up, but he seemed dejected as he answered, "You're the only one who can carry on the family legacy. Everything we've worked for…"

"Clay and Melissa have their own lives too, and pretty darned happy ones as far as I can tell. Everything *you've* worked for is not *our* responsibility. If you don't want to take on more, then don't." My gaze fell to my lap where I smoothed my dress over my thigh.

Daddy shook his head. "You've all done well for yourselves. I know you don't *need* my help. Especially you." He shook his head. "Hell, you wouldn't even let me pay for Harvard. Went to Cornell just because they gave you tennis money. Who chooses Cornell over Harvard?"

There was something satisfying that he was still bothered by that.

"I did. Because it's what I wanted. Just like my job now." The way he minimized my accomplishments always got my goat. "You could be proud of me, of all of us, you know? If you'd stop trying to make everyone do what you want them to and be happy that we've made the lives we want for ourselves."

His hands flew up like it was inevitable. "Well, I guess I might as well. Not like anybody listens to me anymore anyway."

I recognized his ploy. He'd moved into the pleading-for-sympathy stage, but I wasn't going to bite "I guess that's what happens when people grow up."

He chuckled and seemed truly amused. "Maybe that's the trouble. I've tried my whole life to avoid that."

My laugh was dry, and I wished we'd had wine with lunch. I couldn't joke about his galavanting. The sting was still too strong.

"Quite successfully, Daddy."

He laughed, unfazed by my bitterness. "Growing up is overrated. But I know better than to keep on. You've got stubborn in your genes, from both sides, Punkin'." He pushed back from the table. "Wanna hike down to the stream? Beavers built a nice little dam that filled out a swimming hole."

Part of me wanted to pick a fight, but I knew I was better off just to let it go. "It's a little cold for a swim."

"Weather's perfect for a walk. The swim can wait till summertime. It'd be nice if all three of you kids could get out here when it's warm. Maybe you'll be able to fit it in."

"Let's see." I stood to follow him out. "Show me that swimming hole."

~

Daddy steered clear of any talk of business or anything else that might push buttons—which made me think he was devising another strategy to try to convince me. Whatever his motivation, it was a pleasant afternoon trudging the trails.

He pointed out every critter big and small, and marveled over the beaver dam like it was a Frank Lloyd Wright masterpiece. His fascination with nature took me back to the long summer days on the Chattahoochee. And when he put his arm around my shoulder for the walk back to the lodge, I was twelve again.

He squeezed my shoulder on the way up the back steps. "I need to make a couple of calls. Your room is ready if you want to go rest and freshen up for dinner."

My room was the Presidential Suite even though the head of Daddy's bank in Billings was the only president I'd ever known to stay there. While not nearly as fancy as the name implied, the suite's mountain view was fit for a king.

I could see why Daddy loved it here. I'd resented the lodge since he bought it and tried to hate it out here. But it was hard not to fall in love with it.

I pulled out my phone for the first time since I'd landed. There was only a text from Mama asking if I'd made it. Nothing from Hayden. Busy with his aunt, I figured.

I texted him:

I made it to Jackson Hole, all good. You?

After my long shower, there was still no reply. Even if he was busy he could at least say hello. My insecure brain took the doubt baton and ran with it, replaying this morning's conversation with the disappointment amplified from a three to a ten.

Hayden had a legitimate excuse to turn down my offer, but my ego felt it. And worse, my suspicious mind wondered if he just didn't want to invite me into his real life. It felt like we had a good thing going, but he was definitely guarded after I suggested that we go to his place in Breckenridge.

I looked my reflection in the eye after brushing on some mascara. "Stop being so needy."

Needy and negative was how I usually felt by the end of day one with my dad. My mood probably had more to do with him than Hayden. I needed to keep that in check.

My distrust of men started with my dad, but it also seemed to make me gravitate to men who didn't deserve to be trusted. Like some kind of cruel self-fulling prophecy. That wasn't the case with Hayden, I was almost sure.

Corinne said he had issues. Mine were probably just as bad.

I put on a fake smile and mustered my manners to pretend I wanted to be at dinner with Clive and Chester. As long as you smile and nod, men don't usually notice whether you're interested or not. Or maybe they just don't care. Either way, it was easy to be a wallflower for most of the evening.

Daddy flattered me by telling them how well I was doing down in the Keys.

"She runs the whole damn show."

Apparently my position was brag-worthy if beneath me. The bragging was more for Chester's benefit, I suspected. He was tall and handsome and a true gentleman. A real catch for someone who'd be content as a rancher's wife. Fortunately he seemed to know I wasn't the one and didn't bother even casting a line.

After two whiskeys by the fire, I stood up when Daddy reached for the bottle of Glenlivet to pour a third. "I'm afraid I'm gonna have to turn in. I'm still on east coast time."

Daddy frowned. "That's the trouble with you living two time zones away."

"It didn't help that it took me two days to get here." I nodded at Clive and Chester. "It was nice seeing y'all again. Maybe Daddy will invite you back for some of Mama's home cooking."

Chester smiled politely but his father beamed. "We wouldn't miss that." He turned to his son. "I've never had a peach cobbler like hers in all my life."

I could smell it baking at the mere mention of my favorite dessert. "Neither have I."

Chester surprised me when he spoke up. "You take care of yourself if I don't see you again."

"I will. You too, Chester. Good luck with everything."

It's not easy being a full-grown adult, over 30 years old, with parents who think you need help getting a date. We had that in common, if nothing else.

I'd purposely left my phone in my room so I wouldn't be tempted to check it over dinner. My anxious heart thumped when I picked it up, hoping for a message from Hayden while simultaneously dreading not seeing one. My arms felt heavy as I let out a breath of relief when it was there.

Hey gorgeous. Glad you made it. I hope your day was better than you expected. I'm off to bed. Early flight to Dallas. Counting the days until Miami. Sweet dreams.

I clutched the phone to my chest, butterflies swarming in my stomach. My doubts from earlier seemed trivial. Hayden was getting ready for a turnaround trip to Dallas and had a visitor. What did I expect?

The message was from over an hour ago so I hesitated to reply. But I needed him to know I was missing him.

It's never easy but the day wasn't so bad after all. Dreaming about Miami is the light at the end of the tunnel. I CANNOT WAIT. <Kiss emoji>

For fear of sounding too excited, I added quickly:

Hope you had fun with your aunt today. Safe travels.

My heart was so full of want that I felt empty inside. When I reread his message, my eyes fixed on the three words that summed up why.

Counting the days.

CHAPTER 26

HAYDEN

There was only one empty seat in business class when I made it on the plane. I'd missed early boarding thanks to traffic on the highway and long lines in security. After I stowed my carry-on and buckled up, I pulled out my phone to reply to Violet's messages I'd read while still half-asleep after my alarm went off.

It was hard to read how things were really going with her dad from her message. "It's never easy but not so bad" wasn't exactly positive. I felt terrible that I couldn't help her put the visit off another day since she'd obviously been dreading it.

The next message made my stomach knot.

Hope you had fun with your aunt today.

"Idiot." I mumbled under my breath but apparently loud enough for my neighbor in the window seat to hear because she shot me a glance before returning to her book.

I'd blown my chance at another night with Violet and let her down. I was ashamed that I couldn't let her in even though I wanted to, for fear that my reality might scare her off.

The worst part was that I'd told a colossally stupid lie in the process. The sting of guilt was like a needle in my chest.

Good morning, gorgeous. About to take off for Dallas. Sorry I couldn't help you procrastinate the visit with your dad but I'm glad to hear it's going okay. I hope it keeps getting better.

My gaze drifted to my seat-neighbor who was engrossed in a book that she held propped on her long floral skirt. Red roses on a black background gave me an idea. Maybe a nice bouquet would brighten Violet's day.

The captain's voice overhead alerted us that we were preparing for take-off. I hurried to search for an online florist. Nothing caught my eye as I scrolled through the photos on the homepage of the first one in the search. Even the romantic-albeit-cliché classic dozen roses didn't feel right.

Then the poetic verse popped in my mind: *Roses are red, violets are blue.*

I chuckled since they're actually purple, but maybe her namesake flower would make Violet feel less blue.

They offered a potted violet plant with a pretty pink ribbon. I quickly opened another browser window on my phone and googled Dove Creek Lodge. After copying and pasting the lodge address into the order, I typed with my thumbs as fast as I could, adding a note: Violets are blue, like me, without you.

I hoped the surprise would cheer Violet up. And maybe ease my conscience.

As we taxied into the gate in Dallas, I powered my phone on to find a text from Violet.

Good morning! Don't worry, all good. It was better not to prolong the inevitable. Looking forward to Mom coming this afternoon. I know you'll be busy but have a great day in Dallas!

My smile grew wider as I replied.

Crazy busy day here. I'd rather be there. Have fun with your folks.

My phone rang just as I was stepping out of the jetway. Gerald, the IT director at Dallas County General was already waiting outside. When I hung up, I noticed a voice message icon in the corner of the screen.

I smiled when I saw it was from Corinne. I clutched the phone close to my ear to hear as I sped through the noisy terminal, rolling my carryon bag behind me. Her voice was elated.

"Hey there. I just got back on dry land. It was so fucking amazing. But I'm ready for a long shower. Call me when you get a chance. I can't wait to tell you all about it. I hope you're doing great."

That would be a long conversation—one that would have to wait because Gerald was waving from the curb. I tucked my phone into my pocket before shaking his hand.

Gerald gripped my shoulder with his other hand. "Good to see you again Hayden. How was your trip?"

"Not bad at all, thanks. Everything all set for the launch?"

He replied in a boisterous Texan accent, "Ready as we'll ever be."

I nodded as I slid into the passenger seat of his sedan. "I know it's been one hurdle after another. But hopefully we will get all the bugs worked out today." You never know what's going to happen when a new software goes live.

Gerald huffed. "Let's hope there aren't any bugs."

I shrugged. "Minor glitches are to be expected. But that's what I'm here for."

By one o'clock we'd reviewed all the systems and pulled the trigger on the first live test. Gerald instructed one of his IT guys to get busy testing every point of input in some mock patient files. "While he does that we can grab a bite. The hospital administrator wants to take us to Morton's for lunch.

Texans love their beef. I'd almost have preferred chicken myself so early in the day but it somehow felt sacrilegious at a high-end steakhouse.

The administrator was gracious as we sawed into slabs of beef. "While we've enjoyed your visits, I'm hoping we won't be seeing a lot more of you in the near future."

My phone dinged in my pocket as I answered. "Hopefully you won't need to. But I'll be here if you need me, rest assured."

While my hosts went on about how pleasurable the experience with our software company had been despite the hiccups on their end, three more dings sounded from my phone in rapid succession

I held up a hand, embarrassed. "Sorry." I fished my phone out of my pocket.

Gerald extended his palm, understanding. "Of course, do what you have to do."

Four texts from Jenna Dallas TD. The screen was full of Tinder notifications underneath.

Shit. I hadn't looked at Tinder in weeks but apparently I was still logged in. And Jenna had noticed I was back in the area. We'd had a perfectly fine but unremarkable date the last time I was here.

"No, it's nothing important." I powered the phone off after it sounded again in my hand. I felt a little guilty, not for ignoring Jenna, but that another woman was in my phone when Violet was on my mind.

With our bellies full of steak, we returned to the facility. Fortunately the installation had gone fairly smoothly. We still spent the whole afternoon fixing glitches and there were more to go when the IT staff asked if we planned to continue or finish up tomorrow.

I looked up at the clock on the wall. "Oh, wow, it's 6:30. Time flies when you're having fun."

Gerald turned to me with a smile. "Up to you, boss. I can order some food in for these guys if you want to carry on."

I definitely didn't want to spend another day in Dallas if I didn't have to. "I'm game if you guys are. I have an early flight out tomorrow. It was all that was available on short notice."

Gerald nodded. "We might as well. You guys like overtime, don't you."

His employees shrugged. It was obvious that they'd rather go home. But so would I. We powered through, breaking only to eat the boatload of sushi that was delivered two hours later.

It was nearly 10:30 when a full system check finally came back clean. Only then, when I pulled out my phone to call an Uber to my hotel, did I realize it had been off all day.

I started to message Corinne while I waited for the car, but it was after midnight in the Keys. A text probably wouldn't disturb her if she was asleep, but I was more concerned that she might not be and would want to chat. As much as I wanted to hear all about her underwater lab adventure, I was beat.

When I got to my room, I deleted the texts from Jenna that went from *Heyyyy* to *I guess you're busy. Nevermind.*

I messaged Violet.

Long fucking day. But it's over now, and only two more to go before I see you in Miami.

When she hadn't replied by the time I brushed my teeth and washed my face, I sent a goodnight message punctuated with a heart because mine was full of her.

CHAPTER 27

VIOLET

The lodge staff were all running around like chickens with their heads cut off getting ready for Mama's arrival as Daddy and I finished up a late breakfast.

"You'd think the queen of England was coming. Why is everyone in a tizzy?"

"You know how your mother likes everything just so. She sent a grocery list a mile long. If you wanna see a tizzy, go in the kitchen. Ezra's a mess. Clara is upstairs putting on the new sheets your mother had sent." He chuckled, shaking his head. "Whatever makes her happy."

I was surprised they still slept in the same room the few times a year they were together. "Has she been out here since Christmas?"

"No. She's been busy, decorating the new condo, I suppose."

"Have you seen it?"

He shook his head. "Only the pictures. Looks nice doesn't it?"

"Mama wouldn't pick anything that wasn't *real* nice."

"Maybe we can meet out there next time. Get some California sun." He smiled wistfully, pausing to let the daydream play out before he snapped back to reality. "You coming to the airport with me?"

"I need to get showered and changed. When's she land?"

He glanced at his Rolex. "In 20 minutes."

"You better go on without me then. You don't want to keep Mama waiting."

He pushed back from the table. "I know better than that."

I knew better than to ponder how strange it was that my parents led separate lives and yet we'd soon be pretending to be a happy family like we always did. I'd rather think about the California boy who liked to try to talk Southern.

When my phone rang on the bathroom counter while I rinsed my hair, I hoped it was Hayden. But then I wondered if his sister had somehow telepathically connected to my thoughts when hers was the name on the screen.

"Corinne has resurfaced!" I called out as I reached for a towel, even though there was no one to hear.

I hurried to answer before it went to voicemail. "The mermaid is back from the deep."

"I am." I could hear her smile. "It was amazing but I'm happy to be back."

I switched the call to speaker and set the phone on the counter so I could dry myself. "I bet. Was it weird being in such close quarters for so long?"

"Not really. The weird part was being monitored 24/7, but I got used to it."

I caught my surprised look in the mirror. "Oh wow, I hadn't thought about that. I guess they'd have to, to make sure you're still alive down there. But it must be strange knowing someone is watching you sleep."

"Actually, there are no cameras on the bunks. And, honestly, by the third day I was so exhausted I didn't think about anything."

I laughed. "Are you sick of scuba diving?"

"Never!" She laughed. "God, you can't imagine what I saw, Violet. Especially on the night dives. It was fascinating. I'd do it all over again if I could."

"Maybe you'll get a chance again someday."

She laughed. "Pff. I was lucky to have this one. But you never know. So, tell me, how's it going with your dad?"

I sat down on the bed to rub lotion on my legs. "The usual. He tried to talk me into a business idea in Key West, but I politely declined. He didn't push too hard, but I'm guessing I haven't heard the end of it."

"Well, stick to your guns."

"Oh, I will." I carried the phone over to the wardrobe and pulled out a dress. "I can't wait to see you, and I really want to hear all about the lab, but I better go for now. I'm standing here naked and my folks will be back any minute."

She laughed. "You better get your armor on. But hey, before I let you go, I was curious… have you kept in touch with Hayden at all?"

My back straightened and I could see panic in my eyes in the mirror. Why was she asking that? "A little, why?"

"His phone is going straight to voicemail and my texts don't seem to have been delivered."

I focused on keeping a steady voice but it still came out higher pitched than normal. "Oh yeah, he asked me a couple of days ago when you'd be back. He said something about heading to Dallas today after a visit from your aunt yesterday so he was probably on the plane."

"Oh, that's cool. I didn't know Aunt Trish was in Colorado."

"No, I think it was your other aunt… Margaret, I think he said."

After a short silence she said, "It must've been Trish. Margaret died almost four years ago."

I doubted myself for a second but I could hear Hayden saying it clear as a bell. He said Aunt Margaret.

Ice spilled down my spine.

My breath caught and my chest constricted as dawning set in. Hayden had lied.

I couldn't even ask Corinne why he'd lie about a *dead aunt* visiting since she still had no idea we'd hooked up.

"Ah, I guess I mixed it up." I swallowed to stop my voice from trembling. "Anyway, he's probably traveling today."

"Okay, I'll catch up with him later then. When are you back in the Keys?"

I was supposed to be in Miami with her brother until Sunday but now I wasn't sure about anything. "I don't know exactly. Maybe Thursday. But I may stay through the weekend."

"Well get your ass back so we can catch up. There's a great band playing at Sloppy Joe's Saturday. We're due a Duval Crawl."

Three minutes ago, I would have traded a night on the town in Key West for a weekend in Miami with her brother. But that was before I knew he was a liar. I forced a laugh. "It's been a minute. I'll let you know how it goes here."

"Alright. We'll catch up later. Good luck."

The last conversation with Hayden replayed in my mind. He went from cool and relaxed to slightly frazzled after I suggested extending my stay. That's when he'd blurted out the excuse about Aunt Margaret.

First he said he had plans. Then he added that it was a family obligation.

The only reason I could think of to lie about that was that he had other plans he didn't want to tell me about. Maybe "Aunt Margaret" was actually a 25-year-old ski bunny.

My eyes teared up while I brushed on mascara. I stopped to fan them, telling myself in the mirror, "You are not going to cry over that man."

I pushed the pain that brewed in my chest down to the deepest parts where I'd buried all the heartache over Michael when I left New York.

I took a deep breath, rationalizing with myself. Hayden was free to do whatever the hell he wanted. It's not like we were in a relationship.

Even though I didn't like it one bit, I had no right to be upset over him having plans with another woman.

And that didn't necessarily make him a bad guy. But lying about it... That did.

I heard Mama's voice calling my name before the knock at the door. Smoothing the front of my dress, I took a deep breath to quell the seething so I could paint on a fake smile—an art I'd learned from the master herself.

My mother's smile was genuine though. "Violet, darling. You look positively gorgeous." She looked me over before pulling me into her arms.

Her familiar scent and the comfort of her hug threatened to unleash the emotion I'd tried to suppress. I held my breath for a second to try to stop the tears welling up in my eyes. "Thank you, Mama. You look beautiful too. How was your trip?"

"You know how I hate those small planes. But I'm here. That's all that matters."

"Yes it is. And I'm glad that you are." After the hug she'd given me, I realized how much I needed her right then.

We spent the afternoon on the back porch sipping sweet tea and catching up while Daddy went off to help Clive with repairs on his ranch.

Turns out Mama had stayed in La Jolla for a pickleball tournament. She was making quite a life for herself out there. And Daddy had his here.

What I couldn't understand was why they stayed together on paper. They acted like everything was normal, but I guess it was, for them.

"Well, what did they ask you?" Mama wanted to hear all about the Condé Nast interview.

"Pretty much everything you can imagine. Who knows what they'll end up using in the article. They took a million pictures too."

She beamed. "I can't wait to see it. I'm proud of you."

It would've been nice if she'd been proud of my actual position rather than a magazine article, but I'd take what I could get.

"This job has been an amazing opportunity. It's about time that you come visit Paradise Key, don't you think?"

"I'd like that. Your father wants Clay and Melissa to meet us down there. Organizing that is darn near impossible. The way Clay works. And Melissa with two kids."

I nodded with a shrug. "We're all busy." With our own lives that rarely intersected.

"You ever hear from Michael?"

My head jerked in surprise at the mention of my ex-fiancé, from way out in left field. I couldn't mask my scowl. "No, why would I?"

We were over and done, and she knew it, or at least she should have known it. "I think I made it crystal clear that that bridge was burnt when I picked up and moved to an island as far away from that man as I could get."

Her lips drew to one side and she shrugged, like it was debatable. "Yeah, but people change. Minds change. Time can change everything. I was just wondering if anything had changed. That's all."

"Are you suggesting that I might forgive him someday? That I might magically trust him again and want to give him another chance? Not that he wants it. He's still shacked up with his paralegal as far as I know."

Mama might put up with that kind of crap, but I wasn't going to.

"I'm not suggesting anything of the sort. Don't get all worked up, dear. I just hope you meet a nice man someday."

"So do I, Mama." My voice caught in the lump that formed in my throat. I looked away too late to hide the hurt in my eyes.

She reached to turn my chin up and just stared for a long second, reading my pain. "I'm sorry, Violet. I shouldn't have brought Michael up. That was stupid of me. I know it must still hurt."

I couldn't tell her that the tears now streaming down my face weren't about Michael at all. I let her believe they were as she pulled me into a tight hug that I desperately needed.

I sobbed on her shoulder long enough to soak a spot on her silk blouse. I noticed it when wiping my nose with back of my hand, trying to pull myself together.

"Oh, Lord, that's gonna leave a stain. I'm sorry."

Mama rubbed my arm to soothe me. "I have three more like it."

I chuckled, sniffling. "Not in that color."

She winked. "Neiman Marcus does."

And just like that, we left the real talk for chatter about clothes and cooking and her bridge league.

~

Our dinner conversation was light and trivial, at first. The new jacuzzi at the lodge was way better than the last. The horse farm down the road was offering tours now. Ezra's biscuits weren't quite right.

Mama scowled. "I'm making the dough for the chicken and dumplings myself tomorrow. I don't want her messing it up."

Daddy shook his head but was clearly amused. "You'll have plenty of time because me and Violet are heading out ski shooting."

Mama gave him the eye. "You shouldn't be skiing, let alone shooting a rifle in your condition."

"My doctor said it's fine." The finality in his voice was clear. She'd better not bring it up again.

Daddy did whatever he damn well pleased, and nobody better try to tell him any different. I was tempted to snap at him for shutting my mother down, like he always did. But then his tone turned soft.

"Irene, I know you're worried. But I'm listening to the doctors. I'm taking care. Believe me, I want to be around for a few more decades for you, and the kids, and the grandkids." He looked my way. "That should give you time to have a couple of those. Maybe Clay, too." He chuckled.

Sweet as he was trying to be, I wasn't letting him drag me into that topic. "It just might."

Mama had to chime in though. "Well, I sure hope so. We'd love to have a few more young'ns running around."

Trying to deflect, I said, "Clay's your best bet. He's got a lot more baby-making years ahead of him than I do."

My mother didn't veer off on the tangent like I'd hoped though. "That's why I can't understand why you moved to an island, dear. How do you expect to find a nice man there?"

I rolled my eyes. "The odds are as good there as anywhere." Close to zero.

"I suppose you do have some interesting people passing through. They can't be poor if they're staying there."

I counted to five in my head before I responded. "I'm not looking for a man on Paradise Key or anywhere. I'm focused on my career right now."

"Good for you, dear." Mama was trying *not* to sound patronizing, but she still did. "Speaking of which, your daddy told you about the property in Key West?"

"Yes he did." My eye flitted to Daddy who had on his best poker face. "And I told him I think it's a great idea if he wants to do that himself. I won't be able to be involved."

She kept trying to sell the idea though. "At least there, you'd be in civilization. Maybe you should think about it."

I smiled, but she was testing my patience. "I did think about it. And I said no."

"I know, but you can always change your mind. It makes a lot more sense to be working on something of your own than someone else's, don't you think?"

My eyes narrowed. She ought to understand why I didn't want to be under Daddy's thumb. "It wouldn't exactly be my own, would it? It's best not to mix family and business."

She persisted though. "You can trust family more than anybody. And your father's worked hard all his life to build what we have. It'd be nice if one of you would appreciate it."

I wasn't sure if it was her doing Daddy's dirty work or me believing that you can't trust anybody that made my blood boil.

"Why are you going to bat for him? He's barely been around for years."

I regretted it as soon as I said it, when I saw the hurt in my father's eyes. He looked stunned when he said, "I've been around. I've been right here."

"Yes you have, Daddy." He'd been right here in this lodge, two thousand miles away from home. It was a convenient excuse for leaving.

My mother jumped to his defense again. "He's been out here building this place up for all of us."

Why was she always making excuses for him? There was no point in even discussing it. I'd never understand. It was easier just to tell them what they wanted to hear and try to move on.

"I know. And I do appreciate it. I hope you can both appreciate that I want to do my own thing."

"If that's what you want right now, you do what you have to do, Punkin'."

I blinked in disbelief before my eyes slanted suspiciously. "Thanks, Daddy."

My head pounded and I was exhausted from all the pretense. I didn't know what was real anymore.

"I've had a headache for the last couple of hours. I think I need to take a couple of aspirin and hit the hay if we're going to be shooting guns tomorrow."

"I want you shipshape for the biathlon. Get some rest, Punkin." He stood to give me a hug, and Mama followed.

Her mouth turned down in a frown. "I was hoping we could go sit by the fire." She squeezed my shoulders, her face warming with a smile. "But we can do that tomorrow and Wednesday. You fly back to Key West Thursday morning, right?"

I nodded, squinting when it made my headache worse. "Miami. But yes. Thursday morning."

Mama's brow furrowed, perplexed. "Isn't Miami a lot further?"

"The Key West flights were all booked." The lie came out easy but the truth of why I was going to Miami was what hurt.

"Oh, I see. We appreciate you coming all this way."

I forced a smile. "Of course. Goodnight, Mama."

"Good night dear." She kissed my cheek before she whispered, "You take care of him out there tomorrow, you hear?"

"I'll do my best." She knew as well as I did that he'd do as he pleased.

My heavy legs barely carried me up the stairs. By the time I reached my bed I crumpled into blubbering mess.

I cried for the lost hope that Hayden was different. I cried for all the years of wishing Daddy was too. They were all the same, men. You couldn't trust a single one.

I'd nearly cried myself to sleep when my phone sounded from the nightstand.

Seeing Hayden's name on the notification made my heart race and sink at the same time.

Long fucking day. But it's over now, and only two more to go before I see you in Miami.

My first angry thought was who was he fucking in Dallas? And I hated myself for it. I dropped my phone onto my chest and ugly cried until I could barely breathe.

When Hayden texted goodnight with a heart, I threw my phone across the room, cringing when it hit the table leg with a thud.

I might have just broken my phone, but Hayden Kincaid wasn't going to break my heart.

CHAPTER 28

HAYDEN

While waiting in an impossibly long line at the airport Starbucks, I checked my phone again. Violet still hadn't responded to last night's messages. It was only 7:00 am there. Hopefully another text wouldn't wake her.

I'm heading back to Denver but dreaming about us in South Beach. This is the place I booked. Thursday can't come soon enough.

I sent the link for Nikki Beach, the place I'd decided on after hours of research to plan the perfect getaway. Bonus that they had the best Sunday brunch in town, which we'd get to enjoy before we said goodbye again.

When I powered my phone back on after we touched down in Denver, I held my breath waiting for it to connect to the network.

The brief relief I felt at seeing Violet had messaged me dissolved when I read her text.

Miami isn't going to work out. Sorry just bad timing.

I rubbed my eyes before I read it again, hoping I'd misunderstood. But the words hadn't changed.

What the hell?

The other passengers stood when the seatbelt sign went off. The man in the window seat to my right stared down at me impatiently. "I've got a tight connection. Do you mind?"

I grumbled as I shoved my phone in my pocket. "No, sorry about that."

I nearly tripped over my own feet hurrying to my car so I could call Violet to see what had happened. But it went to voicemail after the first ring. I dialed again only to get the same result. What the fuck had happened?

I texted:

Everything okay out there?

I was already through the western suburbs when she replied.

Not really. I can't talk now.

Had two days with her parents gotten to her? Maybe her father's heart condition was worse than she expected. I hoped not, but mostly I worried whether Violet was okay. She didn't seem to be.

I was sick to my stomach and didn't know what else to do. I wished I could ask Corinne if she knew what was wrong. I still owed her a call anyway.

If she'd heard anything concerning she'd probably say so without my asking. I was almost to the pass when I rang her.

She sounded groggy when she answered. "Hey there. It's about time. I've been trying to call you."

"Yeah, sorry about that. Work's been crazy."

"That's okay. Are you still in Dallas?"

I tilted my head. I hadn't mentioned Dallas. "No, I'm driving home from the airport right now. How'd you know I was in Dallas?"

"Violet told me."

Hearing her name made my heart race with hope that Corinne knew what was going on with her. I tried to sound nonchalant though. "Oh, good. Is she doing okay?"

"Yeah, seems like her trip to Wyoming is going better than she expected."

Not what I expected to hear, but I hoped it was true. Why the hell wasn't she coming to Miami then?

"That's good news. She sounded like she was dreading the visit."

"She was. It's a tricky relationship. So, yeah, I was happy to hear it was going smoothly when I talked to her yesterday. I'm hoping she'll be home Thursday like she said. I'll be ready to cut loose this weekend."

I tried not to sound shocked she was planning to return to the Keys instead of coming to Miami. "Thursday, huh?"

"She said she wasn't sure exactly."

I tried to sound upbeat. "Ah, well, I'm sure you two will have a blast when she's back. But you're off today. Why wait? Go have some fun."

Corinne groaned. "I might. But it's not the same without Violet."

My chest tightened. "Everybody needs a partner in crime." I cleared my throat that threatened to close.

"So, tell me about the lab. Was it everything you dreamed it would be?"

"It was everything and more. I'm still processing it, to be honest. It's hard to describe, but life-changing is the best adjective I've come up with yet."

I'd had life-changing moments with her best friend, so I could relate. "That says it all."

"I got some great data on octopuses. They are fascinating creatures."

I kept my eyes on the road that winded into the mountains, forcing a small laugh as I said, "I read about one that could predict soccer outcomes in Spain."

She laughed. "It actually wouldn't surprise me. They're wicked smart. Oh, hey, I have a call with the professor out in Boulder Thursday. Maybe I can finagle another visit soon."

"That'd be great. Did you get everything you needed for him down there?"

I waited but the line was silent. I looked down at my phone on the dashboard. I'd lost her in the pass. I was a little relieved since I was in no mood for small talk.

Corinne obviously had no information to explain what the hell was happening with Violet. I had no idea what her reason for canceling Miami might be, but the sinking feeling in my gut told me it was bad.

I waited until I was almost home to call Corinne back. "Sorry, you know there's no signal in the pass"

"That's okay, I figured."

"You were telling me about coming back to Boulder..."

"Yeah. I'm hoping he will want to invite me out to review all the data with his department. We'll see Thursday."

I couldn't tell her I'd be at a meeting in Miami Thursday because I still hoped that Violet would be there with me, if I could only get through to her.

"That's awesome. Keep me posted. I'm just getting home now. You know you're always welcome here."

I turned into the driveway, where the snowbanks had finally melted down, as Corinne said, "Thank you. And, hey, that reminds me...What was Aunt Trish doing in Breck? I guess I'm totally out of the loop after nearly 2 weeks underwater."

What was she talking about? I turned off the ignition and walked around to the back of the Rover to grab my carryon.

"It's news to me, too, but I'm always out of the loop. Was she here while I was in Dallas?"

Walking up the steps to the porch I spotted a pink ribbon outside the door. When I got closer I recognized the half-wilted purple flowers, delivered to me, not Violet. I must've fucked up the order somehow. So much for that gesture.

That's what I got for trying to ease my guilty conscience--a withered violet.

I realized Corinne had been talking but I hadn't heard a word until she repeated, "Wasn't she?"

"Sorry, I didn't catch that. What did you say?" I pushed my luggage inside the door and went back for the plant.

"I said I thought Aunt Trish was there with you before you left for Dallas. Wasn't she?"

I balanced the phone between my shoulder and my face as I turned on the faucet to water the wilted flower. "No, why? Did mom tell you that?"

I lifted the shriveled flowers to my nose. Still sweet. Maybe it wasn't too far gone.

"No, Violet told me that."

I set the plant on the counter and then put my hand down to steady myself. It landed right beside the photo of me and Jill and Aunt Margaret. This was not good.

"Violet said Aunt Trish was here?"

"Actually, she said she thought it was Aunt Margaret. But since that's obviously not possible, I assumed she meant Aunt Trish."

"Oh."

Corinne was silent for a couple of seconds, waiting for me to elaborate. She finally said, "Oh? What's that mean?"

After another second of silence, her voice was anxious. "Hayden?"

I rubbed my knuckle over my upper lip and drew in a breath. "Tell me exactly what Violet said, please."

Corinne was clearly annoyed when she answered slowly. "She said our aunt was there before your trip to Dallas."

I tried to speak calmly as my stomach knotted. "And what did you tell her?"

Corinne continued in the patronizing tone. "I told her I didn't know Aunt Trish was in Colorado. That's when she said she thought it was Aunt Margaret."

The realization of what must've come next made me nauseous. "And then you told her Aunt Margaret is dead?"

"Yeah, of course."

I looked at the picture that'd started it all. "Fuck."

Corinne asked, confused, "Why 'fuck'? What's going on Hayden?"

My voice came out shaky and dejected. "I fucked up."

"How?"

I couldn't find the words.

"Hayden?"

I took a deep breath. "There's something I have to tell you…."

I came clean about the drunken hookup after her party, and about how Violet and I really enjoyed being together those last couple of days on Paradise Key. I finished with the surprise layover in Denver that led to Violet trying to come to my house.

"I wanted to invite her back here, but I didn't think I could. I haven't had another woman in my house since Jill died." I swallowed to stop my voice from quivering. "I happened to be putting on the sweater that Aunt Margaret had given me for Christmas."

When I paused for a breath, Corinne interjected. "I remember that sweater."

"That sweater is what made me think of Aunt Margaret. I said Aunt Margaret was coming for a visit."

The silence on the other end lasted long enough to make me wonder if I'd lost the connection. But the silence was better than Corinne's ire when it came.

"You're an idiot."

I winced. "I know. Believe me. I know."

"I'm an idiot, too. I thought you guys would be perfect for one another, but I should have known better."

I felt like I might burst into tears as I pushed out the words. "Maybe we *are* perfect for each other."

"Pff. Well, good luck with that."

"I want to make it right." I hated how weak I sounded.

I could tell Corinne was trying to stay calm, but there was still an angry edge to her tone.

"Let's get this straight… you blew her off after a romantic night when she tried to stay an extra day with you at your house. And lied about your plans that were more important than she was to you at the time."

My voice trembled. "But there weren't any plans." Only fear.

Corinne's annoyance grew. "But you *said* you had plans and then lied about them. What do you think she's thinking right now, Hayden?"

Fuck. It hadn't occurred to me until then. "That I blew her off for another woman?"

"I'd say that's a pretty solid guess. Good job. Now she thinks you're as bad as her ex."

“What’s that supposed to mean?”

“Violet caught her fiancé cheating on her. And he wasn’t the first. Basically you’ve just proven that you’re as bad as every other asshole who ever broke her heart.”

Starting with her father. I shook my head at my stupidity. “I would never do that to her.”

“Good luck convincing her of that now.”

I rubbed my hand over my eyes. “Maybe you can help? I think you have a better chance than anyone.”

Her voice rose, perturbed. “Convince her of what, Hayden? That you’re really *not* a liar? That she should give you another chance and that you won’t break her heart?” She paused before the harsh truth came out in a sigh. “I don’t think I can do that.”

“I don’t want to fuck this up. I care about her. Can you at least give me some advice on how to get through to her? You’re her best friend. You know her.“

“My advice would be to tell the truth.”

How the hell was I supposed to do that? “She’s not answering my calls or texts. Even if I get through to her, how’s it going to sound coming from me?” I waited but Corinne stayed quiet. I drew in a shaky breath. “Pathetic. That’s how it will sound.”

“It *is* pathetic, Hayden. The problem isn’t that you lied. The problem is that you had to lie in the first place. You couldn’t bring Violet to your house because you’re living with a ghost. You want me to try to convince my best friend that she might have a future with you? How can I do that, Hayden? How can I do that when you’re living in the past?”

It was the most disappointed and annoyed with me I'd ever heard my sister. "Wow. Don't be afraid to tell me how you really feel, sis."

She finally sounded a tad empathetic. "I'm sorry, I don't mean to hurt your feelings. I don't want to see either of you get hurt."

It was too late for that.

"I understand. I'm sorry. I don't mean to put you in that position."

"I'm sorry, too. I wish there was something I could do, but this is your mess."

The truth stung in my chest. "I know. I wish I knew how to clean it up."

"Start with yourself, Hayden."

After we hung up, I noticed that the petals on the plant had started to perk up. I lifted it to my nose again, but there was no scent. The elusive property of the Violet—here one minute then gone the next.

I couldn't blame Corinne for treating me like I wasn't worthy of Violet. But my heart was bound in a wire cage that tightened around it like a vice. I couldn't just let her go.

I went back to the entryway to retrieve my carryon. As I dragged it through the living room, past shelves full of Jill's trinkets, my house didn't feel like my own.

Passing the door adorned with the floral "A" I caught a chill that made me pause.

I opened the door and flipped the light switch, scanning the crib with its pink rosebud sheets, the name on the wall, and the rocking chair where Jill had cried every day for months after the miscarriage. I'd wanted to take it all down the first week to help ease her pain. But Jill wouldn't hear of it. She said it wouldn't be fair to Annabelle's memory.

I'd stopped insisting. Jill was too fragile in her grief. But the grief was her undoing.

I walked over and sat in the rocker, looking around the room full of memories never made. I'd recognized the unhealthy pattern, and yet I'd repeated it.

Guilt washed over me, for letting Jill sink so low and for thinking I could make up for it by preserving her memories like a museum. I knew the pattern, and I knew the result if I kept on this course.

The definition of insanity came to mind—doing the same thing over and over and expecting different results. Einstein might not have said it, but he'd surely have agreed. It was fucking crazy.

I pushed up from the chair and trudged across the rug

I was a subject in many, if not most, of the photos that lined the hallway—pictures of me not my own. I set my luggage on the bed and looked around my bedroom. None of it was me. It was all Jill. It always had been.

I supposed that's what made it so hard to let it go. But I didn't feel the same attachment I always had when I scanned the bedroom now. I felt the burden of memory keeping, the weight of the task. It would crush me if I let it.

I didn't resent the photos and all the other reminders of Jill. They weren't unwelcome intruders. They were beloved friends who'd overstayed their welcome and needed to go.

I brought two large boxes in from the garage. An hour later I'd filled one with mementos and the other with empty frames. The stack of photos I had removed was three inches tall, and that was just from the bedroom.

I carried the box of frames out to the garage and returned for the second box.

The room felt different, empty in a way. But now there was space for someone else.

An ache throbbed in my chest. Violet was the someone else I wanted there. I needed to let her know somehow.

I wasn't surprised that she still hadn't responded to any of my messages. And I wouldn't be surprised if she didn't answer, again, but I had to hope she would.

She didn't. It didn't even ring.

Her battery might be dead, or she might be in the mountains with no signal. I wished for either of those to be true, but it was more likely she'd turned off her phone.

I could hear her say it, in that thick drawl that drove me wild. She didn't want to hear my excuses.

I might not deserve her, but I couldn't let Violet think that I'd blown her off for another woman.

CHAPTER 29

VIOLET

Daddy sat on a stump, his rifle and skis standing in the snow beside him. He was breathing harder than he should've been. "You doing all right?" I handed him a water bottle out of my backpack before I pulled out my phone. We'd already been at it for two hours. "Good run so far."

"I'd say good run. You're shooting sharper than I've ever seen."

I might have pictured Hayden's face in the bullseye of one or two of the targets. "You're not shooting bad yourself. But you've seemed winded all morning."

"I'm okay. I just need to rest every now and then. They said I'll be back to normal after the procedure."

I smirked. "You've never been normal a day in your life."

Daddy laughed. "Thank God for that."

My phone rang in my hand. The rush of panic when I saw Hayden's name stopped my heart. I hadn't heard from him since I'd sent the message calling off the trip to Miami earlier this morning. He must've landed in Denver.

I pushed the red button as fast as I could and looked up quick like it hadn't even happened.

"You might not be able to do everything like you used to."

Daddy's eyes darted toward my phone when it rang again. When I hung it up just as fast, he asked who was trying so hard to call.

"No one important. It can wait." I turned the ringer off.

He nodded and went back to what he was saying. "I might not ever be a hundred percent, but I'm not gonna stop doing what I love to do just to try to be here longer, not doing what I love to do."

He was obstinate. There was no point. "I know, Daddy, you'll do whatever you want to do. So I'm gonna stay out of it."

My phone buzzed with a text from Hayden.

Everything okay out there?

Daddy continued, undeterred by my distraction. "We ought to all do whatever we want to do. Don't you think?"

I held up a finger before I typed quickly,

Not really. I can't talk now.

This time I powered the whole damn phone off before I tossed it in my bag.

I bit my tongue but it still lashed into my father, softer off my lips than it was in my head. "When you have obligations, commitments," my emphasis on that last word sounded bitter, "sometimes what you *want* to do isn't what you *need* to do, or what you *should* do. You can't always think only of yourself."

He chuckled. "Is that what you think of me?"

I shook my head and sighed. "I don't know what to think, Daddy." Of him, or anyone.

"Well, I'll tell you one thing, even though I was out here a lot of those last few years you were home, I was always thinking of you and your mama back home, and your brother and sister away at college. Everything I've ever done I've done with every one of you in mind."

It sure as hell hadn't seemed like it, but out skiing with a heart condition was not the time for Daddy to discuss it. I had to nip the conversation in the bud or I'd get him riled up. "Thank you for saying that."

"I only say it 'cause it's true. You all mean the world to me."

I tried to hold back, but I couldn't just let him carry on with his delusional act.

"I guess it might've felt more like it if you'd stuck around. But that's water under the bridge." My gaze drifted to the snow.

"I stuck around as long as I could. As long as your mama would let me. "

I looked up, glowering at his deflection. "Let you? Are you blaming her for you leaving?"

"I'm not blaming anybody. It takes two to tango, Punkin'. Your mother is as strong-willed and hardheaded as I am. Sometimes you just can't have two bulls in one pen. She and I butted heads until we knocked ourselves silly. And neither one of us let up."

I didn't remember any knock down drag out fights. Cunning jabs, yes. Vicious stabs, no. "It didn't seem that way to me."

"Good. We tried to keep our troubles from you kids. The first time things got especially tense between us, I came out here and stayed on Clive's ranch for a few months. But then your mama and I got to missing each other, and I missed you kids something awful. So we gave it another whirl and lasted five more years, most of them good."

He drew in a deep breath. "When things turned south again, we both knew if we kept on it was going to get ugly. But it was your mama who put her foot down. She sent me packin'." He chuckled almost like it was a fond memory.

I blinked at him trying to assimilate the new story that didn't fit the narrative I had written for it. "Mama sent you across the country?"

"Not exactly. I'd had my eyes on the lodge since that first time I stayed with Clive. I had a pipe dream of spending summers out here, all five of us. That's why I snatched it up as soon as it went on the market two years later. We had a couple good summers before things went sideways again between your mother and me."

The fishing summers. Daddy dragged me and Clay to every stream in the hills. I outfished them both the second year.

Daddy continued, wistful. "Getting the lodge running smooth was rough, but it was easier than trying to smoothe things out with your mother. I ended up spending more and more time here. After Clay graduated high school, you and me had a pretty good summer just the two of us."

The summer of blame. When you're 15 it's easy to hate the world. I hadn't exactly been kind a lot of that summer, but I had good reason after he'd picked up and left. There were some good times though.

Remembering fly fishing got me choked up over the memories I'd never make with Hayden. "I was a bear that summer. I'm glad you remember it fondly."

"One of the best ever. That was the last one you came and stayed. Once you had a car, you blazed a trail." He seemed unaware that it was my resentment that kept me away, continuing, "I didn't blame you, of course. That's what happens. Kids grow up."

A smile spread on his face as he paused, nodding toward a bunny who'd come out of hole a few yards away. "I hated to miss out on your last couple of years of high school, but it seemed like the only way to keep the peace. Truth is, back then I still thought your mama would end up here with me after you finished school."

I stared at him, still not convinced. "What changed?"

"Turns out living apart most of the time made us happier than when we were together."

Which was pretty much limited to family holidays anymore. "That doesn't seem like much of a marriage."

"Well it's a darn sight better than divorce. Neither of us wanted that. Still don't."

My mouth turned down in a frown despite trying to keep it relaxed.

"Why not? Wouldn't you rather find someone you can stand to live with most of the time."

They weren't that old. Too young give up on happiness.

"We both have our lives apart, but the one we made together is the one that means the most. That's why."

You could have knocked me over with a feather. I sat down beside Daddy on the stump, eyeing the lines in his face as he watched the rabbit foraging for food.

He looked nothing like the picture I'd painted of him half my life ago. I'd seen my mother as the victim for all these years.

As ridiculous as it seemed, I was kind of angry that she wasn't. Holding onto false beliefs was easier than tearing them down.

The man I'd thought was a lying cheat, wasn't. And the man I thought might be different, wasn't either. I had it all wrong. I pushed the angry thoughts of Hayden out of my head.

It was mind-blowing that the image I'd had of my parents' marriage was so completely skewed. They hadn't been acting like everything was normal. Everything *was* normal for them.

"I guess if it works for you and you're both happy, who am I to judge?"

My father shrugged. "Live and let live. Might as well. People are gonna do what they want to anyway." He slapped my knee and laughed. "Are you ready for the next leg?"

I stood and offered him a hand. "We'll take it nice and slow."

We had plenty of time, which was good. It was going to take a while for this to all sink in.

The hodgepodge of smells that met us on our way into the lodge brought back memories of the flavors of my childhood.

Mama had prepared a feast of all of my favorites. Chicken and dumplings, soup beans, turnip greens, cornbread, and broccoli casserole.

I'd picked at my breakfast and only eaten a few bites of the sandwich Mama had packed for lunch. I'd been too mad at Hayden to even think about food, but my mouth watered now.

We served plates from the assortment of dishes in the center of the big round table. My taste buds exploded with the first bite of dumpling. There was nothing like Mama's cooking.

When we dug into the steaming plates, manners went out the window. Daddy bragged on my marksmanship with his mouth half-full. "She beats all I've ever seen. Hasn't touched a rifle in a year and shot spot on."

Mama smiled, dabbing her mouth with a cloth napkin before she spoke. "Violet's always been good at everything she does."

Except choosing men.

I smile half-heartedly. "Thank you. It's more like I only do the things I'm good at."

"You do a little bit of everything, and you do it all well, dear."

"Well, you both had a lot to do with that." I never took my privileged childhood for granted.

Daddy smiled as he buttered a piece of cornbread. "We tried to give you kids all the opportunity we could. You never really wanted it though. But you didn't need it either. You've always been the one I worried about the least."

Maybe that helped explain why he didn't seem to care what I did half the time. I wasn't exactly grateful back then though.

"You don't need to worry about any of us any more. We're all doing just fine. I can't speak for Melissa and Clay, but I'd bet the farm that they appreciate everything you ever did for them as much as I do."

"If you ever have kids of your own, you'll understand. You never stop worrying about every one of them. But I'm proud of you, Punkin'. You're forging your own path."

I took a long gulp of sweet tea to wash down the lump that formed in my throat. In all my independent rebellion I still sought his approval. "That's good to hear."

"We've got to get down there to see that island of yours sometime soon."

"It's not my island" I chuckled. "But one of the two owners—the non-silent partner—is there a lot. Clifton is the best boss ever. You two'd get on like a house on fire." Polishing off a bottle of Macallan Reserve, no doubt.

My mother chuckled. "Well, I wouldn't be surprised if you end up with your own island someday. And kids of your own, like your daddy said."

I took a deep breath, focusing on the food I scooped onto my fork. "I've got plenty of time to decide that."

Finding someone I'd want to have them with was the most complicated variable in that equation, but I didn't want to get her started on men so I kept my mouth shut.

She was already on it though. "You do have time. They say forty is the new thirty. But I can't help but hope that you'll find the right man and settle down sooner than later. We'd love another grandbaby to spoil."

"It'll happen when it happens." If it happened.

"Irene, she doesn't have to worry about finding Mr. Right. He'll come along when she's ready for him."

My brow slanted at Daddy coming to my defense. "If he's out there, he'll have to find me. 'Cause I'm not looking."

Mama spoke up, confident. "Mr. Right's out there. I have no doubt. You don't have to *look* for him as long as you're willing to let him in when he comes knockin'."

I smiled up at Clara as she cleared our plates and set a pyrex of peach cobbler in the center of the table. I waited for her to walk away before I replied.

"Even if the right guy never comes along, it won't matter if I'm living the life I want on my own. That's what I'm focused on right now."

Mama laughed. "You're preaching to the choir, dear."

"I'd say you both do your share of living the life you want on your own." They say you shouldn't poke the bear but I was eager for Mama's perspective on Daddy's account of their marriage. "I think your arrangement is great as long as you're both happy."

Mama's shoulders drew back, her head turning slowly to side-eye Daddy.

If faces could shrug, his did.

She turned back to me with a smile, but the uncomfortable kind. "It hasn't always been an easy road, but it got us here."

Those last few bitter years before I left home had been hard on us all, but we'd made it through. I sighed, sorry for us.

"Here is not a bad place to be." Although she was elsewhere most of the time. "If you two are happy living like you do, I'm happy for you. Life isn't a fairytale." I'd stopped believing in knights in shining armor or Prince Charming a long time ago.

Daddy handed me a plate. "Fairytales don't have your mama's peach cobbler."

I thought back on those last years, of how she'd withdrawn, kept it all in. I'd felt powerless and in the dark. And I'd blamed Daddy all the while. I was surprised at the hurt in my voice when I asked my mother, "Why didn't you tell me? Or any of us?"

She stared at me for a long second like she was choosing her words. "Tell you what? That we were trying to keep our family together? But the best way we found for that was being apart."

"Yeah, if that was the truth, that would have been a good place to start." The pain of harbored resentment burned in my chest.

My mother answered, prim and proper. "You shouldn't speak of those things to children."

I rolled my eyes. "We were practically grown."

She smiled apologetically. "It's hard to explain something you can't understand. We were feeling our way, dear. I suppose we still are."

I sighed. "Aren't we all?" Just feeling our way through the maze of life.

I pushed back from the table, patting my belly. "That is by far the most delicious meal I've had in years.

Daddy chuckled. "I'm glad you still enjoy the taste of home."

I nodded, warm inside. “The best there is.”

Mama laid her napkin on the table as she stood. “Should we move to the fire for a digestif? I brought a bottle of port.”

I chuckled. “A farmhouse meal followed by a digestif. Country couture.” That was Mama.

Daddy looked up from stoking the fire. “I think I’m gonna take your advice and buy that condo hotel in Key West.”

I laughed. “I don’t have a dog in that race. You do what you want to do, remember?”

He grinned as he put the poker back in the stand. “I know, Punkin.’ I like the idea even if you won’t get involved. It’s a good investment, and close to you. I figured it’d be a nice place to all get together.”

He really was doing it for us. “Sounds perfect as far as I’m concerned. Hopefully it’ll make a boatload of profit too.”

“It’ll do just fine in appreciation alone. I might get down there to see it in the next couple weeks. You mind if I stop by and see you?”

“Mind? I’d love if you’d come stay for a few nights.” I turned to my mother. “And you, too, if you want.” Two visits in a month might throw them out of equilibrium.

“I wouldn’t miss that.”

Clara cleared her throat behind us. “Miss Violet there’s a delivery for you—flowers.”

I looked at Mama and Daddy who both seemed to be thinking the same thing I was. "Flowers at this time of night? "

Clara nodded. "They said the order was mixed up—delivered to the wrong address—that's why it's so late. They want to give it to you personally, with their apologies."

"Alright…" I looked to my father who simply shrugged. Mama jumped to her feet, though, as uneasy and suspicious as I was. "We're not letting you go alone. Too many scary movies start like that."

Daddy chuckled as he stood to follow. "You worried about Jack the Ripper in Jackson Hole?"

My parents were on my heels as I made my way to the foyer. I whispered back over my shoulder, "I'm not worried about a killer."

I twisted the knob timidly before cracking the heavy wooden door.

It took a second for my brain to process the image because I didn't believe my eyes.

My breath and all time stopped as I took in the navy blue parka and wrinkled khaki pants. My knees felt weak under me when I looked into the turquoise eyes that'd done me in from the start. There he stood, holding a potted violet plant that'd seen better days.

The man who'd slayed me.

CHAPTER 30

HAYDEN

Seeing Violet took my breath away. I had no air in my lungs to answer when she finally spoke, confused.

"Hayden?" She opened the door further, blinking in disbelief.

I stood there, watching the light disappear into her long black hair, dumbfounded.

Her eyes locked on mine, searching for an explanation. "What are you doing here?"

I glanced at the flower in my hand and wondered if this was dumb idea. It was the only one I had. I tightened my grasp around the pot so it wouldn't tremble in my hands as I stammered, "I sent you this—or I tried to—from the plane on my way to Dallas. When I got home it was on my doorstep." I paused, holding her gaze. "I guess I screwed it up."

The regret of all I'd screwed up made my chest tighten. "So I thought I should fix that."

Violet's eyes narrowed. "You thought you could fix that by driving eight-and-a-half hours to bring it?"

I forced a grin. "I was hoping it might." I swallowed down the fear that it might not. "I made it in seven." When she looked confused, I clarified. "Seven hours."

Her tone was colder than the night air. "Driving like a maniac, no doubt." She didn't seem impressed.

"Pretty much. I didn't know what else to do. I tried calling—a few times. I thought maybe your phone was broken."

Violet held me in an angry stare. "No, I shut it off earlier."

She seemed to remember we weren't alone, turning toward the couple I assumed to be her parents behind her, exchanging glances.

"Mama, Daddy, this is Hayden. He's my friend Corinne's older brother from Breckenridge. You remember Corinne, the marine biologist I told you all about?"

Her mother clasped her hands in front of her chest, head tilted to the side like she'd just witnessed the sweetest thing she'd ever seen.

"Of course I remember." She turned to me. "She just had a birthday, didn't she?"

I nodded. "She did. In fact, that's where I met your daughter. At the birthday party."

Violet's face was beet red.

Her father extended his hand. "Jim Monroe. Pleased to meet you, Hayden. Come on in and take a load off. You must be tired after that drive."

I looked at Violet. She didn't seem thrilled to invite me in, but she held her hand out and stepped aside. "Please."

The obligatory buck head over the hearth stared down on us when we sat around the fire, but it was Violet's father's eyes that made me uneasy. He was sizing me up, I could tell.

Taking a glass of port from Violet's mother, I asked him, "Did you shoot that?"

"Nah. I only shoot at targets. I'm not much of a hunter."

A smile spread on my lips when I glanced at Violet. "You certainly taught your daughter to fish."

Jim smiled. "She told you about that, did she?"

Violet interjected. "Hayden came along to check out a couple of different charter companies when he came to visit his sister."

Her father stroked his chin. "Fishing on the clock. You might just have this thing figured out after all."

I was relieved to see Violet fairly relaxed, shrugging with a smile. "Perks of the job. I'll take you, too, when you come visit."

Her mother hadn't stopped grinning. She clapped her hands three times fast. "How exciting."

I asked, "Are you planning a Keys trip?" Seemed soon for another visit considering Violet's reticence to come out for this one.

Her father answered. "Nothing official yet but probably soon. How'd you like it down there?"

My gaze lifted to Violet whose dark eyes were hard to read. "Beautiful."

Our eyes locked for long enough for her mother to take note. She patted her husband's knee. "It's been a long day. We'll leave you two to enjoy the fire."

"Nice meeting you." I stood to shake her hand but she pulled me closer to kiss my cheek.

"Likewise." She turned toward Violet. "Goodnight, dear. See you in the morning."

Jim shook my hand firmly. "I believe room number 14 is clean and ready if you need a place to sleep."

I wasn't sure if that was an order, as in I better not be thinking of sleeping in the same bed as his daughter.

"Thanks so much. Sorry to barge in. I appreciate the hospitality."

He squeezed my shoulder with a smile. "Hospitality is our business."

CHAPTER 31

VIOLET

Being alone with Hayden was dangerous. I couldn't let those apologetic aquamarine eyes cloud my judgment.

They stared, as pitiful as a puppy dog as he said hesitantly, "I wanted to explain what happened in Denver."

I raised my brow, anger churning in my belly at the reminder. A deep breath helped to keep my cool. This wasn't the time or the place to lay into him for lying, but he could keep his excuses. I wouldn't believe him anyway.

"You don't have to explain. That's your business, Hayden. You can do what you want. You don't owe me anything."

"I owe you an explanation, so, please, hear me out. I *wanted* to bring you home with me when you suggested it in Denver, but I didn't know if I could."

He swallowed but his voice still quivered. "I lied about having plans. There were no plans."

I hadn't expected him to admit his lie so readily since liars usually try to explain them away. Admission of guilt didn't absolve him of it, though. I shot back, "Well, you clearly didn't have plans with Aunt Margaret."

He looked physically pained. "No. Corinne told me she let that cat out of the bag. I'm sorry. I'm a terrible liar."

The hurt in his eyes tugged at the heartstrings I thought I'd wound tight enough to sever. My tone softened a touch. "Being an expert liar isn't something to aspire to." I'd almost married one.

"That was a monumentally terrible lie, though. I mean, your *dead aunt*?" I squinted, incredulous and still angry he'd lied.

He shook his head, ashamed.

"I know. I said the first stupid thing that came to mind when you caught me off guard." Hayden rambled, desperate to explain. "I'd seen a photo of Aunt Margaret when I was getting dressed to come see you in Denver, which was ironic since I was putting on the sweater she'd given me just before she died."

He paused for a deep breath that was meant to calm him. "Then I was putting on that same sweater when you suggested staying for an extra day, and that's what came out."

I was anything but calm though as he continued, my anger boiling inside at his ridiculous explanation. I pressed my palms into my thighs to still my trembling hands. My voice cracked and tears stung in my eyes at the hurt he'd caused.

"Why did you have to lie? If you wanted to take me home, why didn't you?" If he was keeping me at a distance to keep it casual, he should just come out and say so.

His gaze fell to his lap where he picked at his cuticle. His words finally came, barely more than a whisper.

"I'm sorry, Violet. I should have just told you the truth. I guess I was too afraid it would sound strange, or crazy, and I'd lose you over it anyway."

"What truth?" I squinted, annoyed and hurt that he still couldn't say it. "You came all this way. You might as well spit out."

He ran his fingers through his hair, forcing his regretful eyes to mine. "The truth is, I haven't had a woman in my house since my late wife passed. I haven't been able to. Hell, I never even wanted to before you. But when you suggested it, I choked. I didn't think I could do it." Tears welled in his eyes. "I'm sorry. I didn't mean to lie."

From the jet-setting bachelor persona he'd projected, it hadn't occurred to me that Hayden was still so broken up over his wife's death. But I knew about hiding pain and I could see it now in his eyes. My heart ached for both of us.

"Oh. Wow. You said it's been a couple of years, I just assumed..."

His voice trembled despite obvious effort to keep it steady. "No. I haven't even had a date in Breckenridge."

I narrowed my eyes, still leery. "You only date away from home?"

"I wouldn't call what I do away from home dating." His head shook as he hurried to correct himself. "Did. What I *did* away from home, before."

"Before what?"

"Before you." He wiped the tears that spilled down his cheek as he gathered his breath. "For nine months after Jill died, I barely left home. I didn't want to see anyone or do anything. Thank God I had to travel for work. That's all that kept me from going over the edge."

I nodded for lack of words while he paused.

He seemed relieved to get it off his chest as he continued. "When I was away from home, the fog of depression started to lift. I could go out and not be worried I'd run into anyone I knew, that *we* knew. I started to feel like myself and have a more normal life again while I was away, so I stayed away from home more and more. I even started dating, if you can call it that. But I certainly wasn't looking for love, or any kind of a relationship, really." He shook his head. "And I thought I was happy with that life. But all that changed when I met you, Violet." He stared with expectant eyes that melted the icecap on my heart.

It figured that the first potentially trustworthy man I'd met in half a year would be loyal to a dead person. I couldn't fault him for it, but that was a lot of baggage to unpack.

Even if Hayden was honest most of the time, he was completely unavailable. Getting tangled up with him was a bad idea from the start and I cursed myself for not listening to my gut.

"You're a very bad liar, but that's not a bad thing. I get it. I won't hold it against you. We can just pretend like it never happened—like everything else. There's no hard feelings, Hayden."

He rubbed his lips together, drawing in a deep breath. "You don't have to pretend like it didn't happen. I own it. I'm sorry

I lied and I'm sorry I hurt you. But we can't pretend like we didn't happen, Violet."

"We can't pretend like it's something it's not either. You are clearly not ready for a relationship. To be honest, I don't know if I am either."

He stared back with sympathetic eyes. "Corinne told me you were engaged."

I straightened, surprised. "Turns out he wasn't ready for commitment either. Apparently that's my type." I let out a dry chuckle but it wasn't the least bit funny.

"I'm not that type of guy, Violet." His words seemed as sincere as his eyes, but he'd run for the hills at the first sign of feelings.

"Judging from the fact that you just drove four hundred miles to tell me you're sorry, I suspect that you're a good guy deep down. I understand that you feel bad about lying, Hayden. And I appreciate that. But be honest with yourself. Your default was to keep me as a side fling for a reason."

"There was a *reason*—that I'd never slept with a woman more than twice before I met you—ever. Not once in the last two years, Violet. It was a rule. I didn't want to string someone along when I knew there was no future. But with you, all the rules went out the window because all I can think about is the future and how I want you in it."

As much as I wanted to believe him, my heart didn't want to hear it. "It doesn't sound like you're ready for that."

He hooked under my chin to force me to hold his gaze.

"After I left you in Denver I realized that the life I was afraid to let you into was just a big empty house full of memories.

I've lived there, but I haven't been living. You make me feel alive, Violet. You made me start living again. I want you in my life—my real life. Come back to Breckenridge with me."

My stomach did cartwheels, the acrobatics of love and fear grappling for a foothold. Taking a chance on Hayden was what got me in this mess in the first place. My mind told me no, don't do it, but my heart knew he was sincere.

He'd come running to try to keep from losing me. I didn't know where it might go, but I didn't want to lose him either.

"I wanted to know you better, that's why I wanted to stay an extra day." I laughed to stop myself from crying. "I wasn't supposed to like you like this."

His fingertip traced my lower lip, his stare so deep I thought I might drown as he said, "That's funny, because I'm pretty sure I was supposed to love you like this."

His soft lips met mine with a tenderness I'd never felt from any man.

The warmth in my chest took my breath. He'd said "love" and meant it. I could see it in his eyes and feel it in his touch. The kiss took me back to that first drunken night, the memory of the fire he lit in me from the start clearer now than ever.

The passion we'd tried to deny raged like a summer wildfire. The longing ached deep in my core as we fell deeper into the kiss. When his hand slid up my thigh I threw my knee over his lap and slinked up his chest, straddling the bulge that pressed into his zipper.

It seemed he was trying to slow himself down when he pulled away, pressing his shoulders back into the sofa while he held me at bay.

His eyes smiled as he softly brushed my hair off my face. His finger trailing down my cheek set off fireworks in my chest. My breath was heavy with want as I waited.

Hayden's gaze turned serious. "If you want to know me better, you should come back to Colorado."

I smiled, not wanting to think about tomorrow or anything other than how badly I needed him that very second. "If you want to know me better, you should come to my room."

Hayden cocked a brow. "Do you think your father expects me to stay in Room 14?"

I chuckled at him worrying over what Daddy might think. "My father knows I'll do what I want, and he wouldn't have it any other way. It's in the genes."

"I will be eternally grateful for the genes both your parents gave you, gorgeous." He scooted forward to the edge of the couch and hoisted himself to stand, holding me tight. I locked my ankles behind him while our breath steamed between kisses as he crossed the den.

When we reached the lobby, Hayden stopped. "I just realized I have no idea where I'm carrying you."

I laughed, flushed from his heat pressing against me as I slid down his front. "My room's upstairs. Probably better for us both if I walk."

He scooped me right back up, holding my hips tight as he shimmied to shift my weight up to his waist. "I've got you." He kissed my neck and whispered, "Just trust me."

The heat in my chest made me melt in his arms. Trust was easier said than done, but Hayden made me want to try.

I clung to him, giggling after he almost dropped me while fumbling to open the door. "That doesn't inspire trust."

He hurried to hush me, chuckling. "Shh. You'll wake your father."

After he lowered me slowly to the bed and gently kissed my lips, Hayden said, "I may stumble but I'll never let you fall."

My breath stopped under his deep turquoise gaze before his mouth covered mine. My lips parted to let him in. I was so full of him there was no room for doubt. I was already falling.

Hayden kissed a trail down my neck while he worked my dress up over my hips. I moaned in anticipation while he rolled my panties down. He tossed them to the ground, taking in the sight of my sex with a grin.

His palm covered my mound, warm and firm. "When I thought I might not ever see this again…" His pressure increased as he rubbed over my clit. "I came running."

I laughed. "You couldn't live without my pussy?"

He leaned over, scooping under my shoulder to lift me to sit. "All of you." He pulled my dress over my head. "I can't live without all of you, Violet."

He tore his shirt off and threw it in the pile, exposing the rippled chest and abs that most men have to spend hours a day in the gym for. He was blessed with the body of a god, and I, the lucky beholder. .

My heart raced as our mouths crashed together, hungry and desperate for what we'd almost lost. I fumbled with his button and zipper while he unhooked my bra, neither of us wanting to pull away to shed the last of our clothes.

He shimmied his legs out of his khakis as he pushed me back onto the pillow. When our bare chests met, I could feel his heart pounding as fast as mine.

I gasped when he slid into my wetness. "God you feel so fucking good, Hayden. I didn't want to live without this either."

"You don't have to, beautiful. I'm not going anywhere you're not. And I'll never lie to you again." He thrust into me, looking so deep into my eyes I was sure he saw clear into my soul. "Ever."

The miracle was that I believed him, without a doubt. My body was so charged I thought my heart might burst as he pushed harder and deeper, faster and faster. The friction on my clit every time he reached my limit sent a surge through me that built with every pass.

I moaned, louder and louder until I called out, "Yes, Hayden. God, yes." His thrusts continued but he covered my mouth to muffle my moans until they subsided.

He held still, his face twisting with restraint. The urge to come must've passed because his mouth curled into the easy smile that had melted me from day one.

"Your father is going to hate me if you carry on like that."

"My father is going to love you." My nails dug into his firm butt as I lifted my hips, but he didn't move.

Throbbing inside me, he paused to trace my lower lip with a fingertip. "You never answered. Are you coming home with me? If you don't want to cut your visit with your parents short, we don't have to go tomorrow. But I want you to come home with me, more than anything."

I had to chuckle at how chatty he was in the heat of the moment, but the butterflies that swarmed in my stomach took my breath. He was already out on a limb and I trusted him enough to join him.

The weight of all our baggage might break the branch, but at least we'd go down together. I had to take the chance. He felt so right.

My words came out in a sigh. "Of course I am."

His grin spread, the green in his eyes sparkling in the lamplight. "That makes me a very happy man."

I wrapped my legs around him, clenching his thick girth as he finally slid slowly in and out of me. "And this?" I gripped him harder. "Does this make you happy?"

"Fuck. How do you do that?" An astonished fire lit in his eyes. "You are amazing, woman. Where have you been all my life?"

I whined with a sigh, "Waiting for you."

He pushed harder and deeper, groaning. "We were worth the wait."

We. Us. Undeniably connected.

My face flushed with the heat that spread up from my core again, hips lifting in rhythm with his as the tingling intensified. His hand returned to cover my mouth, muffling my moans that grew louder with his thrusts. I bit into his palm to keep from screaming his name as the surge shot through me.

I was still writhing when he pulled out. His stifled groan rumbled through me as he spilled onto my stomach. He stared for a long moment before lowering himself to my chest. We laid still in the moment I knew neither of us wanted to end, both of us trembling.

After he caught his breath, he whispered. “I couldn’t hold back.” He pushed up onto his elbows and looked me in the eye as he sighed. “I don’t want to hold back with you.”

CHAPTER 32

HAYDEN

A tickle pulled me from a dream that I'd already forgotten. My eyes fluttered open to the most delicious sight. Violet laid facing me, running her fingertip down my forearm, biting her lower lip with a grin.

She glowed in a halo of light from the window behind her, too beautiful to be real. In my sleepy daze I wondered if it was all a dream, but her sweet Southern voice coaxed me awake.

"Good morning, handsome."

"Good morning, gorgeous."

A playful grin lit in her dark eyes. "Did you have nice dreams?"

Her hand moved over the sheet between us to grip my cock, which only then I realized was rock-solid morning wood.

"I don't remember what I was dreaming, but it couldn't be better than this."

She slinked closer, squeezing me harder in her hand. "I know how we could make it better right now."

I smiled, tempted, but I was shell-shocked after the way she wailed last night. "Your folks are awake, I presume."

She rolled her bottom lip between her teeth. "So…?"

"I sense a rebellious streak." I chuckled, mustering resolve. "But that's not a great first impression on my part."

"We're both over thirty, Hayden. I think that constitutes grown."

I gave her a warning stare. "Babe, I want to stay in their good graces."

Violet cocked her head before her smile spread. "They'll see how amazing you are." Her grip around my dick released and she slapped my hip softly. "But you're right. We should get moving. It's a long drive."

"So you *do* want to go today? I don't mind staying."

She nodded. "I'm ready to get out of here. It's been a great visit but it's better to end on a positive note. Besides, I can't wait to see your place in Breckenridge."

A nervous knot tightened in my stomach, but I let the fear go before it could take hold. The truth was stronger than fear. "I can't wait to show it to you."

I gave her lips a soft peck. She smiled as she pushed up onto an elbow before rolling over to fling her legs off the bed. "I'll get packed up—it won't take me long."

Watching her prance around the room nude, I felt like I'd died and gone to heaven, but more alive than ever at the same time. With great reluctance I pried my eyes to search for my clothes.

Violet had her bag packed by the time I'd washed my face. She nuzzled in next to me wearing jeans and a fitted turtleneck and reached for her cosmetics bag. I was mesmerized by the sight of her in the mirror, brushing on mascara that she didn't need. I shoved my hands in my pockets to keep from touching her.

Her dark eyes sparkled as she smiled back at me in the mirror. "I hope you're hungry. I bet my mother has a feast prepared."

I was hungrier for Violet than I was for food. Resisting the urge to ravage her wasn't easy, but we had to get moving.

"I'm starving."

Violet's mother looked up from setting a steaming plate of biscuits on the table. "Good morning sunshine." She leaned in to kiss Violet. "And good morning to you, Mr. Kincaid." She smiled curtly, extending her hand. "Did you two sleep well?" There was a playful edge to the question that made me think she'd heard Violet's late-night vocal performance.

"Very well, thank you. And you?"

"Like a rock. I always do. It's Jim that has a hard time sleeping sometimes."

I shot Violet a worried glance, hoping he hadn't suffered a bout of insomnia last night.

But she was unfazed. "Where's Daddy?"

Her mother answered, cheerful. “Clive came by to drop off some tools. He’s outside with him.”

Jim’s deeper voice boomed from behind us. “I’m right here. Just waiting on you night owls to wake up so we can eat.”

I forced a smile. “Sorry to keep you waiting.” I quickly shifted my gaze to his wife who looked less skeptical. “Breakfast smells delicious.“

I surveyed the smorgasbord. A heaping platter of sausage and bacon sat beside bowls of hashbrowns, scrambled eggs, and white gravy.

Jim slapped me hard on the shoulder, maybe a little too hard. “I’m just kidding you, son. We’re in no hurry. As you can see, Irene just got the food on the table.”

Violet strummed her fingertips together, grinning after she sat. “I haven’t had biscuits and gravy since… well, since Christmas I guess.”

Her mother smirked. “Not everything’s better in the islands, is it now?”

Violet rolled her eyes after her mother had turned away.

“I hope you’re hungry, honey.” Irene held up the plate of biscuits.

I rubbed my stomach. “Famished.” I hadn’t eaten anything but a bag of pretzels on the road trip yesterday. I took a biscuit, placing it on my plate to wait for Violet to assemble hers since I’d never actually eaten biscuits and gravy.

I wondered if Jim purposely waited until my mouth was full to ask, “What do you do back in Breckenridge?”

I washed down a delectable bite with orange juice. "Project management for a software company."

"Ah. So you sit behind a computer all day?" He said it like it wasn't real man's work.

"Unfortunately, yes, most of the time. I don't get out fishing nearly as much as I'd like." Work wasn't really to blame but I hoped the change of subject would remind him we had something in common.

"So much tech work these days keeps folks indoors. I think I'd lose my mind." Jim crunched down on a slice of bacon.

Violet's mother piped in, chipper. "It's the way the world is. What've you kids got planned for the day?"

Violet blurted matter-of-factly, "Actually we're heading back to Colorado. I'm going to fly out of Denver instead."

I could have choked on the bite of biscuit in my mouth at her lack of tact, which I suspected was intentional. I looked tentatively at her father, preparing to dodge the crossfire.

Jim raised a brow. "Is that so?" His eyes narrowed at Violet. "I guess one night there wasn't enough."

"It wasn't long enough to go see Hayden's place in Breckenridge, so no." She quipped with a defiant satisfaction that made me sweat. They were going to hate me for sure.

But then Irene smiled as she glanced Jim's way, and he smiled too as he answered. "Well, that sounds like fun. I'm glad to hear it."

Violet blinked, incredulous. "I'm glad you're not disappointed." For some reason I doubted that was true.

Jim's lips spread in a genuine grin. "Lord, no. I'm happy you're having fun. Life's short. You gotta live it up."

Her mother also took the news in stride. "By the sound of things we'll see you down in the Keys soon anyway. Unless I can convince your father to have his surgery beforehand."

He waved off the suggestion. "That can wait. The condo deal might not last that long."

Irene looked skeptical. "You might be biting off more than you can chew, Jim. It'll be hard to keep up with all that after heart surgery."

Jim laughed off her concern. "Nothing worth doing is easy."

I wasn't sure what they were talking about but I couldn't argue with his assessment. Everything worthwhile I'd ever done had required great effort.

Violet climbed up into the Range Rover, waving at her parents on the porch.

After we'd turned toward the road, her face relaxed and she let out a deep breath. "That was weird. I guess they like you."

I laughed as we pulled out onto the winding mountain road. "Why's that weird?

Her eyes narrowed. "What was weird was how happy they were that I was taking off a day early with you."

I grinned. "Seems like they want you to be happy."

Violet started to say something but then just chuckled and lowered her sunglasses down onto her nose.

I reached over to put my hand on her knee. "You want to be the deejay?"

"Sure. What are you in the mood for?"

"Whatever you like."

Her head fell back as she laughed. "You might be sorry. Taylor Swift has a hundred albums."

"We've got four hundred miles to get through them. Bring it on." Love songs seemed appropriate.

Violet crooned every word of over a dozen songs.

In the middle of yet another chorus about a breakup, I said, "I'm noticing a pattern. Makes you wonder if Taylor Swift will ever find the right guy."

Violet laughed. "She's built a brand on unrequited love. I guess people can relate to heartache."

Violet and I had both seen our share of that. I chuckled. "Yeah, but don't people want the happy ending?"

"Those don't happen near as often as heartache." She fiddled with her phone. "But maybe something more upbeat is in order."

We sang along to nineties songs on Spotify until the fuel gauge was in red. After a pit stop, we were back on the road. Violet bit into a piece of fried chicken. "God this is dry. I should've known better."

"Better than to buy gas station fried chicken?"

She grimaced. "Gas station fried chicken in *Wyoming*. The gas stations in Georgia have some of the best fried chicken in the world."

I laughed at her indignant stance on the subject. "You're quite the connoisseur, I take it?"

"I grew up on that stuff, from the country store near our farm."

"It's funny, we *never* had fried chicken except when Dad took me out sailing."

"Best boat food there is." Violet tossed the chicken leg into the paper sack, sticking out her tongue in disgust. "Not this one though. Mama makes it with buttermilk batter—delicious like everything she cooks."

"Do you cook like your mother?"

Violet laughed, shaking her head. "I wish. Melissa—my older sister—was the one in the kitchen while I was out digging worms with Daddy."

I didn't want to pry but her contentious relationship with her father didn't seem to add up. "Just tell me it's none of my business if you don't want to talk about it, but I have to ask. When did things go sour with your dad? It sounds like you had a good relationship."

Violet didn't hesitate in blurting it out. "He left when I was in high school. Bought the lodge and moved out to Wyoming."

"Right, you mentioned before that your parents hadn't been living together for years. They seem happy now, though. Then again, I suppose anyone can seem happy for an hour."

"What's strange is that I believe they *are* happy now. Apart, but somehow still together." She shook her head. "I had a long talk with my dad yesterday. Turns out I was mistaken about a lot of what happened back then. Since no one told me *anything*, I assumed things then that I now know weren't true."

I could tell she was hurt by it all, but it felt like she wanted to share. "Things like…?"

"Things like my mother was the one who kicked him out. He wanted to come back but their marriage was too rocky. She basically banished him to the ranch."

I cocked my head, trying to understand. "And you thought he'd left her?"

"Left *us*." She looked out the window for a few seconds. "I took it very personally, but it had nothing to do with me."

I reached over to rub her knee. "Blame is a nasty dagger." Especially when you turn it on yourself like I had.

"No kidding. I'm still processing it all. I resented my dad for things he didn't even do. It might take a while for all that to work itself out."

"It may take a while, but it will. For what it's worth, your dad seems genuine."

She inhaled, doubtful. "It's hard to tell. When he's trying to get what he wants, he's sweet as pie. I'm sure he's still hoping to rope me into that condo hotel somehow."

I nodded, glad she'd brought it up. "I was wondering what that was about."

Violet rolled her eyes in a huff. "A business venture that I refused. That's what he dragged me out here for, to try to sell me on a property he wants to buy in Key West. Sounds like he's going to do it on his own, or so he says. Fine by me if he does. I don't know why he'd want a property in the Keys if I'm not going to run it for him though."

I wasn't sure why she seemed so irked by it. "Maybe he's trying to be closer to you."

Her sour expression softened. "I was so mad that he was trying to manipulate me that I hadn't even considered benevolent motives. But knowing what I know now, that may be true."

I waggled my brow. "I certainly wouldn't blame him for that. But I just drove four hundred miles to win your heart so I'm clearly not objective."

The sparkle returned to her eyes as she grinned. "That was pretty impressive. And the flower. Nice touch." She glanced at the plant on the dash.

I squeezed her knee. "I'm glad it worked because I didn't have a plan B."

She picked up my hand and laced her fingers through mine. "Good thing you didn't need one. But you won't be able to drive to Paradise Key in a day to surprise me."

"No, but planes are faster. And I'll be on one to Key West every chance I get if you'll have me."

"If my father acquires the condo hotel, you'll have no shortage of places to stay in the Keys anytime you want."

I grinned, loving that we were talking about the future like we might actually have one. "Your little bungalow on Paradise Key would be my first choice, but making a habit of that might be frowned upon."

She narrowed one eye with a smirk, a *Yeah, right* look. "I can have visitors whenever I like. So you can stay with me anytime you want."

I liked the idea of spending weeks in the Keys with her. "You may regret that offer. I can work from anywhere."

She rubbed the back of my hand tenderly. "You are welcome anytime, mister."

"You think you'll stay in the Keys?"

She shrugged. "Forever? I haven't stayed anywhere forever yet. But who knows? I'm happy there for now."

"Happy for now is pretty damn good."

The afternoon sun glimmered through the windshield, freckling her nose with light. She was a sight, biting her lip before she said, "Now's all we have."

And all that mattered was that she was beside me. She was my now. She was my moment. "I'm pretty fucking happy right now."

"Good." She smiled, head tilted. "You still happy in Colorado?"

The question caught me off guard—probably because I was contemplating how damn cute she was when she asked it. So I answered without thinking. "I don't think I've been happy in Colorado for years."

She looked surprised. "No? I thought you loved Breckenridge?"

"I do. It's awesome. But it doesn't feel like home anymore."

Her head nodded slowly like she already knew the answer when she asked, "Since your wife died?"

"Since before, really. But it certainly got worse after Jill's accident."

She rubbed her thumb over mine. "What happened—if you don't mind telling me, of course?"

The truth came easy with Violet. She made me want to open my trunk of secrets and bare them all. "She had a skiing accident and suffered a fatal head injury."

Violet's face twisted in shock. "Fuck. I'm sorry."

After her reaction, I was sorry I hadn't said it a little more tactfully. "It's okay. I've done a lot of healing, especially lately." Even if my house didn't show it.

Violet's dark eyes were pained. "I can't imagine losing someone you love so suddenly—and so tragically."

Everyone always said they know it's hard. That they know I miss her. That they know I'm strong. I loved that Violet admitted that she didn't know. I reached across to squeeze her hand.

"I think that was also why I panicked and lied to you in Denver. You suggested coming to my house *and* going skiing. I choked."

Violet's free hand covered her mouth. "I'm sorry. I had no idea. Corinne mentioned she'd died in an accident. I guess I just assumed it was a car accident."

"Of course you didn't know. But that's life. And even if you're not so great at it, it goes on."

CHAPTER 33

VIOLET

Hayden wasn't kidding. There were pictures *everywhere.* Lining the walls of the entryway in geometric clusters. Scattered on tables and shelves. Everywhere.

A large diamond shaped arrangement of wedding photos covered the side wall of the living room.

I tried not to stare at the pretty blonde bride. She was my polar opposite physically. Fair skinned and petite, she couldn't have weighed more than a hundred pounds soaking wet.

"That's Jill. Obviously." He shoved his hands in his pockets nervously, but his smile was warm.

"I kind of figured. She was pretty."

"She was."

He laid his coat over the back of a dining chair and picked up a frame off the kitchen island. "Here we are quite a few years later, with Aunt Margaret."

"Ah." I took the frame, chuckling as I studied it. Hayden started laughing too, and a fit of giggles took me over until tears were streaming down my face. I fanned myself with my hand, trying to catch my breath.

"I'm actually glad you're such a bad liar. I've been with some good liars and I'd rather not do that again."

He slipped his hand around my waist. "I'm good at lots of other things."

"You're good at everything that counts." I set the frame back on the island, my gaze roaming the high rafters and settling on the stone fireplace, the mantle full of photos. "Thank you for bringing me here. This is a really great house."

He smiled into my eyes. "It's way more house than I ever wanted. But it is great."

I looked around the cavernous open room, hallways branching off both ends. "It is a lot of space for one person."

He chuckled. "I told you, I'd be happy living on a Catalina 21."

My nose wrinkled. "That'd be a little cramped for me."

"Well, if you were going to join me, I'd spring for a Lagoon 42."

"Now you're talking." My hand rested on his chest, a big grin on my lips. "There's a great spot to moor a big catamaran, right outside my front door."

His grip tightened around my waist. "Now *you're* talking."

It was a daydream we both liked to imagine, but the reality pulled him back.

"You can see why I don't have visitors. I know this is way over the top."

I tried to keep judgment off my face and out of my tone. "It's a lot. But everybody has their thing."

"This was certainly Jill's thing. And unfortunately it became my thing when I couldn't bring myself to get rid of any of it."

Hayden seemed to recognize that holding onto the past wasn't necessarily healthy. He might've even been ready to move on. But he had a long way to go.

"It's hard to let go of things you've held onto. I understand."

"It's ironic, though. It became this …obsession almost, for Jill. Chronicling our lives on the walls. It started normal, a few photos here and there, but then it grew and grew." His chin dropped, like he might be embarrassed by it.

"Don't feel like you have to apologize for the memories you still have scattered around."

"Thank you. They're not really my memories, though. I mean, some of them are, but having them on display like this"—he waved his hand—"this was never my idea. It's time to change it, for my sanity."

"You do what's best for you. Don't do anything for me."

He chuckled, almost smug. "It's for both of us, babe." His chin dipped to brush my lips, his short whiskers sending a shiver through me. "Are you starving after throwing the fried chicken out?"

I grinned. "I kind of am. You?"

"Let's go get a bite out. The Mexican down the street isn't bad."

My eyes grew wide. "God, not margaritas."

Hayden patted my butt, laughing. "If you want to freshen up, I'll show you to the bathroom."

"Yes, please." Some water on my face and some mascara were in order if we were going out in public.

I followed him down the hallway, past a closed door with a carved wooden "A" painted white with pink flowers.

The bedroom was starkly different from the rest of the house in that the walls were empty. I thought there were no photos at all until I spotted a stack of pictures on the dresser.

Hayden called from the other side of the room. "Here's the bathroom." He flipped a light switch. "Take your time, but hurry. I'm starving."

I lifted my chin for a kiss. "I'll be right out."

I eyed the empty walls while I washed my face. Had he taken down all those photos I'd seen on the dresser? On my way out, I stopped, tempted by the tall stack of memories. I looked around like someone might be watching as I picked up the first few pictures. Jill and a pretty brunette with a dimple. Jill and Hayden in Rocky Mountain National Park. Hayden, Corinne and Jill with a Christmas tree in the background.

Packing up the memories surely wasn't easy, but it couldn't be harder than living with them. Hayden had been through a lot, but it seemed like he was moving forward. Better late than never.

Hayden was waiting by the fire, smiling. "I'm seriously going to die if I don't get a burrito in the next fourteen minutes."

The burritos were fantastic, as was the pitcher of margaritas, which, technically was only two margs each. Not so bad.

I was smart enough to decline when Hayden suggested a beer afterward. "I'm too full for that. And if I drink any more I'll fall asleep on the way home."

"Well, we can't have that." He signaled the waitress to ask for the check. "Let's call it an early night."

On our way to the car, an attractive brunette with a big baby bump waved frantically from across the street. "Hayden!"

The man with her trotted to catch up as she crossed the street. She grinned as she got closer, showing the cutest little dimple I recognized from the photo with Jill.

Hayden straightened for a second but then he pulled me closer to his side as she approached. "Melanie. Wow. Twice in a week." He didn't sound overjoyed.

She didn't seem to notice, or to care if she did. She beamed, "That's what happens when you get out of the house. You see people." Her smile spread as she looked me over, sticking out her hand. "Hi, I'm Melanie."

Hayden spoke up. "Oh, sorry. Violet, this is Melanie. Melanie, this is Violet. She lives down in the Keys."

Melanie shook my hand enthusiastically. "Ah. Nice. Did you two meet down there?"

I was hesitant to be the one sharing details so I answered as short and sweet as I could. "Yes we did."

Hayden explained further. "When I went down for my sister's birthday party a few weeks ago."

Melanie touched her chest. "That's awesome." She finally took note of her husband beside her. "Honey, this is Violet. Hayden's new friend."

I didn't like the sound of that, but I wasn't sure what a more appropriate term might be. I wasn't sure until Hayden said it aloud.

"My girlfriend, you'll be happy to hear." Hayden grinned at Melanie.

She bubbled over with excitement. "I'm *very* happy to hear that." My cheeks blazed when she turned to me. "Hayden's a great guy."

I leaned into him as he squeezed me tighter in a side hug. "I get that impression."

Melanie wrapped her arm around her husband's waist. "You two enjoy your visit. I hope to get to see you again soon, Violet."

"Thank you. I'd like that."

I waited until we were in the car to comment. "That was weird."

Hayden chuckled. "What? That she liked you?"

I didn't want to let on that I figured—from my snooping earlier—that Melanie was one of his late wife's friends. "Ha! Well, yeah. I mean, she *really* liked me."

Hayden smiled, drinking me in with those turquoise eyes. "Of course she did. She also *really* liked seeing me happy. Kinda like your folks."

I wondered what happy must look like if it had been so obvious to everyone who saw us. It must look beautiful. That's how it felt.

CHAPTER 34

HAYDEN

My stomach knotted as we rolled into the driveway. Maybe I wasn't as ready for this as I'd thought.

The moment had come, and I wanted Violet more than I'd ever wanted anything. But I knew my strong urge to ravage her in the car came, at least in part, from my reluctance to take her back in the house.

I pushed down the fear that tried to rise in my chest as I slid the key out of the ignition. It was new and a little scary, but it was time to break out of my old pattern and bring my new love into my real life.

Violet was oblivious to my hesitation. Hopping down to bound up the steps of the porch, she wrapped her arms around herself while I unlocked the door. "It's freezing. How'd that happen?"

"Cold front, I guess." I hadn't paid attention to the weather forecast all week.

"I'm glad we don't get many of those down in the Keys."

I took off my heavy jacket and flung it over the back of a dining chair. "I'm kind of over the cold, to be honest."

Violet stepped in close, her palms sliding up my back. "It's not so bad when you have someone to keep you warm."

Her lips, soft and warm, felt like home. In the sweetest of kisses, my eyes fluttered open to be sure it was real. My gaze was drawn to the largest wedding photo on the wall behind her.

I barely recognized the man in the tuxedo staring back with a big grin. It was another me, in another life. And my life right now was standing in front of me, in my arms.

"Let's go to bed, beautiful."

Violet tucked under my arm, close to my side as we made our way down the hallway. She glanced down at the stack of photos on the dresser. "I noticed you took the pictures down in here."

I slipped my hands around her waist, pulling her close. "It was time."

With the photos in a neat stack, Jill wasn't staring from every angle. But I had a strong feeling in my bones that she'd be happy that I finally felt love in my heart. There was room there for the memories and for new love.

Violet's arms draped around my neck as she smiled into my eyes. "They say timing is everything. If I'd met you a few months earlier I wouldn't have been ready either."

I stepped a foot between hers, palms sliding over her ass to pull her crotch onto my thigh. "Are you ready now?" Any doubt that I was ready had faded.

She sighed, swooning in my arms. "Fuck."

Our lips and hands moved in a familiar rhythm, clothes dropping in a trail to the bed.

I pushed her down onto the mattress, nudging her higher on the pillow before I slid her black lace panties down her long, tanned legs. She bit her lip, drawing in a fast breath as my mouth moved between her thighs, hovering there to breathe in her sweetness.

She opened to me, knees spreading wide, clenching my fingers that pushed into her depths. I stared into her fiery dark eyes as her face twisted in bliss, my mouth full of her, her fists full of sheets.

I swallowed her up like the first drink after a long drought while her hips writhed in climax.

She stilled, whining through breathy moans, "What you do to me, Hayden. Fuck." Her eyes drifted closed as her head fell back.

I slid my fingers out of her silky warmth, lifting my face that dripped with her scent, squeezing her thigh.

"Look at me, Violet. I want you to watch me make you come again."

Her dark lashes blinked open as she panted, staring directly into my soul while I ate her up. Her moans turned desperate as her hips bucked wildly. My fingers dug into the crests of her pelvis to keep my tongue trained on her clit. I wanted to finish her off until she disintegrated into a whimpering pile of pleasure.

Soon the song of her pleasure reverberated, her shrill longing filling the room.

When the quake finally settled, her body trembled as much as her voice. "You can't keep doing that to me. I can't handle it."

I wiped my mouth on the back of my hand before I climbed over her. "Too many orgasms?"

She squirmed under my gaze like it was hard to admit it. "Too many feelings."

I brushed the hair from her face, sliding into her warmth. "If there's a limit on feelings I'm probably way over it." My chest was so full of them I thought it might burst.

A month ago I couldn't imagine letting a woman into my heart. But now that Violet was there, I couldn't imagine ever letting her go. The feelings I'd tried so hard to avoid spilled from my chest, pulsing through me in waves that would take me under if I didn't stay focused. I moved in measured thrusts, trying to hold back. "But I don't know limits with you. Every taste of you only makes me want more."

She sucked in a fast breath, whining with a sigh as I pushed deeper. "You can have all you want, Hayden." She gripped me from within, wild eyes staring into mine. "I'm yours."

And with that, any semblance of control I thought I had, came unglued. The orgasm came on like a flash flood. I pulled out just in time, grasping my shaft.

"Fuck. You do this to me, woman. I can't control myself with you."

She smiled up. "I feel out of control with you, too. But I kinda like it."

I touched her face, smiling into her eyes. "But I want to fuck you all night, goddamnit."

"Well, the night is still young." She licked her lips as they spread in a smile. "Maybe we should shower first. I definitely need it."

I chuckled as she looked down at her cum-splattered belly. "Good plan."

Under the warm shower stream, I ran my hands through her long black tresses. After we were both soaked, I turned and pumped my hand full of body wash. Her head fell back under the stream as I rubbed over her flat stomach, but her eyes blinked open as the scent filled the shower.

"Is that *Caudalie*?"

I smiled at her Southern accent in French. "It is. I ordered it as soon as I got home from Paradise Key—to remind me of you."

She stared up at me, clearly touched as she wrapped her arms around me, sliding her slippery chest over mine. "That is so incredibly sweet. And really fucking hot." Scooping suds off her chest, she massaged my cock.

"You're fucking hot. Look at that." I nodded at my dick growing steadily in her hand.

She grinned, tugging harder. "Looks like you might be almost ready to go all night."

However long it lasted, it wouldn't be long enough.

CHAPTER 35

Violet

I pulled on Hayden's T-shirt I found on the floor before wandering down the hallway toward the clanking noise that awakened me.

The door with the floral A was ajar. Hayden was stacking white wooden rails against a small mattress leaning on the wall.

Pink letters spelled out ANNABELLE above where the disassembled crib stood. A nursery. *Had there been a baby?* A chill spread through me.

Hayden looked up with a smile when he noticed me in the doorway.

"Good morning, beautiful. I hope I didn't wake you."

I rubbed my eyes, forcing a smile. "It's okay. What are you doing?"

"Something I should have a long time ago." He wiped his hands on his flannel pajama bottoms. "You ready for some coffee?" He led me by the hand to the kitchen.

I took the mug he pushed into my hands, sniffing the air that smelled of fresh-cooked something.

His hand slid up my back, tracing circles over his T-shirt as he spoke. "Jill had a miscarriage a year before she died. She insisted on putting the nursery together as soon as she found out she was pregnant. After she lost the baby, she refused to take it down."

I lifted the mug to my lips, blowing to cool the coffee, trying to process what I'd seen and what he'd said. "Too painful?"

"Yes, but having the nursery there wasn't good for her mental health. I knew it. I said it." He squinted, shaking his head like it hurt to remember. "But she wouldn't hear of taking it down."

He chuckled dryly. "The crazy part is I did the same thing after Jill died—keeping all this stuff here."

His gaze drifted to the stack of frames on the dining table at least two feet high."Reminders of death."

I cringed, recalling the words I'd used at the Buckhorn Exchange. "Don't beat yourself up. You had to do what felt right."

"Holding onto the past never felt right, but packing up everything she held dear felt just as wrong." He filled his mug. "But it was time. And I think she'd understand."

I didn't know what to say, but I had to say something. "If you're doing what's right for you, then I bet you're right."

"I never realized it until you came along. I needed to make space in my life for you."

"Hayden, please don't do anything because of me."

He stepped closer, tipping my chin up so he spoke directly into my eyes. "I told you last night, I'm doing this for us."

"This has been a long time coming. I just didn't realize how urgent it was until I almost lost you because of it."

He lowered his mouth to mine for a quick kiss. "You're saving me from myself, beautiful. Thank you."

I fought the urge to look away. "As long as you're sure…"

He kissed my forehead. "I'm sure."

I knew right then I was staring my future in the eye. I swallowed before I said the the words I'd doubted I ever would again.

"I love you, Hayden Kincaid."

His gaze reached my deepest parts, and I knew he spoke from his, when he said, "I love you, too, Violet Monroe."

My knees went weak when his soft lips met mine.

He pulled away, grinning. "We better eat before the eggs get cold."

I'd heated up inside, but I knew he was right. "What can I do?"

He turned to take toast out of the toaster. "Get some forks and knives." He motioned toward the drawers to my right.

I opened one drawer that was full of stuff, including another photo of Jill. There was something about her smile that struck me. "No forks here, but this is a great picture."

He stopped, surprised before he nodded with a smile. "

It was the day she had the first ultrasound—the happiest I'd ever seen her."

"You might want to keep this one in a frame then."

He took the photo from my hands, sad eyes not matching his smile. "I think you're right. It's good to remember the happier times." He chuckled as he set it on the counter. "I'm sure I can find a frame that fits."

I lifted the infamous photo of Aunt Margaret from the kitchen counter. "I'd say that one is another keeper."

Hayden laughed. "I guess it's also good to remember your biggest mistakes." He picked up the frame. "And your favorite aunt. Don't tell Aunt Trish I said that when you meet her."

My chest warmed with the thought of meeting the rest of his family. It also made me think of Corinne.

"Shit. I haven't spoken to your sister since she told me about Aunt Margaret. Have you?"

"Nope. She was pissed at me for fucking this up. Should we call her?"

I wondered if she was pissed at me for not telling her I'd been secretly dating her brother. But he had his phone out before I could answer. "I suppose."

Hayden propped the phone against the photo of his aunt.

Corinne scowled when she answered. "It's about damn time."

Hayden grinned, turning the phone so I was in the picture. "Sorry, we've been busy."

Corinne's eyes widened, a smile spreading across her face. "Holy shit! Violet? You're in Breckenridge? How the hell did that happen?"

"Your brother drove to Wyoming to get me."

Her mouth dropped open as she clutched her chest. "Hayden, I didn't know you could be so romantic."

"I couldn't let this one get away." His arm slipped around my shoulder to pull me into his side.

My face flamed, embarrassed I'd kept it from her. "I'm sorry I didn't tell you before. I didn't know how."

"Don't be sorry. I understand." She grinned. "You've always felt like the sister I never had. If my brother doesn't screw it up again, maybe it'll be official."

I chuckled. "Let's not get ahead of ourselves." But I could see her being my sister-in-law in the not-so-distant future if he asked.

Hayden laughed too. "One day at a time. Today we're hitting the slopes so we can't talk long."

"You're taking her skiing?" Corinne blinked, incredulous.

"Thanks for making it weird, sis. Yes, I'm taking her skiing. All the way to the top if she can handle the double black diamonds."

My competitive side bristled. "I can hold my own on the double blacks."

Hayden chuckled, squeezing me closer to his side. "Knowing you, you can ski circles around me."

"I'd rather ski beside you." I grinned before I bit into my toast.

Corinne beamed. “Gah! You two are too fucking cute. Go have fun. I’ll talk to you soon.”

Hayden’s phone dinged as soon as he ended the call. “That’s the client I was supposed to meet in Miami today. He says he’s happy to reschedule for next Friday. Can you meet me there?”

My stomach fluttered with hope. “I wondered when I’d get to see you again. I didn’t expect it to be so soon.”

“If I have my way, I’ll be in Florida so much you might get sick of me.”

If I had my way he’d be living there already. I smiled up at him.

“Like overdosing on Haagen Dazs, I’d love to try.”

EPILOGUE

Violet let the mainsheet out a few inches. I watched the speed climb a full knot on the GPS, patting her ass. "You're not supposed to show me up on my own boat."

Her black hair streamed in the breeze. "I'm not trying to show you up. Do you want the helm?"

I shook my head. "No, I'm perfectly happy letting you take the wheel."

She smiled. "And I'm perfectly happy with you being the captain. I'll be your mate any day."

I stepped in behind her, sliding my hand around her waist to pull her hips tight. "You're the best mate, in more ways than one." I rubbed myself against her perfect little ass.

"Don't start that now. We're almost there. Are the bow lines set?"

"Yes ma'am."

She laughed at my poor impression of her accent. "You want to take us in, Captain, or shall I?"

"Up to you."

She bit her lip. "I'd rather let you dock this beast in this strong wind."

"It's tricky." I was sure she'd manage just fine, though.

I turned us upwind to take down the main sail as we approached the channel marker.

Violet climbed up on the deck, stopping to tell me, "The basin is the first right, I believe. I haven't been there from the water yet."

I peered out at the only building I thought it could be. "Fuck, this is it?"

"That one over there." Violet pointed to the sprawling coral-colored building I'd been admiring before climbing up onto the deck to head to the bow.

Violet's father waved from the concrete dock and caught the bow line when she tossed it. "Morning, Daddy."

She hopped onto the dock and ran back to the stern, grinning as I tossed her a line. "Great job, Captain."

Jim walked back to meet me as I stepped onto the dock, gawking at the catamaran. "That's quite the yacht you've got there, son."

"Thanks. And that's one hell of a condo hotel."

"The penthouse is yours anytime you want to stay. 'Course Violet already knows that."

Violet planted her hands on her hips and shook her head. "I still think you should rent it when you're not here. You can get fifteen hundred a night for that, all year long."

Jim patted her on the back. "Money's not everything. I'd rather know that we all have a place to stay anytime it tickles our fancy."

He turned to me. "Let's head up there so you can see it, then I want a tour of your boat before we head out fishing."

"Sounds good." I slipped my arm around Violet's waist as we headed down the dock. She looped her other arm through her father's elbow.

"You're right, Daddy. Money's not everything. Thank God you still have your health. Did the doctor give you the all clear last week?"

"He said the procedure was a success, and that I'm healthy as a horse."

Jim swung the lobby door open "Your mother insisted on cooking even though I told her the fishing boat will be here at ten."

Violet chuckled. "That doesn't surprise me." She scanned the sleek lobby on our way to the elevator. "This turned out nice. I love the epoxy art." She nodded toward an enormous piece on the wall, its swirling blues reminiscent of the sea.

"Of course it turned out nice. You have a great eye, Punkin'."

Irene answered the door with a smile, stretching out her arms to hug me first. "Hayden! It's so nice to see you here."

Violet beamed. "I smell biscuits and gravy."

Her mother pulled her into a hug, kissing her cheek. “Your favorite, dear.”

Jim waved us to follow him across the expansive living room decorated in chic modern furniture to the dining table. “We need to hustle.”

After we’d started eating, Irene asked, “So how’re you liking your new boat?”

I finished chewing the bite in my mouth before I answered. “I’m loving it. We both are. Violet’s a natural, of course.”

Jim laughed. “I hope so. Most financial types would tell you it’s crazy to sell a house to buy a boat.”

I chuckled. “They wouldn’t be wrong. Even sailors say that a boat is just a hole in the water you pour your money into.” I shrugged. “But, like you said, money isn’t everything. And I only used half my house money on the boat. The other half is invested to make up for the depreciation and expenses, so it should work out.”

Jim nodded. “I’m sure it’ll work out just fine. You’re a smart feller.”

“Smart enough to marry your daughter. Thank you for your blessing.”

Irene looked up from buttering a biscuit. “It was so sweet you called, Hayden.”

Violet did a double take. “You what?”

My mouth was full so Irene explained. “You didn’t know? He called us both before he proposed.”

Violet contained her grin, but I could tell she was touched. “How very gentlemanly of you.”

I washed down the bite with a swig of OJ. "I figured that was Southern protocol."

Violet stared for a long second before her lips curled in a smile. "Not bad, California boy."

Jim picked up his phone that buzzed on the table. "Y'all hurry. The charter boat is turning down the channel and I want to see that catamaran of yours before we head out."

Violet laid down her fork. "I've had enough to eat already. It's going to be bumpy out there with this wind."

She had a good point. "Me too. We can go tour the boat now if you like."

We headed toward the dock. Irene followed along, trotting to keep up with Violet. "Are you gonna be back in time to go talk to the baker?"

"Gus will meet us there even if it's after hours." Violet looked at me to explain. "He's the one making the cake." She turned back to her mother. "But the wedding's not until March. We have plenty of time for all that."

"I know it's still seven months away, but I want to see what you have in mind."

Violet rolled her eyes, but her soft smile seemed touched by her mother's excitement.

I didn't care what kind of cake we had. After she said yes on the deck of the catamaran the day I bought it I knew I could have my cake and eat it too.

Violet's mother read the teal letters on the side of the hull. "Aunt Margaret? Was that the name that came with the boat?"

"Nope. That was my doing. It's an inside joke." I chuckled at Violet's amused look.

She stepped aboard first, offering her mother a hand. "You're going to love the galley up design."

Irene clutched her hands in front of her chest, admiring the galley. "My, yes. I've seen a couple of these with the kitchen way down there." She pointed toward the port hull.

I led Jim down the steps into the starboard hull to give him the tour of the main cabin.

He called up to Violet.

"This is a darn sight better than that Morgan 30 we sailed to Jekyll Island, isn't it, Punkin?"

"It's certainly got a lot more room. And doesn't heel in the wind. But I loved that Morgan."

"Me too. Best trip ever." He smiled proudly.

Irene turned to Violet. "Jim tells me you two are planning a trip to the Bahamas soon?"

Violet grinned. "Yeah, next month. September is low season for the resort."

Jim clicked his tongue. "High season for hurricanes." He sighed with a shrug. "But I bet this fancy vessel has all the bells and whistles to track storms."

I pointed to the screens at the navigation station. "It does. Don't worry. We'll be careful."

"The only thing I worry is that you'll like it over there and decide to stay. I want you back here for Christmas."

Violet smiled. "We'll be back long before then."

Violet's mother said with relief, "Good." She turned toward Violet. "You know Clay and Melissa and all the young'ns are coming."

"Yes, I know, Mama. I also know that the charter captain is not going to be happy with us if we keep him waiting. We should go. We'll give you a full tour later when we take it out for a sunset sail."

Jim moved toward the door. "We don't want to make the best fly fisherman in the Keys mad."

I rubbed my hands together. "No we do not."

I stepped onto the charter boat after Violet, already being greeted by whom I figured to be our guy. His sun-streaked tousled hair and mischievous look—like he'd just gotten away with something—was fitting for his name.

"Hi I'm Trevor Rodman, but they call me Trouble."

Violet didn't miss a beat as she nodded, giving him a once-over. "Well, you look like trouble, so that's not at all surprising."

He looked clearly thrown off his game that she had no interest in. "I'm not really trouble. Don't let the name fool you."

"I can assure you that I'm not easily fooled, Mr. Rodman. But with a name like that, you've got a lot to live up to." Violet smirked as she pulled me into her side.

"This is my fiancé, Hayden. He's been chomping at the bit to meet you for months." She nodded toward her father who was stepping down into the cockpit. "And my father Jim, who hired you."

Violet wasn't swayed by Trevor's local notoriety, or the Rodman family name that was so prominent in the Keys.

One of the many things I loved about Violet was that she could put anyone, anywhere, in their place. She'd certainly put me in mine when I was dishonest.

I was a lucky man that she forgave me, and that my place—now and forever— was beside her.

****

If you're guessing Corinne's story will be next, you'd be correct! And if you picked up on the hint that she get tangled up with the worst kind of man (in her book)—a fisherman!—you get extra points. Yep…it's Trouble in Paradise. Who doesn't love an enemies-to-lovers adventure??

You can be the first to hear out about this, and all my releases, by signing up for my newsletter. You can find that link on my website too. My reader group on FB is a good time as well.

If you're new to the Paradise Key series, you can also catch Tessa's and Gavin's story, the one that started it all, in Paradise Found. And Simon and Delaney's swoony Keys to Paradise. All are true standalones and can be read in any order.

ACKNOWLEDGMENTS

As with the others before it, this book would not have come to be without the love and support of my two amazing sons who cheer me on despite their personal embarrassment that mommy writes sexy books.

Thanks to my editor, Ann Rachelle, who helped make this book so much better.

And my BFF, Keri Peyton, for all the listening and talking about my characters like they're our friends.

I am eternally grateful to the plethora of fellow authors who continue to offer advice and support. I'm constantly in awe at how some people want to lift up others around them. I'm doing my best to be like them and pay it forward.

ABOUT THE AUTHOR

Macy is a foul-mouthed tennis addict whose sweet side comes out with her two teenage sons. Strong, smart heroines inspire her as much as hard-bodied heroes with hearts of gold.

When she's not on the tennis court or locked in her writing cave, you'll find Macy on the beach with a sunset cocktail or out on the boat near their home in the Florida Keys.

Connect with Macy, and get exclusive content and special offers at www.macybutler.com

ALSO BY MACY BUTLER

Happier Ever After Series

Unholy Trinity- Romantic Suspense Duet

Taming Kate

Trinity's Trust

Made in the USA
Middletown, DE
19 April 2024